ONE TO LOVE

By Tia Louise

This book is a work of fiction. Names, characters, places, and incidents are products of the author's imagination or are used fictitiously. Any resemblance to actual events or locales or persons, living or dead, is entirely coincidental.

For Mr. TL, who helped me find Kenny and then approved of Slayde.

Yes, this one is for us.

Contents

Chapter 1: "The pain you feel today is the strength you feel tomorrow."
Kenny

Left, left, left, right jab.
Left, left, left, right jab.
Switch.
Right, right, right, left jab.
Right, right, right, left jab.

My fists slammed into the canvass bag, hitting it over and over with a satisfying *THUNK!* I was a rockstar, a badass. Rocky. No—I was Wonder Woman, blocking bullets with my wrists. *Ten more seconds...*

Left, right, left, left, left. Roundhouse kick.
Right, left, right, right, right. Roundhouse kick.
BUZZ!

"Woo!" I yelled as I jumped up and down, clapping my gloved hands together before raising them over my head.

My muscles were burning and spent, but I felt amazing. I glanced at the motivational poster on the wall—a superhot, ripped woman in a black bikini running over the caption: *She's the gazelle. Be the tiger.*

I pointed at it. "Fuck that! *I'm* the tiger." *Boom!* I gave the bag another roundhouse kick. "Take *that,* gazelle!"

Then I exhaled a laugh and stepped back. Post-workout adrenaline was crazy. I grabbed the white towel off the bench along with my water bottle and took a long drink. I wasn't very good at kickboxing, but it was so much fun. The idea hit me (ha ha) cleaning out my boss Rook's old VHS tapes of celebrity workouts. I popped in Tae Bo, and immediately I wanted to do it.

Being self-taught, I'd have to do a certification class if I wanted to train or teach a class of it here at the gym, but I didn't care. Right now I was simply getting stronger, punching out the stress. A brief glance at the speed bag, and my lips twisted into a frown.

That little fucker was a whole other matter. I'd looked like an idiot trying to keep time with it my first try. It ended up bouncing back and hitting me in the head, which made Rook howl with laughter. Embarrassment burned my cheeks, but I swore I'd master that guy.

I just wasn't doing it this morning. In thirty minutes my first and only client of the day would arrive, leaving me enough time to shower, put on fresh yoga pants, a sports bra and tank, and have my morning power smoothie.

Fridays were light days, but I had to help run the juice bar for Mariska and hang around in case any new clients walked in or existing ones decided to rearrange their schedules. Mariska was my best friend and self-appointed Mistress of Smoothies. We'd met in art class at Ocean County College. I had taken fall semester off this year, but she arranged her schedule so all her day classes were on Fridays. Pete, the other trainer, wouldn't be in until lunch. Rook, and his wife Tammy would arrive in the next hour.

Rook was an ex-NFL player, forced to retire after blowing out his knee. It was pretty life shattering from what I'd pieced together. He'd almost fallen apart, and ended up working as a bouncer, a bodyguard, a mover, pretty much anything requiring muscle, until he met Tammy.

She was a bombshell of a former pageant girl and got him into professional fitness. She taught most of the group classes here, from Pilates to Zumba, but they started out doing bodybuilding, nutrition, and videos before opening The Jungle Gym in Toms River, right next to Bayville, where I lived, and close to where all the MTV reality-TV kids liked to misbehave.

They kept it flush with product endorsements and reviews, and the vibe was very sexy, "Where the wild things are." We never got any celebrities in the gym, but we got a lot of suburban wannabes, which was just as good if not better.

Rook made all the hiring decisions, and he paid his trainers a decent wage. I was lucky I'd moved back to Bayville right when he'd needed a new juice bar attendant. I'd quickly moved up to personal trainer. Now I was toying with adding kickboxing to my resume. He wanted all of us on the cutting edge of new class offerings. Currently, I was planning out a regimen that combined BodyCombat, Animal Moves, and Rhythm Hit.

Making my way through the large exercise room, everything smelled like Windex and new carpet. It was actually a nice space for a small, unincorporated gym. I grabbed my key out of my cubby and heading to the female locker area in the back of the building.

Cool metal met my hand as I pushed through the door and rounded the painted cinder-block wall. The floor was concrete, but it was scored with a diamond pattern and stained aqua blue. Stopping at a locker, I slipped in a small key and opened it. My black tank was soaked as I pulled it over my head, but it was good sweat, not perspiration. I'd worked hard this morning, and a hot shower was calling my name.

Pushing off my capri-length black workout pants, I stuffed everything into the plastic bag I kept for sweaty clothes and slammed the door. A few steps and I'd be relaxing under the spray. Towels were stacked in neat rolls at the entrance to the long row of showers, and I grabbed one just as I heard the sound of water going.

Tammy must've decided to shower at the club this morning. It was unexpected, but I wrapped the towel quickly around my body in case she stepped out as I passed. Not that I was so modest, but who really walked around a locker room totally naked? Plus, I didn't want to hear her exclaiming about the lines on my torso or how nicely I was "filling out" since I'd started doing CrossFit.

Tammy was in amazing shape, and a full-figured hourglass. As such, she made it her mission to fight "negative body image," and she was always encouraging me to eat more. It would've gotten on my nerves if she weren't so nice.

Shaking my head with a smile, I rounded the corner and almost screamed. The curtain was open, and Tammy was on full display under the steady stream. Her eyes were closed and her back arched against her husband's dark chest. He held one of her legs up as he pounded her from behind, and with every slam, her moans grew louder.

"Oh god! Yes, Yes, *YES!!*" she wailed.

Rook gripped one of her breasts in an enormous hand before reaching down and throwing her other leg over his arm. He was actually strong enough to lift her that way, slamming her up and down against his pelvis as the muscles in his dark legs flexed.

Shock and awe had me glued to the spot with my mouth open. Heat flared between my thighs at the live show.

"So... fucking... good," he groaned, gripping her thighs and bouncing her up and down his long shaft.

"Right there! Right there! Oh YES!" Tammy cried, holding his neck and frantically pumping her legs to help him. She yelped like a puppy, over and over as her entire body began to shake.

Glazed eyes slit open, meeting mine, and I snapped out of it. I spun on my heel and ran all the way back to the lockers, clutching the towel against my chest. I was panting, my heart was flying, and my whole body trembled. Moisture was slick between my thighs, and Tammy's orgasmic yelps still echoed in my ears. *Shit!*

It was the second time I'd caught them going at it in the gym. The first time was six months ago when I'd been doing my final, nightly sweep before locking up. I'd busted them all the way in the back in the men's weight room. That time, Rook was straddling the weight bench and Tammy was straddling him.

Her white-blonde head flew and her back arched as she held on behind her. Every time he pounded her, her large breasts circled with his mouth chasing them. I'd never get that image out of my brain.

That time I'd run all the way to the juice bar snorting. This time I was pissed. *Dammit*. They knew I was here, and worse—they knew I'd been alone a long time. It was completely inappropriate and insensitive to parade their insatiable sex life in front of me. Before long, I'd be afraid to round any corners after hours.

Sitting on the bench, I waited until my breathing calmed, and after what felt like forever, I cautiously stood and crept back toward the showers. My client would be here in just a few minutes, and I had to get ready.

My long, dark hair was still piled on top of my head, and the towel was secured around my body. The stalls were all empty and quiet. The only signs anyone had been here were the water droplets on the curtains and the wet floor. I figured Tammy had hustled them out after seeing me.

With a deep breath, I reached for the handle to turn on the hot water.

* * *

Tammy was alone, flipping through a fitness magazine behind the juice bar when I went out front. She had a Zumba step class at nine-thirty, and she was dressed in black booty shorts and a loose, hot-pink tank over a camo sports bra. Her hair was now up in a ponytail, and she was a festive contrast to my all-black trainer gear and low-ponytail.

"Good morning." Her voice was quiet and had the faintest hint of remorse, but I didn't respond.

Instead I went straight to the smoothie machine and loaded it up with almond-coconut milk, a banana, Dino kale, and two scoops of crushed ice.

"You're the one ordering all the kale?"

I glanced up to see her pert nose wrinkled. "I didn't order it," I said. "The girls over at Veggie-Smooth asked me to try this recipe for a week and send them clients. If I like it, of course."

"I can't even imagine."

Hitting the button, an irritating *WHIRR!* filled the space, mirroring how I felt inside. "I'm leaving at noon today," I shouted over the noise. "When Pete gets here."

Her light brows clutched together, and I could tell she was working out a response. She knew I was pissed, but to be honest, I wasn't really sure why. I didn't begrudge them a healthy, married sex life, and it was their club, after all. Still. They should've at least closed the damn shower curtain.

She took a step closer and leaned against the bar beside me. "I'm sorry, Ken. About earlier. Your key was in the cubby." It was her way of saying they didn't think I was here, and she watched me a few moments waiting for my response. "Are you very mad?"

I released the button on the machine and poured the green mix into a cup. Exhaling, I took a sip of the surprisingly tasty drink. She had a point. Leaving my key in the cubby *was* the internal code I hadn't arrived, but I wasn't convinced she hadn't heard me in the small boxing room. I was being pretty loud.

Clearing my throat, I nodded. "A little. I mean, Jesus! Weren't you just in bed with him at your house?"

"You're right, of course you're right." She held a hand up in agreement. "It's just... Rook had to be up here early this morning, and well, I guess... He heard me showering?"

"Why were you even showering here? What's wrong with the shower at your house?" One look at her face, and I knew the answer—she was as horny as he was. "You know what? Just forget it."

I shook my head and did a little growl. "I'm feeling tense. I'll take off early today, decompress over the weekend, and we'll just forget the whole thing."

Her hot-pink lips pressed together, and she gave me a little smile. "I'll try not to let it happen again."

I suppressed an eye-roll before taking another long sip of my breakfast. "I would *really* appreciate that."

The women were filtering in for her class, all dressed in booty shorts and neon spandex just like their instructor. They were as bubbly and festive as she was, but a few steps behind them, a short, slightly stooped elderly woman followed. She was dressed in cotton sweats, very old-school and real, and she wore small glasses.

"Mrs. Clarkson!" I called, giving her a wave. "Over here."

Confusion left her face when she saw me waving, and she smiled. "Kendra!" She held a hand straight up, and I laughed, thinking of Rook's silly motivational posters. We were signaling each other across the Amazon—familiar tribe here.

14

"Come on." I caught her hand and led her in the opposite direction, toward the free weights and the machines where I'd work with her on strength training and balance. We got started with our first circuit: curls.

"Keep your elbows in line with your shoulder." I lightly touched her joints as Mrs. Clarkson curled the four-pound dumbbells toward her chest. "That's right."

She exhaled a laugh as she lowered the weights. "I'm such a weakling. I don't know how you have the patience for me."

"No way, you're doing great!" I easily lifted the small purple hand weights she used, but as I turned, I caught the shimmer in her eyes. "Are you okay? Was that too heavy?"

She hastened to reassure me. "Oh, I'm fine! I'm fine." But her voice trailed off on the second *fine*.

Guiding her workout had eased the irritation… *frustration?* simmering in my chest over this morning's shower surprise, so I gently tried again. "It's okay if you want to talk."

Mrs. Clarkson was about the same size as I was, five foot, just at one hundred pounds. She was also forty years older than me, and while I was basically all muscle, she was working to get hers back.

She gave me a tired smile. "It's Friday. I don't want to spoil your weekend fun with my old problems."

Blinking down, I helped her lean forward, her knee on the bench, as she slowly extended her elbow behind her, dumbbell in hand.

After I was sure her form was correct, I answered. "My fun weekend will most likely consist of lying around on the couch watching television."

"Boyfriend out of town?"

"No." I shook my head, exhaling a laugh. "No boyfriend. Not for me."

Switching the weight to her other hand, we rearranged her position. She didn't say anything, but I could tell the wheels were turning in her head.

I gave her a little wink and a smile. "So tell me why your *fine* doesn't sound so convincing."

She shook her head. "It's just an anniversary. George and I would've been together fifty years today."

Taking a step back, my eyebrows rose. "Fifty?"

A smile softened her face at my look of shock. "People got married younger back then."

"I'll say. You must've only been, what? Eighteen?"

She nodded setting the weight on the rack. "That's right. And we had forty loving years together."

The idea of that teased an old ache in my chest, a fantasy I thought I had moved past clinging to — what my life might have been like if only... My inner masochist forced me to ask, "Do you still miss him?"

"Every day." Her scratchy voice was just above a whisper.

Sitting on the bench where we'd been kneeling, I only half-realized I was leaving my one client of the day hanging. It didn't matter. She turned and sat beside me, looking at her own shoes the way I studied mine.

"Now your turn." She sounded like the grandmother I didn't have.

"Why would your *fine* not be very convincing?"

"I am so sorry." I stood then, starting to move past her to the next machine, but she caught my arm.

"It's okay to talk." Her smile was warm, soothing. I turned my palm up and ran my finger over the black teardrop I'd inked there years ago.

"It's not my anniversary or anything. But sometimes I feel like my life will always be this way."

She held my hand. "What way?"

I blinked up at her and did a little smile. "Alone. Missing... I was only twenty-one when Blake died, but it never seems to get easier."

Compassion was all over her face, and for the first time in a while, it didn't make me want to clam up or run away. "Was Blake your boyfriend?"

I thought about the question as I looked at the small window above us. "He was my first real boyfriend. When he said he was leaving for Princeton, I couldn't let him go, so I married him and went with him."

"Oh, dear!" She stood up and pulled me into a hug. "I'm so sorry."

Shaking off the bad memories, I forced a real smile. "Now who's spoiling Friday? I'm sorry. Let's work on your balance."

She followed me over to the large ball in the center of the room. Facing each other, I held her hands as she slowly lowered to a sitting position on top of it. Her gray eyes were full of concern as she watched me.

"You lost him... five years ago?" Her voice was quiet, and I nodded.

We were talking softly, although the only other person in the club was a man on the treadmill running hard, earbuds firmly in place.

"Was he the father of your sweet little boy?"

At that question, my cheeks warmed. "Umm... no," I stammered. "That was somebody else. Sort of a random thing that turned into something more permanent, I guess. But we're not together or anything. Patrick's just my friend."

It was hard to explain my relationship with Patrick Knight to anyone who didn't know him. We'd had a stupid, drunken hook-up that turned us into parents. It didn't change the fact that we were completely wrong for each other. Now he was blissfully engaged to someone else — to Elaine — and I was... alone.

Still, that encounter had given us Lane, my beautiful little golden-haired boy with the big blue eyes. He lived with Patrick and Elaine, but I visited every chance I got, and when I hugged him and buried my face in his soft skin, I could almost believe it was enough.

Mrs. Clarkson was strangely reassured by my news. "That is a *very* good sign."

I almost laughed. "The fact that I'm an irresponsible person who shouldn't be allowed to shoot Tequila is a good sign?"

"The fact that you were willing to open your heart again. Maybe you handled it poorly, but you're too young to give up on love. I'm glad your heart knows it even if your head has to be checked out for it to happen."

"Head checked out. That's a great way to put it. I should've had my head checked out." I did laugh then.

18

We were finished with her routine, and I walked with her back to the juice bar. Before we parted, she took my hand and gave it a squeeze. "You have a kind, loyal heart. It's not a betrayal to Blake's memory to live your life."

It was the same thing everybody always said, but for some reason, hearing it from another survivor hit me hard. I had to clear the thickness in my throat before I was able to answer.

"Thank you." I whispered, nodding, and she was gone.

A quick glance at the clock told me it was almost eleven. The women were filing out of Tammy's class, laughing and making noise. Zumba was one of the few fitness classes where participants came out more excited than when they went in. My irritation started to return, and I collected my things.

Eleven was close enough to noon, and I really needed a break. Stopping at the cubbies where we stowed our personal items, I saw a small, white box in Mariska's. Pulling it down, I recognized Pete's handwriting and shook my head. As many times as she said No, he still gave her little gifts. It was sweet and heartbreaking at the same time.

It also reassured me that he was in the club somewhere. I grabbed my keys and my hipster bag and headed out the door.

Chapter 2: "Inhale the future; exhale the past."
Slayde

Rook Callahan was not what I expected to meet at my job interview at the Jungle Gym Friday afternoon. He was a head taller than me and built like a mountain. Black tattoos showed faintly on his ripped arms, which rested in front of him on the desk as he studied my resume. A heavy, stainless watch was on his wrist.

I'd spent two days poring over the Help Wanted section, looking for anything that didn't require a lot of background information—restaurants, garages, cranberry bogs. Most places wanted references, and I was lucky to have Doc, even if he wasn't always available to take phone calls.

"You say you've never worked at a health club before?" His black eyes cut to me.

"No." I held his stare a moment before I looked down at my hands, running my thumb over the bold 21 inked on the back of my right one. A blue, red, and green network of vines and a skull covered my forearm above it, and I was glad he had ink as well. That was one additional bit of prejudice I didn't need. "I've used gyms quite a bit, but I've never worked at one."

"You've got one reference listed. This somebody related to you?"

"No." Looking up again, I met his gaze head-on. "References are difficult. If I can speak for myself, I'm a hard worker, and I'm only looking for honest work. Nothing more."

He chewed the inside of his bottom lip as he looked back to the sheet in front of him. Then he leaned back in his chair and ran a large hand over his close-cropped hair.

"You used to be a fighter?"

My insides clenched, and I wanted to push us quickly through this part of the conversation. "Years ago. I had to… I was forced to quit."

For whatever reason, that admission changed him. The hard intimidation softened, and he leaned forward to stand, circling the desk so that he was in front of it, facing me.

"When I played ball, I knew a lot of guys forced to quit for whatever reason." He paused and looked at the door as if reliving it. "They'd get mixed up in some shit or the other. Couldn't let it go."

His words were probably meant to build a bridge, but I could feel the heat rising in my chest, that old anger sparking to life. I tightened my jaw, searching my brain for one of Doc's mantras, hoping to head off whatever he might say next.

"I just need a job." My voice was flat.

Bridge unbuilt, intimidation back. I was far more comfortable with that arrangement.

"Any of your shit going to come to my gym?"

"No, sir," I answered fast. "It's in the past. Over."

He nodded once. "I'll give you a shot, a probationary period. You show me we need you up here, that you won't cause any problems, and I'll see about making it permanent."

"Fair enough." I stood and held out my hand.

He stared at it before pushing off the desk and going to his office door. "I'll give you the tour."

I put my unshook hand in my pocket and followed him down the short hall. He paused at a set of double-glass doors to the right. "Through here are racquetball courts and on the other side is the group fitness center. The women's lockers are behind that. You'll take care of them after hours — mornings, evenings, you decide. *Not* when the women are present."

I nodded. "Understood."

He continued a few steps, and we were near the center entrance, where a large juice bar was situated.

"Mariska works the bar. She's off Fridays, but we can usually handle the traffic. Keep the floors mopped and the trash emptied back here. She can handle wiping down the counters."

I nodded, and a very blonde, very stacked female stepped into the center of the bar area. She had the kind of body that made any guy's dick twitch, and by the way she moved, I could tell she knew it.

"This is my wife Tammy."

She was also officially off-limits, not that I was interested in romance of any kind. I did a quick nod before looking down.

"Nice to meet you." Her voice was smooth and friendly. "You our new maintenance guy?"

"Yes, ma'am."

Rook lingered, and when he spoke again, his voice was low. "Where's Kenny?"

"Left early. Said she wasn't feeling well." The way she answered, it seemed they were communicating something else.

I glanced up at them and noticed my new boss's frown.

"She'll be in on Monday?"

"Yeah, I talked to her. She'll be okay."

I couldn't tell what was going on, but Rook started moving, resuming my tour.

"What's your name, maintenance guy?" Tammy called out.

"Slayde," I answered.

"Good to have you, Slayde." She gave me a friendly smile, but I stuck with a nod in response. I wasn't looking for friends either.

The Jungle Gym was bigger than it looked on the outside. Rook led me through an enormous, open room filled with free weights and machines on one end and treadmills and stair climbers on the other. The men's locker room was off the back of it.

"You can get in here and clean whenever it's slow. Our busiest time is after work hours during the week." He stopped and looked around the empty room. "I don't care when you clean it, so long as you hit it once a day."

"Yes, sir." I followed him back out and around a corner to a room that stopped me in my tracks. It was a small boxing area. A strike bag hung from the ceiling in one corner, and in the center was a speed bag. A smaller strike bag was on a pole weighted to the floor.

"What's this for?" I instinctively reached out to touch it, but the onslaught of memories was almost too much—the sound of the whistle, the barked orders of my coach, the hours upon hours I'd spent working, chasing, dreaming. I'd gotten so close, and I'd lost it all.

"Cardio strike bag." Rook answered, oblivious to my discomfort. "Kenny's working up a routine for group fitness. I like to keep things fresh."

It was the second time this Kenny person had come up, but I was less interested in her than in getting out of here. Clearing my throat, I nodded down.

"You still keep your chin tucked." A grin was in his voice.

I didn't even realize I was doing it. "I guess. It's good protection."

"Old habits. I know." He chuckled. "Come on."

As I followed him back toward the front, we met a guy who looked about my age. He had light brown hair and was dressed in nylon pants and a thick brown tee with a Nike swoosh on the shoulder.

"Slayde, this is Pete. He's one of the trainers here."

I nodded as per usual, but he stopped me. "Hey, nice ink. What's that?"

The short-sleeved shirt I wore didn't quite cover the pair of boxing gloves on my right biceps. I didn't want to talk about it, but I didn't see a way out.

"Just something I did a while back." Briefly pulling up the fabric, I allowed him to read it before I dropped the curtain again.

"*Never stop fighting.* Cool. You a fighter?"

Rook interrupted. "That your three o'clock walking in?"

He glanced over his shoulder before turning back. "Yeah, okay. Take it easy, man."

We were back at the front, and Rook faced me.

"I've got a few forms you have to fill out, then you want to start today?"

"Sure. Thanks."

He handed me the paperwork, and I folded it lengthwise, putting it in my back pocket.

"The supply closet is here." I followed him to a small door, which he opened to show shelves of cleaning supplies. A heavy, plastic bucket on wheels was inside holding a mop. "The cubbies on the wall have a master key for everyone. When you're in the club keep it around your neck. When you leave, put it in your slot. That's how we know who's here."

"Got it."

I reached forward and rolled the bucket out. This was my life now. Cleaning up other people's shit. Keeping my chin tucked, guarding my vulnerable spots. It wasn't about my dreams or what I'd lost. It was about taking the first step. Then taking the next step. Before long, I would have walked away from the past and found my new normal.

Chapter 3: "Life goes on."
Kenny

The restless, angry feelings slugged it out in my chest as I wandered through the drugstore. I'd come here straight from work specifically to get a bottle of wine, and Mrs. Clarkson's words echoed in my thoughts. *It's not a betrayal to live your life.*

I wanted to live my life. I really did, but whenever a guy approached me, everything inside me shut down. The only time it hadn't happened was with Patrick, but we were so shit-faced, that didn't count.

Mrs. Clarkson's theory was interesting, though—maybe she was right, and my heart was ready. I just had to learn to switch off my brain and let go. Either way, it didn't matter because there wasn't anyone waiting to catch me.

It was early, but I grabbed the bottle of wine anyway. Then I wandered to the cards and gifts aisle, stopping in front of *American Ink* magazine. The model on the cover had long, straight-black hair like mine, and her arms were covered in a colorful pattern that twisted and flowered up her biceps. It looked like the artist had used a watercolor technique, and the year I'd been at Living Arts Tattoos with Carl crept across my memory.

Carl had done elaborate tattoos like these, ones that took multiple sessions to complete, and I'd watched him closely, learning how to take blank skin and turn it into a canvass. I wasn't there long enough to get as skilled as he, but I'd enjoyed the few works of art I'd created. Most of them were on my own body, from the tear in my hand to the star on my hip. The only one I hadn't done was the butterfly on my ribs. It was my first ink, and Carl had done it for me after I lost Blake.

When I moved back to Bayville, I'd let that part of me go. I was pregnant, and I needed allies. I couldn't be the rebellious teenager who'd run off and married the delinquent everybody hated.

Something in me twisted at the loss, and I added the magazine to the basket on my arm. From there, I went to the hair care aisle. Walking slowly, I saw a box for deep violet-colored dye. It had been years since I'd done anything interesting with my hair, and the urge to change everything pulled hard at my insides. The bottle went into the basket, and I headed to the front.

The cashier didn't even blink when I placed a bottle of wine, a tattoo magazine, and a box of purple hair dye in front of her. As far as she cared, she saw shit like this every day. Whatever. I was shaking things up, seeing if a little change would release the tension.

* * *

Sitting in front of the television with my hair wrapped in plastic, I sipped a glass of wine as I thumbed through the magazine. I traced my favorite tats into my sketchbook and tried to decide which I would do if I still had a gun.

Men's tattoos were so straightforward, tribal bands or broad Samoan patterns across shoulders and over backs. I stared at a photo of a pale, skinny guy with spikey blond hair and a square jaw. He had gauges in his ears and both arms were covered in green and black sleeves that were a mixture of skulls and chains. His light eyes pierced out from the pages at me. *Trouble* was written all over his expression, and the muscles low in my belly tightened. Of course, this was the type of guy Kenny the Tigress wanted to maul. Or was I Wonder Woman?

One thing was for sure, I was buzzed. I pulled myself off the floor, stumbling to my closet, glass of wine still in my hand.

All the way in the back was a box I never opened anymore. Lifting the lid, I dug through the napkins and cigarette books from clubs we'd visited, dried flowers and a diary. I shoved them all aside trying to find it. *Was it all the way at the bottom?*

A hard cube met my fingertips, and I pulled out a cheap, red-vinyl box that opened with a squeak. Inside was the thinnest gold band anybody had ever seen. It was all we'd been able to afford. I think it cost twenty dollars. Pulling it out, I slipped it on the third finger of my left hand, and my breath hiccupped.

Going back to the box, I dug some more until I found the one picture I still had of us together. Blake had his skinny arm thrown over my shoulder, and I was leaning forward laughing, clutching his waist. A cigarette hung out of the corner of his mouth, and his eyes were half-closed while he flipped off the photographer with his other hand.

God, we were so young—not that I was so old now, but when this was taken, I'd only been eighteen. Mrs. Clarkson was eighteen when she'd married her husband. But they'd had forty years together. Blake and I only had two.

Staring at the faces, I waited for the tears to start. I braced myself for the gut-wrenching sobs that used to double me over and have me silently screaming. It always happened when I looked at these mementos. How long had it been since I'd done this? A year?

Nothing happened. I sat in silence staring at these artifacts from my past, and that was exactly how they felt. Distant.

My phone rang in the other room, and I pushed myself off the floor. Wobbling back to the living room, I took another long sip of wine, still amazed I wasn't crying. On my phone face was a girl with a wide smile and light-brown curls flowing over her shoulders. A garland was across her forehead. Mariska.

"Why didn't you tell me Rook hired a new guy today?" Her voice was loud and taunting.

"Probably because I was too pissed at catching them fucking again." My voice was a little slurry, but she didn't seem to notice.

She screamed a laugh. "No. WAY!"

I put my wine glass on the coffee table and fell back on the couch with a loud exhale. I needed to eat something.

"Way," I muttered, reaching up to touch the plastic cap still on my head. I still had dye in my hair. Great. Dragging myself off the couch, I headed to the bathroom.

"They are *so* inspiring." Mariska's voice had gone dreamy. "Imagine being married to someone that long and still wanting to fuck their brains out all the time."

My eyes rolled. "It's more shocking than inspirational, actually."

"I'd love a sneak peek. Rook's hot. I bet he has an enormous dick."

"Please. Don't. He's our boss." The fact was, he did—and I didn't want to think about it.

I leaned toward the mirror and lifted the plastic, checking my color. It looked ready. "But if you really want to see it, you could try working longer than two hours in the middle of the day. That seems to be their down time."

"Looks like I'll have to if I'm going to see Mr. New Guy." She was back to scheming. "Pete said he's clearly got a backstory. What did you think?"

Turning, I leaned against the sink. "I didn't see him. I left early."

"What's wrong? Are you sick?"

The tiny wedding band was still on my finger, and I stared at it for a few moments. Still nothing.

"Kenny?" Mariska's voice was a little louder. "You okay over there?"

"I don't know." I turned my hand over and studied the small, black tear I'd inked in my palm. "I mean, Yes! Physically, I'm fine. But something's different."

"What do you mean? What's different?"

"I'm not sure, but I tried to come home today and sort it out. My feelings are all mixed up, and I just feel this tension inside, like I'm going to bust open." Whoa. I never talked this much about my feelings. No more wine tonight.

"Go out with me tomorrow night!" She was almost shouting with excitement. "Just say yes for once and don't think about it. We can dance all that bad juju away!"

Images of me with her in a dance club flickered through my mind. "I'm going to Wilmington. I miss Lane."

"You were just there last weekend!" she cried. "You've got to go out and be around guys your age."

"Tell you what." I pushed off the sink and walked back to my room. "Next week, I'll go out with you." I took the small band off my finger and returned it to the vinyl box.

"Promise?"

"I promise."

We disconnected, and I returned everything to the larger box and pushed it all the way to the back of my closet again. Switching off the light, I headed to the bathroom.

The water ran deep violet as I washed out the dye, massaging my scalp with my fingers. Once it was clear, I shut off the tap and squeezed out the excess. Then I grabbed the blow dryer and turned my back to the mirror. I hadn't bleached it first, so no telling how it would look. When it was completely dry, I turned around, and gasped. It was perfect—dark, blackish-violet, cascading over my shoulders like a cape. I turned to the side and shook my straight hair down my back. I couldn't wait for Lane to see it.

Running back to the living room, I scooped up my phone and shot a quick text to Patrick. *Is it okay if I come for a visit tomorrow? You busy?*

I waited, wondering if it was too late to order take-out when my phone buzzed in my hand. *Sure! Lane misses Mommy.*

A smile broke over my face, and I quickly replied. *Will be on the road before eight. See you soon!*

If anything could break me out of a funk, it was chubby little hands and a heaping dose of baby scent. I couldn't wait to cuddle my little boy.

CHAPTER 4: "LIVE LIFE. NO REGRETS."
KENNY

By mid-afternoon I pulled my car up to Patrick and Elaine's place in Wilmington. The eight-hour drive was exhausting, but dashing up the stairs, I couldn't wait to see everybody. Patrick had the door open before I'd even knocked twice.

"Hey, get in here." He kissed my head before heading back to the bar where he was working. "Elaine and Peanut ran to the store to get more supplies."

His back was to me, and for a moment, I took him in. His faded jeans were slung low on his slim hips and his green tee stretched across his broad shoulders. I dropped my overnight bag on the floor inside the door and walked over to where he was cutting onions, carrots, and potatoes into quarters.

"Digging the purple hair." He hooked a long strand over his pinky and tugged before going back to his work. "But you're still a bone. I'm making giant cheeseburgers, and I expect you to eat two."

"Either your memory is for shit or you never listen to me." I pecked his scruffy cheek, the warm, faintly citrus scent of him filling my nose before I hopped up onto the counter.

"What are you talking about? I always listen to you." He only paused a moment to squint at me then he dropped the knife and pulled out several long, bamboo skewers.

"I'm lactose intolerant, dumbass. You know this. Now hand me one of those."

"Well, shit." His tone was teasing, and he passed me a skewer. "I can still make you a plain burger. Of which you'll eat every bite."

"Sounds great! Just no bun. And no kebobs for me."

His lips pressed together as he moved the cutting board of vegetables between us. I grabbed a potato and speared it.

"That's your problem. Why no carbs?"

"I teach low-impact, strength-training classes. Protein is what I need. Look how bulked up I am!" Pulling back my sleeve with my pinkie, I flexed my bicep proudly. I'd never had muscles before.

He shook his head. "I've seen bigger lumps in Lane's oatmeal."

"What the hell!" I kicked his thigh. "Don't give my baby lumpy oatmeal!"

"Ow!" He laughed, which made me laugh.

"Just because you're all Mr. Muscles."

"Muscles need fuel. You need to eat right." He grinned, and for a moment, we only slid vegetables onto bamboo spears. I didn't feel like old arguments.

"So what's going on?" He finished his and moved around me to wash his hands then leaned against the counter still holding the towel. "You usually plan your weekend visits on Monday, not Friday night. Want to talk about it?"

I finished my kebob and reached for the towel to clean my hands. In the time it took to do so, my eyes went from his light brown hair touched with the faintest caramel highlights to his smoky hazel eyes. Patrick was so good-looking. *Why didn't I feel more for him?*

"I dunno." I hesitated, feeling just the slightest bit nervous. "I haven't been myself lately. I feel like something's wrong with me."

"Like what? You sick?"

"No," I said, crossing my arms. Now I wished I hadn't brought it up.

"Then what's this about? What's on your mind?"

Squinting my eyes closed, I thought about the pressure in my chest, about how it was so hard to take a deep breath. I thought about Patrick and me, and why a no-good punk in a magazine captured my attention when this sunny, Captain America didn't.

"I feel like somehow I'm destined to make bad choices. I mean, I'll get these opportunities, and then it's like I run away or screw them up somehow." Hopping down, I walked to the table, my back to him. "Like just for example, why didn't I stay with you? You were sweet to me, and we had great chemistry. Why did I run?"

He walked over to where I stood, and I turned to study his thoughtful face. "It's probably because you knew, deep down inside, that if you'd stayed with me, you'd be in jail right now."

"Dammit, Patrick!" I punched him hard—left jab to the shoulder.

"Shit," he laughed, rubbing the spot. "You really are bulking up! What was that for?"

"I thought you were being serious." My brows pinched. "I need you to be serious for once."

"I'm serious as a fuckin' heart attack. If we'd stayed together, with how we both are... you'd have ended up sticking a fork in my head or something."

Even though he was joking, I knew he was right, and it felt like a huge weight off my shoulders. "It's only because you're ridiculously sunny all the time. If you weren't so obnoxiously good-looking, we wouldn't even have Lane."

"I guess that's a compliment." He leaned back against the table, crossing his arms and giving me The Smile. *Panty-melter.* "So why the sudden attack of self-doubt?"

"I don't know." Rubbing my stomach, I started to pace. "Back then, I was so afraid of being disloyal to Blake's memory. I felt like if I even acknowledged a man was attractive, I was somehow cheating on him. When I slept with you, I thought I'd die for hurting him like that."

"I remember." His voice grew quiet. "But Ken, Blake is dead."

"I know!" Pushing my hands into the sides of my hair, my mind went to last night and my experience with the box. "Yesterday I was looking at his things—at our things—and it was the first time I could do it without breaking down. I'm scared of what that means, Patrick."

He exhaled deeply, and for a few minutes he only stood there, rubbing the back of his neck. "Like what? That you could have feelings for someone else?"

"No." I was still figuring it out myself, but I pushed on. "I think, maybe I'm scared… like even if I don't feel the pain anymore, I still remember how bad it hurt to lose him. I can't go through that again."

"Why would you have to?"

My chin dropped, and a curtain of dark purple slid over my cheek. Strong arms were around me at once, pulling me against his chest. His chin rested on my head as he stroked my back. "Love is a risk, babe."

"If I'd stayed with you it would've been easy. I was safe, and we had Lane..."

"Now you're fucking with your own head. You don't like safe, and you don't love me."

I stepped away from him, embarrassed. "I do..." *Just not like that.*

"Look at me." He caught my shoulders, and I lifted my chin. "You made the right call. You knew it then, and you know it now. We would've eventually killed each other."

I tried not to laugh, but I couldn't help it. He was right.

"What's worse is I wouldn't have Elaine, and she is perfect for me. Just like there's someone out there perfect for you."

"If I don't manage to screw it all up."

"Don't." His voice was calm, a direct order.

"Don't." I repeated. "Just like that."

"Just like that. Don't borrow trouble, and don't go looking for it. Put one foot in front of the other and stay open to what might happen."

My lips pressed together as I thought about it. "And if I ruin everything again?"

"You won't ruin anything. You couldn't. When you find him, he'll be right in every way. No forks needed." He caught my hand and held it. "Will you try?"

The smallest hint of a smile tugged at the corner of my mouth, and I nodded. "I'll try."

At that exact moment, the door burst open and a tiny, golden tornado blustered straight at me. "Mommy!"

I dropped to a squat just as chubby arms flew around my neck, filling every part of me with roaring love and happiness.

"Peanut!" I cried, as he hit me with such force, I sat back on my ass.

"I couldn't get him out of his car seat fast enough." Elaine laughed as she put two bags on the counter. Patrick had gone to meet her, and she kissed him on the lips briefly, still talking. "He kept squealing 'Mommy!' like there was no tomorrow."

I hugged Lane tighter, kissing his little neck and burying my nose in his sweet baby scent that always soothed whatever was bothering me.

"Mommy," he said, patting the sides of my head, his baby blue eyes filled with wonder. "Purple."

"That's right!" I stood, hauling him up with me. "Mommy's hair is purple. You like it?"

"I love it!" Elaine had just finished pouring him a sippy cup.

"Mommy." He reached for her, and she handed it to him. She was as beautiful as ever dressed in a simple white tank and jeans, her straight blonde hair hanging loose down her back.

Patrick sidled up behind her, sliding his hands around her waist. "How long before Lane can say he has two mommies?"

Her eyes narrowed as her elbow shot back into his stomach. "Shut up."

"Hot," Patrick mouthed with a wink, but I only shook my head, hugging my little boy.

"Wish I could get away with crazy colors at school." Elaine was back in the kitchen, unpacking the bags.

Lane pulled the cup away with a smack and plunged a chubby hand into my hair. "Purple," he said again.

"You are so smart! You know your colors." Rubbing my nose against his, I carried him over to the table, glancing back just in time to see Patrick kissing Elaine's neck as she put the groceries away.

If I ever doubted staying with his daddy was the absolute best choice for Lane, seeing the two of them together always erased it. Here he had a stable home with two people who loved each other as much as him. I was still trying to figure my shit out, and I earned just enough money to cover my bills. It was hard, but this way I could see him as often as possible, and it felt like I had a family, too.

"Why don't you guys go out tonight?" I called back. "I'll stay home with Lane, and you can have a date night."

Patrick was saying something low to Elaine, but he stopped to yell at me. "You'll do anything to get out of a decent meal."

"I'll have my dinner with Lane."

He finished whatever he was saying, and her eyebrows rose before she hopped over to where I was sitting on the couch.

"I have a better idea. Let's have a girls' night!"

My brow lined, and I couldn't help being suspicious. "I don't know. I didn't really bring anything for going out."

"Are you kidding? We're in Wilmington. It's completely casual. We'll just go to one of the little bars and have some girl talk and flirt."

"Hey!" Patrick called from the kitchen.

"Kenny will flirt." She shouted back. "Mel and I will merely judge her choices. It will be a very judgy evening."

Squeezing my baby closer, my initial impulse was to say no, but I caught sight of Patrick's encouraging face. I *had* just promised him I'd try.

"But I came here to see Lane." It was a weak last attempt, and my little boy was already resting his head on my shoulder.

"He'll be asleep before we leave the house," Elaine said, rubbing his back. "You're staying in his room, right? You can snuggle with him in the morning, too."

With a deep exhale, I surrendered.

* * *

Derek Alexander met us at the door dressed in a navy tee and jeans with a tiny infant perched on his shoulder. His muscles stretched his shirtsleeves, yet he was so careful with his little son—I silently acknowledged few things were sexier than the sight of a giant man cuddling a baby.

"Hey, Elaine. Kenny." He pulled my companion into a hug, but I hung back.

It wasn't only because he was ridiculously gorgeous. He was also the man Carl had gone to for help. The night I lost Blake, Carl also lost his little brother Max. It was a bar brawl, and the prosecution needed help building their case against the killers.

As a private investigator, Derek agreed to help us *pro bono*, which was a fancy way of saying *free*, and Carl always said it was because of Derek his brother got justice. I'd only met him once, because I wasn't able to attend the trial. I'd pretty much fallen apart after Blake died, and it took a month before I even had the will to crawl out of bed. I'd heard the beginnings of what had happened that night and thrown up. After that, I didn't want to know anymore—I just wanted it gone.

Carl sort-of adopted me as a little sister. He took care of me, bringing me food and even giving me a job when I was finally able to get on my feet again. I was eternally grateful to him and to this man standing in front of us for getting me through one of the toughest times in my life.

"Look at Dex," Elaine cooed, taking the infant from his daddy's arms. The dark-haired baby rooted into her neck but didn't wake, and I watched as Derek rubbed his little back, eyes brimming with love.

He was like this gorgeous, giant mountain of perfectness, and my stomach was so tight, I couldn't even face him to say Thank You.

All I could manage was a quiet, "He's really cute." I blinked quickly to meet Derek's intense blue eyes and then away just as fast. "How old is he?"

"Six months, next Tuesday." His voice was deep and soothing, and while it was difficult to hold eye contact with him, I could tell he was an amazing dad from the way he touched that little guy.

Melissa breezed into the room, and his expression changed again. The look that passed between them was enough to make anyone envious.

"You're sure you'll be okay here without me?" She smiled, rising on her tiptoes to kiss his lips.

Derek leaned forward and swept her into a huge hug. "Yes, now get out of here and have some fun with your friends."

She laughed, squeezing his massive arms. "You make it sound like it's such a prison sentence being here."

A low rumble, and she took Dex from her friend's arms. "Goodnight, my love," she whispered before kissing his baby ear and carefully handing him back to Derek. "Let me know if he wakes up or cries or *anything.*"

"He'll be fine." Derek cuddled his little boy. "Now go before I change my mind."

His eyes twinkled, and I knew he was teasing. Regardless, Melissa hesitated until Elaine grabbed her by the wrist.

"Good lord, you two are going to drive me crazy. Enough with all the hermit behavior." She dragged her friend out the door with Melissa still glancing back at her gorgeous husband and darling infant.

Following, I couldn't even criticize her. I remembered when Lane was that age. He'd stayed with me at first because I was nursing him, and I didn't want to leave him for anything. Of course, I didn't have any reason to leave him—he was all I had.

"He'll only be an infant once," Melissa argued, going slowly to the car. "I can't help it if I hate to leave him."

"I know how you feel," I said giving her a smile. "I understand it a lot."

Her blue eyes met mine, and she ducked, crinkling her nose. "I'm sure Elaine's right, though. It's good to get out of the house."

The Dancing Gypsy was a small place with beaded curtains and colorful accents. A stage was in one corner and a bar in the other. Several wooden, diner-style booths were peppered around the room. I ordered a cosmopolitan while Elaine had a margarita. Melissa got a glass of white wine.

It didn't take long to get our orders—the place was pretty empty. Still, we were decked out. Elaine had changed into a bright red top over her jeans, while I'd pulled on khaki jeggings and a long-sleeved black tunic. Melissa wore a sleeveless black dress with a fun, flippy skirt and heels.

"I really shouldn't drink, since I've got to feed Dex," she apologized, taking a small sip from her glass.

"And now you're done!" Elaine used best teacher voice. "No more baby talk! It's a Saturday night, Kenny's getting laid, and you're having nothing but adult conversation."

My mouth dropped open, and Melissa burst out laughing. "I got the better end of that deal!"

Glancing around the room, I couldn't help agreeing with her. The place was pretty empty, and it didn't look to be filling up anytime soon. Even less encouraging, I was pretty sure the elderly couple in the back corner ordered waffles.

"Get talking, Jones," Elaine continued. "We'll figure out the guy situation when the lights go down."

"Define adult conversation." Melissa sipped her wine. "Vajazzling? Penis rings? Prince Alberts?"

"I knew a guy with a Prince Albert." I lifted my drink as Elaine bounced in the seat beside me.

"*Now* we're having a girls' night! What did it feel like?"

She caught me mid-sip, and I almost snorted vodka up my nose. "It was my boss," I coughed, and her eyes grew wider. "No! I mean, I didn't see it or sleep with him or anything. Carl at the tattoo place was licensed to do piercings. I knew he had one."

"What a letdown that story was!" Elaine flopped back against the booth and frowned at me before licking the salt off her glass. "I would love to try sex with metal."

"If you convince Patrick to impale his peen, I'll... I'll—"

"Don't say anything too outrageous." Elaine took a big gulp of margarita.

"Get him convinced, and I'll figure out something," her friend finished.

I attempted not to snarfle as I sipped my cosmo. The waiter appeared, and Elaine waved her finger in a circle over our heads. "Another round for the table!" Then she turned back to her friend, green eyes narrowed. "You'd better think fast, Jones. Patrick is refreshingly open-minded. As opposed to some people I know."

"I know you're not talking about Derek." Melissa sipped her wine, eyebrows raised. "There is nothing wrong with my man."

I could believe that. Elaine gulped the last of her margarita. "You know who I'm talking about, and he isn't Derek."

"It takes a really long time to heal," I jumped in.

"How long are we talking?" Elaine rested her head on her hand as the waiter placed drinks in front of all of us.

I lifted mine and took another sip, shaking my head. "Depends, but at least two months."

"Two months!" She flopped back against the booth again. "Kenny, you are officially the little black cloud at the party."

My face fell, but Melissa laughed. "You are such a pill! She can't help it if you're a nympho."

"My friend Mariska would love this place," I tried, going for a more optimistic topic. "I bet it gets really busy... at some point."

Melissa laughed more and rested her forehead on her hand. "I'm sorry," she said with a sniff. "It really doesn't."

Elaine's eyes narrowed, and she turned to me. "Hey! Are you still doing tattoos?"

"Oh, yes!" Her friend sat up. "I would love to get something with Derek and Dex's names or birthdates. Help me think of something."

Tracing my finger around the rim of my glass, I thought of last night. "I've still got my license, but I don't have the equipment. "

"Well, shit." Melissa frowned. "I loved what you did with Patrick's ink."

I smiled up at her. Melissa was really nice to me, but I'd never been certain of Elaine's feelings. She seemed okay with Patrick's and my past, but it was hard to tell.

"You have mine." Melissa slid her second wine glass across the table. "I'm the designated driver, and with Dex nursing, I—"

"Baby talk!" Elaine held up a hand then she leaned into my ear. "Don't worry. Once the band starts, they'll dim the lights and this place will get crazy. Ish."

My eyes drifted to the elderly couple now eating waffles in the back corner. "I can't wait."

At that moment Elaine squealed, "Ow!" and I almost spilled my cosmo. "That's my leg, thanks!"

Melissa's eyes were round, and she shot forward, leaning against the table, her mouth partially covered with her hand. "Brrnnn. Twrrrf o'crock."

"What?" Elaine's voice was too loud, but it was too late.

A tall, nice-looking guy with brown hair and eyes stopped at our booth, and her body went rigid. Standing next to him was a shorter fellow with floppy brown hair and dark eyes that drifted over each of us, pausing on me. He wore a green tee, and I could see a little ink peeking from under both shirtsleeves. *Interesting.*

"Hi, Elaine." The tall guy said. "You look great as always."

Melissa's eyes were on her wine glass, and she fiddled her fingers along the base. She seemed to be holding her breath, which made the muscles in my stomach clench uncomfortably. *Why were they both freaking out?*

"Hello, Brian." Elaine's whole demeanor had changed, and her voice was cool and controlled. "I hope you're not planning on causing another scene."

"I said I was sorry for that." Brian's eyes went from us to sweeping the room. "I was a little drunk, but I've accepted that you've moved on... still?"

"That's right. I have." Elaine was ticked, but when I glanced at the shorter guy again, he was smiling at me. He was cute, so I gave him a little smile back.

"This is my cousin Gabe. He's new in town and wanted to come over and say Hi. He works at the body shop with Ed."

Melissa's chin snapped up, and she seemed to be inspired. "Hi, Gabe, I'm Melissa. You know Elaine, I'm sure, and this is our friend Kenny."

"Hi, Kenny." His tenor voice was shy, which I decided was cute. A tatted-up shy guy was something new to me.

Smiling, I pushed a strand of purple behind my ear. "Hi."

Elaine's expression changed as well, and whatever issue she had with Brian was forgotten. As if on cue, a tall, slender girl with gorgeous, spiraled black hair and bohemian clothes took the stage followed by two guys similarly dressed and carrying guitars. The lights dimmed, and the girl started singing in a voice like silk. Elaine jumped out of the booth, grabbing my arm and pulling me right behind her.

"Come on, Gabe!" she shouted over the music. "Let's dance!"

Gabe appeared as stunned as his cousin, and I couldn't help laughing—the two cosmopolitans helped. Perhaps my brain was taking the night off? I followed Elaine out to the floor, where she started twisting her hips to the sultry rhythm. Her silky, blonde hair swished over her shoulders, and Melissa shook her head, smiling into her wine glass and keeping her seat.

I followed Elaine's lead, swaying to the beat of the exotic music. The song was something about meeting a guy in the desert, and it didn't take long for Gabe to come up behind me and hold my waist as we moved together, facing the band.

He was shorter than most guys I knew, and in my purple stacks, his mouth was right at my ear when he spoke. "I like your hair."

The vibration of his voice tingled my skin, and I turned to face him. His hands were still on my waist, so I put mine on his shoulders and studied his dark eyes, blinking to mine and occasionally catching the colorful lights from the stage.

"Thanks," I said and smiled.

We couldn't really talk over the music, so we just danced. I thought about what Mrs. Clarkson said about my heart versus my head. I thought about my conversation with Patrick today and my feelings last night with the box. I thought about my feelings right this minute, and I realized I didn't feel a thing—no guilt, no fear. Sorry, Gabe, still no attraction, but it didn't matter. It was over! I wanted to laugh and spin around. I was free!

Tonight, I wasn't Blake's widow or the runaway who'd taken a chance on love and lost. Or even the careless dropout who'd gotten drunk and pregnant with a guy she didn't love. I was just a girl in a silly club dancing with a cute, shy, inked-up mechanic.

The song changed to a faster tempo, and everyone started jumping around us. Brian walked up and tried to dance with Elaine, but she left the floor, going back to where Melissa sat. I didn't care, I wanted to jump around, too. It was like a celebration in a way. I was enjoying myself, and I wasn't buried in an avalanche of guilt. I was dancing again, and I loved it.

Gabe's smile grew bigger, and we twisted around in front of each other, occasionally bumping hips. At some point, he caught my wrist and pulled me closer.

"Would you go out with me Friday?" His dark eyes glowed with interest, and I hated what I had to tell him — he'd done such a great job losing his shyness.

I made a wistful face. "I'm so sorry, Gabe, I live in Bayville."

His brow creased. "What?" He shouted over the music.

"Bayville!" I said louder in his ear. "It's in New Jersey. I'm only visiting."

Leaning back, our eyes caught, and the side of his mouth went down. I shrugged and then leaned forward again. "But you're really cute. Thanks for dancing with me."

The song was ending, and he caught my chin before I pulled away. "You're really beautiful. Let me know next time you're in town."

Chewing my lip, I smiled and agreed before taking off back to our booth.

Elaine was swaying in her seat, and Melissa slid toward me. "He was really cute."

I picked up my drink and polished off the last few sips, my whole body buzzing with happiness. "He really was. Too bad I'm heading home in the morning."

We stayed an hour longer, dancing occasionally; Elaine and I having one drink more until Melissa called it. Her blue eyes were tired, and I remembered how the early days with babies were — exhausting.

I grabbed my bag just as Elaine swerved up with her margarita. "We've got to get you laid! What happened to Sage?"

I snorted then, and Melissa shouted over the music. "Gabe! And it's time to head home."

"What did I say?" Elaine looked at me confused.

"Sage," I said, unable to stop laughing. I couldn't help it—I was buzzed and giddy.

She laughed, too. "That's not even close!"

Melissa gave us a push, and we made our way to the exit. An overwhelming feeling of freedom had me floating on air, and I held Elaine's arm. "Thank you." I could see her confused expression as I continued. "For being so cool about everything and so sweet to Lane and for taking me out. It's been an amazing night."

She shrugged, looking at her feet as we walked. "I love Lane. He's Patrick's baby boy."

"I know, and it's so cool. You've never been angry with me or resentful."

Her lips tightened. "I was resentful. And pretty angry with you, too."

I stopped walking, the high I'd just been on plunging straight into the gravel. She continued a few steps toward the car and then stopped when she realized I wasn't with her.

Melissa cleared her throat softly, but didn't say anything. I got the feeling she was waiting to see what might happen next.

"I-I'm so sorry." I was such an idiot. Of course she hated me—I'd had Patrick's baby and nearly broken them up. Now I had the nerve to show up unexpectedly at her house.

But she wasn't finished. "Then after Lane was born, and you asked me to keep him, it was like everything changed."

I studied her face, waiting, unsure what to say.

Her brow relaxed, and a tiny smile appeared. "Lane is the sweetest little thing, and he looks so much like Patrick. How could I not love him? It's still hard sometimes, but I know Patrick loves me."

"I would never come between you and Patrick." I wanted to cry, and I meant every word. "I don't feel that way towards him. I don't know why, but I don't."

She exhaled a laugh. "I believe you. I can't say I understand you, but everything about Patrick says he loves me. I love him, and I love Lane."

Melissa suddenly charged forward, catching us both in a hug. "Oh, you two!" She cried. "It's so good to clear the air finally!"

The *finally* made my face burn with shame. I'd been so self-absorbed. "I'm so sorry, Elaine. I won't come here ever again without your permission, and I—"

"Stop it!" Elaine shook her head and put her arm over my shoulder. "That would be terrible for Lane, and like I said, it's getting better all the time."

My chin dropped, but she gave me a little squeeze. "Friends?"

"Of course!"

The rest of the way back, the windows were down and the music up. Melissa and Elaine discussed the appearance and disappearance of Brian, who apparently was Elaine's ex-boyfriend and lost his shit when she started dating Patrick. Mel dropped us at the condo, promising to bring Elaine's car back tomorrow, and we whispered goodnight before I slipped quietly into Lane's room, over to where he slept sideways in his crib.

Resting my chin on the back of my hand, I reached down and slid a lock of soft blond hair off his little forehead. He sat up at once, causing me to jump, but his eyes were still closed. With an exhaled laugh, I gathered him into my arms, going to the small bed on the other side of the room and crawling beneath the sheets with him in my arms. Three breaths of snuggly, baby scent, and my body relaxed completely into sleep.

CHAPTER 5: "CHANGE IS THE ONLY CONSTANT."
SLAYDE

Breakers crashed on the sandy shore, and every day the air grew a little cooler. The one-room studio apartment I was able to afford had the sole perk of being close to the beach. Make that two perks — the double bed was comfortable.

Inside, a track with hooks ran along the ceiling, so I hung a curtain to separate the sleeping half from the living half of the square I now called home. At two-fifty a month, I couldn't complain, and I was used to smaller quarters these days.

Walking along the shore before work, I thought of Doc's advice to take it one day at a time. It was a good system, even if I wasn't an alcoholic. No pressure, positive. My hands were shoved in the pockets of the same jeans I'd worn since I arrived in Bayville. Next payday, I'd have to buy another pair. Then I'd have the start of a wardrobe.

For now, I stood watching the waves hit the shore with all their force. The strike sent my mind reeling into the past, to the few bright years of luxury, the days when I was on top. As a rising star, I had the best rooms at every hotel, a different girl in every city, and designers sent me clothes for free. All they wanted was for me to walk around wearing them.

A low burning in the pit of my stomach brought me back to reality. Those days were long gone. I was living in the real world now, and I had to get used to it. I repeated my personal mantra: *This is my life now.*

Heavy black boots waited for me at the edge of the boardwalk, and I reached inside to pull out one of three pairs of socks I owned. I'd have to buy more of those as well—and underwear. For now I usually went commando.

Walking back, I climbed into the beat-up, rusty truck I'd managed to purchase. It took the last of my money, but I needed transportation. Cheap white bread and even cheaper generic peanut butter would have to get me to payday. If anything else came up, I'd get creative.

Doc had a saying for starting over: *Change is the only constant.* For me, change was not only constant, it was good. If it weren't for change, where would I be?

Rook was alone at the gym when I pulled into the parking lot. It was Saturday, my first full day on the job. I went inside and made my way straight to the supply closet when the scent of eggs, cheese, and sausage assaulted my nose.

My mouth instantly watered, and I gripped the door handle, waiting for the dull ache of hunger to release my midsection. I'd felt this way before, and I knew from experience to wait a few days. It would pass, my body would adjust to eating less.

The stinging scent of disinfectant erased the good smell of my boss's breakfast as I prepared the mop bucket, and I wheeled it out and started down the hall toward the women's locker room when he stopped me.

"You're awfully early for a Saturday." I paused and looked back, but all my eyes could focus on was the last of what looked like a sausage biscuit in his hand.

"Yeah," I blinked and rubbed my midsection, looking down. "Figured I'd hit the women's locker room early like you said. Then I can take care of the men and be done mid-afternoon."

He nodded watching me. "We're only open a few hours on Sundays. It can be your day off."

"I can work a few hours." My eyebrows clutched, and I tried to meet his eye. But my stubborn gaze wouldn't go past his breakfast. Licking my dry lips, I forced my sight back to the bucket. "I need the money."

Rook didn't speak for a few moments. I couldn't tell why or what he was thinking, until he suddenly spoke. "I'll up your weekly pay to cover it. Everybody needs one day off."

I did meet his dark eyes then. "Thank you."

"Well, you'd better get busy. Sometimes the trainers come in early to exercise before it gets crowded. Mostly it's just Kenny, but still. She'll need the locker room when she's done."

He turned back to his office, and I took the bucket, guiding it through the large, open workout space and through the metal door. The locker room was large and empty. Showers were in the back behind a cinder-block wall, and small, beige lockers lined what was the dressing area. Benches filled the center, and sinks and large mirrors were around the perimeter. I tried not to look at myself as I pushed the mop.

I'd gotten skinny. The lines were still on my arms, but until I ate regularly, I wouldn't have muscle mass. My eyes were different, too — ice blue and slightly wild. I needed to work on my expression or I'd scare people.

Bending my arm, my bicep still peaked. The boxing gloves inked there extended past the bottom of my shirtsleeve—*Never Stop Fighting*. I wasn't sure how I felt about that phrase now. The bold *21* stood out on the side of my hand, and I made a fist, thinking of its meaning, the year my life changed.

A metal-door scrape grabbed my attention. Tammy pushed through it, and when she saw me, she stopped in her tracks. She was dressed in calf-length black pants and a skin-tight, hot-pink tank top. Her body was impressive, but I wasn't checking out the boss's wife. I wasn't checking out any women.

"Hey, Slayde is it?" Her tone was sharp, and it irritated me. But my days of being a badass were over. I was a fucking janitor now.

"Yes, ma'am?"

"For starters, don't you dare call me *ma'am* again." The smile in her voice made me glance up. "Second, you've got to put the signs up when you're in here. The yellow ones and the flag? We don't want the members complaining about a man in the ladies' room."

Rook hadn't mentioned anything about signs, but it made sense. I pushed the mop into the bucket. "Right. Sorry. If you'll tell me where they are—"

She let out a little growl and rolled her eyes. "I know, Rook forgot to tell you. He isn't the best when it comes to details. Follow me."

Back at the juice bar, a white bag in my cubby caught my eye. I didn't have time to investigate.

Tammy came out of the supply closet and pushed a plastic sign and a flag on a suction cup at me.

"Take this and this. Prop that on the floor and attach the suction cup to the door."

"Yes, ma…" I didn't finish, and she laughed. I started to head back to the locker room when she stopped me.

"There's something in your cubby you'd better get."

Stopping, I went back and pulled the white bag out. The scent of sausage, egg, and cheese again hit my nose as hard as a left jab. A note was taped to the outside: *Bought too much. Have my extra biscuit. – R.*

My brow creased, and I glanced up at Tammy, but she was loading ingredients into a blender. A guy the size of Rook probably ate five of these for breakfast. I didn't understand.

"You'd better hurry up before the ladies start showing up for Zumba," Tammy called without turning around.

I decided not to question it and carried the food back with me to the locker room. Flag on the door and sign in place, I pulled back the wrapper, and the minute that savory cheese, spicy sausage, and buttery egg hit my tongue, I leaned against the wall and let out a low groan. In three bites, it was gone.

* * *

Everything was cleaned and squared away by early afternoon, and I headed back to the front to return my key and check out. I'd done my best to avoid members, and I'd only passed a brief greeting to Pete, who seemed to be the only trainer working this weekend besides Tammy. He was nice enough, but I didn't take it any further.

A slender girl with light-brown hair pulled up in a long, messy ponytail was behind the bar now, and without even looking, I could feel her watching me closely.

"Hey." She spoke fast, like a short order cook. "It's Slayde, right? What brings you to The Jungle Gym?"

I was tired and hungry and not in the mood to answer questions, so I didn't.

Without looking up, I went to my slot, where I found another bag waiting for me. Pulling it out, I shoved my key in its place, catching another whiff of what smelled like food in the mystery package. I wanted to go to the truck and open it right away, but when I turned around, the girl was doing something with her hands.

My brow lined as I watched her. She waved her hands in a sweeping motion then circled one around her finger. The entire time her eyes bored into mine as if they were attempting to communicate silently.

"What are you doing?" My voice was husky from not talking all day.

She straightened, blinking fast, and her cheeks flushed slightly. "I was asking if you spoke sign language."

"Why would you ask me something like that?" I surveyed her appearance—long, tie-dyed smock over a white tank and jeans that were shredded at the knees. Around her neck were several necklaces in addition to the lanyard holding her key, and her fingers were covered in rings.

"You didn't answer when I spoke to you, so I thought maybe..." Her light-brown eyes traveled down to my throat. "I just finished this novel about a guy with no voice. It was really hot."

"I can speak just fine. I'm also tired and hungry. I've been here since seven, and I don't feel like answering twenty questions." Even that much explanation was pissing me off.

Her eyebrows rose, and she leaned forward on the bar, giving me a little smile. "I can make you a matcha-tea smoothie if you want. It's my newest specialty. Very relaxing and full of protein."

"I don't like smoothies." It was a lie. I didn't have money to pay for it.

"Oh, I'm a wizard at them. You'll love it." She leaned back and eyed me up and down. "I'm Mariska, by the way."

"I'll take a pass, Mariska. I'm heading out."

Her pink lips pressed together in a thin line. She was pretty. Hell, she was really pretty, but I wasn't interested in female drama, much less from a hippie-chick who spoke sign language.

"You're going to have to try one at some point. I'm here every day but Friday." She gave me a wink, but I kept going. "See you tomorrow!"

My truck waited for me like an old, rusty dinosaur in the parking lot. I didn't even bother to lock the door. If somebody wanted to steal this piece of shit, they got what was coming.

Sliding across the cracked vinyl seat, I lowered the visor and caught the silver keys as they fell. Opening the white sack, I found a bacon club. Fuck, it was like sex in a paper wrapper. I sat in that back parking lot and inhaled all of it in less than five minutes.

I knew what this meant—Rook had my number, but I didn't give a shit. I was hungry. I'd deal with the fallout later.

I didn't care to have Sundays off. I didn't have any money to do anything, so I basically milled around the box I called home looking for things to repair. After a while, I went down to the water in the only pair of shorts I owned and sat on the beach reading a crap paperback I'd found on the bus.

The book was called *Remembrance of Things Past*, and it was about two thousand pages long. It was boring as hell, but I stayed with it. I couldn't afford a television or even a radio, so I had to make do with what I had—some French kid worried about his mom kissing him goodnight. I couldn't even remember the last time I'd been kissed. *Shit*, like I even cared. I needed to find a better book.

When the sun was gone, I put it aside and listened to the waves hitting the shore as hard as I used to hit the bag. I looked down at my fists. People didn't understand boxing. They thought it was just idiot brutes punching each other's lights out, but it was more than that. It was choreography of the feet and hands. It was knowing when to hit your opponent and when to wait, when to wear them down and when to drive it all the way as hard as you could until they hit the mat. It was art.

Rubbing my face with both hands, I pushed those thoughts aside. I had to quit torturing myself with these fucking memories. I looked across the distance to a brightly lit bar. The music was soft, but it still reached me where I sat. Somewhere over there, people were having fun. They had lives to live. They would have love and adventure.

I, on the other hand, would put one foot in front of the other and stay out of trouble. What brought me to this town was the definite possibility of a very dull life.

From all the way across the shore the sound of a woman's laugh made it to my ears. I sat, looking back at it, thinking of what I'd lost. Until I finally called it a night and went home.

CHAPTER 6: "WHAT DOESN'T KILL US MAKES US STRONGER."
KENNY

For the first time in a while, I didn't wake up before my alarm on Monday. I still wanted to exercise, of course, but I didn't feel the driving urge to hit the bag like before. Calm had settled over me following the giddy happiness I'd found Saturday night. It was still with me, and it meant I was surviving the grief. I was making it through.

Yesterday, I'd stayed as long as I could with Lane, hugging his baby body, relaxing into his scent until I had to get in the car and drive back to Bayville. Elaine had been extra nice to me, and I figured she was feeling bad about her drunken reveal. Honestly, I was glad she'd said it. I was a lot more conscious of how I interacted with Patrick now, and I included her every chance I got.

Patrick had followed me out to the car he'd helped me buy. "Everything else okay back home? Rook treating you right?"

I squinted up at him holding my door as I tossed my stuff on the passenger's seat. "Yeah. I just wish he wasn't so horny all the time."

At that, Patrick completely changed—his fists clenched, brow lowered. "Is he sexually harassing you?"

"Oh my god, no! Not at all!" I grabbed the side of my hair. "It's more… he and his wife are sloppy with public decency laws, you know?"

"No." Patrick frowned as he watched me, still all riled up like my own personal guard dog.

Leaning forward, I dropped my voice. "I caught them having sex a few times."

"Oh." His shoulders relaxed. "Well, I can't hassle him for that."

"Patrick!" I punched his shoulder.

Elaine joined us smiling. "What did I miss?"

"Your fiancé was giving my boss a pass for having sex all over the gym."

"Oh, well..." Elaine looked down, and I rolled my eyes.

"You guys are too much. Still, I like this whole... crazy big-brother-bodyguard thing you're doing."

He pulled me into a quick hug. "You let me know if anybody doesn't treat you right."

"Thanks, Dad," I laughed, then turned to Elaine, holding out my hand. "And thank you again. For everything."

She stepped forward and gave me a squeeze. "You're welcome." Stepping back, she touched my chin, smiling. "You don't need a guard. You're doing great."

* * *

Mariska was waiting at the juice bar when I arrived at ten. It was later than I'd ever gone into work, but I didn't have a client until ten thirty. My best friend was dressed in a black bodysuit with a long, red handkerchief-print skirt wrapped around her waist. I was in my usual all-black trainer gear.

"Dammit, Ken!" She cried as I rounded the corner to get my key. "You just missed him! I've been holding my breath all morning… Oh! Love the purple hair!"

Nose curling, I put the lanyard around my neck and went to fix my not-disgusting green smoothie. "Thanks! I got the urge to change everything Friday. I actually think I might've done it, too. I didn't even feel like getting out of bed this morning!"

"Is that a good thing?" She bounced over to lean beside me on the bar as I threw in the simple ingredients followed by two cups of crushed ice. "Okay, that looks disgusting."

"It's really kind of sweet." The loud *WHIRR!* of the blender forced me to yell. "But yeah, I've been having trouble sleeping."

"You need a matcha shake," she shouted back. "It's a whole-leaf green tea I've been using in my newer smoothies. Full of antioxidants, protein…"

Nodding, I shouted. "After the kale regimen. Why are you holding your breath?" Her expression was confused, and I released the button, continuing in a normal tone. "You said you were holding your breath."

"Oh! Oh oh oh!!!" She bounced on her toes. "I'm so ticked at you, though."

I took a sip of the sweet concoction and smiled again. "Then I guess I'll never know."

"You're really happy today. It's weird. Did you get laid?"

I almost choked on green smoothie. "*Shh!* Jeez, there are members right over there." I nodded my head toward the open workout room.

She only passed a glance in their direction. "Well? Did you?"

"Sadly, no."

"Don't worry. The clock will be ticking on that problem once you see him... Only, *dammit!* Rook sent him on some overnight errand to Scranton."

Jerking her ponytail, I leaned forward. "What are you talking about?"

"The new guy Slayde! The one you never told me about."

"I never met him."

Her eyes sparkled. "He's not a trainer, he's like a maintenance-handyman-janitor-badboy-sexgod. Rook's got him doing all sorts of things, I guess 'cause he has a truck, and his aura is totally smokin-red-hot."

"Good for him." I took another big gulp, as she studied me. I could tell she was thinking, but I wasn't sure I wanted to know what.

"I think you're patronizing me. Anyway, he hardly ever speaks, and when he does it's usually something grumpy." She reached for my cup, and I handed it over. Taking a sip, her eyebrows rose. "That's really good. I need the recipe."

"It's on the notepad there. If you make it for anybody, you have to mention Veggi-Smooth. They donated the ingredients, and I'm not patronizing you. I can't wait to meet this maintenance-badboy-janitor-nontalking-sexgod."

She grinned. "Okay. But you *are* going out with me tomorrow night. You promised."

"Who goes out on a Tuesday night?"

"Everybody! There's this hot new bar that just opened on Water's Edge." She swept her long brown curls into a high ponytail. "We need to go there before it closes. You know Bayville can't support a place like that. By the way, *your* aura is as purple as your hair… although it's drifting toward red. You're going to get lucky."

My client, a new mother I was helping lose the baby weight, waved to me from the other side of the bar. She was fun, and I liked swapping baby stories with her.

I waved back, passing Mariska my smoothie. "Here, drink the rest. You know I love you, and I don't believe a bit of that aura shit."

"Tomorrow night. You wait. It's going to change everything."

* * *

The Cay was a brand new club that shined like a penny. Most of the dance clubs were in Toms River or Seaside Park, so it was a double bonus to have a place so close to home, even if Mariska predicted it would be closed in a month. I decided to live in hope. Inside, everything caught the light, from the new brass hardware behind the bar to the red vinyl on the barstools.

An enormous dance floor filled the center of the space, with disco lights and strobes bouncing off everything. Thick brass railings framed dancer cages suspended at the four corners of the floor, and a DJ booth was in the back center.

A second level housed rows of red-vinyl booths with small tables leading to balconies where patrons could look down on the floor below. It was impressively posh, and when we arrived at ten, it was steadily filling with Ocean County singles. It was also a far cry from the dusky, antique-beaded-curtain style of the Dancing Gypsy, which reminded me.

"Elaine took me to this amazing bar in Wilmington." I shouted over the thumping dance mix as I took a sip of my Tequila Sunrise. "It was called the Dancing Gypsy. You would've loved it."

"Sounds like it." Mariska took a long sip of her Mojito. Tonight she was dressed in a short-short black sheath with a long, sheer spider-web-patterned overlay and ankle boots. "But wait—you said Elaine? I thought you didn't think she liked you."

"*Ugh!*" I shouted. "I was right about that, but I think we're all good now."

I turned my back to the bar and surveyed the crowd. I wore a short, smoky-blue dress with mile-high black stilettoes. A few potentially dateable males were scattered around the room, and I loved the return of my feelings of freedom. It had been so long since I'd gone out dancing with a friend and enjoyed myself without being wracked by guilt.

"You have *got* to tell me what happened this weekend, but first we need to enjoy this place." I noticed Pete enter the club with two other guys. They were all dressed in jeans and short-sleeve polos, and they all went in different directions once they got inside.

Leaning into her ear, I spoke just over the music. "Heads up—Pete just walked in the door."

Her lips pressed together, and we both turned to face the bar, moving our heads close together. "Did he see us?"

"Don't know, but I'm thinking we're kind of hard to miss. It isn't that crowded yet." I couldn't resist teasing her. "I bet Pete's *loving* your crush on the new guy."

Straightening up to face me, she shook her head, eyes round. "Oh, no. It's not a crush at all." I frowned, but she continued. "I mean, Slayde's definitely doable, and you know I love the wounded ones."

"But?" I took the last pull from my drink as the bartender placed Number 2 in front of me.

"I like my injured ones sweet." She took another hit of mojito while I paid for my second Tequila Sunrise. "Slayde seems like more of a biter."

Snorting, I shook my head as I sipped my drink. "You probably said something about his aura, and it ticked him off."

"It's not true! I think I ticked him off when I tried speaking sign language to him."

"What?!"

A swirl of warmth to my left, and Pete was with us, smiling down at Mariska. "Hey, sexy. I didn't know you were going to be here tonight."

The desire in his voice almost killed my buzz, considering what I knew about his chances. It was a shame, too, because Pete was hot—tall, muscular, with light brown hair and nice eyes.

"Hey, Pete, I'm going to dance," I said, ignoring Mariska's variety of facial expressions trying to get me to stay.

"Hey, Ken," he called after me. "Like the hair."

I did a little wave over my shoulder and plunged right into the sea of gyrating bodies. The DJ was playing loud dance music, and I closed my eyes letting it wash over me and take me out on a sea of techno. It wasn't long before I felt the warmth of a body behind me. Glancing over my shoulder, I met a perfectly white smile in a tanned face.

His eyes were a little hard to make out because of the brim of his cap, but he wore a black tank that showed off all his muscles and ink. He was straight-up sexy.

Turning to face him, I noticed he was wearing jeans and a loose gold watch on one arm. My eyes went back to his face. Bad-boy grin. I could work with this.

He leaned forward near my cheek. "I've been watching you all night. You're like a pixie with that hair."

Lifting my chin, my voice was coy. "Would that make you Peter Pan?"

His sexy grin grew a little bigger across his face, and large hands moved to my waist, pulling me closer. We were moving against each other now. It felt good, and I slid my hands up to his shoulders. He smelled good, like that after-shave everybody wears. Lemony. The song changed, and we kept dancing, our bodies rubbing together in a delicious way.

"I'm Grif. Or Griffin, whichever you prefer."

I leaned forward so that my lips touched the skin of his ear. "You live around here?"

When I moved back for his answer, I saw his eyes sweep my body.

"Nah, I'm just passing through. But maybe I'll be back."

The idea of traveling, just leaving everything behind and going, felt so seductive right now. "What do you do?"

"I'm in sales." His hands moved up my ribs, and when they slid back down, his thumbs drifted across my stomach, sending a tingle through my core to my toes.

It was hot, and I was starting to feel sweaty, but I didn't want to stop dancing. I took a big gulp of my drink instead. The song changed again, and a guy came up beside us.

Grif's head snapped toward him. "Get lost."

I didn't like his tone, and somewhere thorough the haze of my tequila-soaked brain, it nudged a little trigger of caution. I chose to ignore it. *Check out, brain!* I was dancing with a hot guy with nice hands and a nice smile, and I wanted to taste those lips.

Mariska appeared out of nowhere to dance beside us. She leaned into my ear. "You okay here?" Wobbling back up, she looked straight into my eyes.

"Yeah!" My voice was maybe a bit too high. "I'm having fun. Thanks for taking me out tonight!"

She gave me a squeeze and started dancing with both hands over her head. I turned back to smile at Grif and caught his eyes moving over her body as well. I didn't like the way he was checking her out, but at the same time, Mariska was a beautiful girl. Guys would be brain dead if they didn't notice. I didn't want to be with any brain dead guys. That made me laugh, and a third Tequila Sunrise magically appeared in my hand. I took a big gulp, and one of my favorite dance mixes came on. I jumped up and down squealing, only spilling my drink a little, when I noticed Pete was back.

He was so good-looking. He caught my friend's hand, and I saw the way she blinked up at him. I wasn't sure what number mojito she was on, but it looked like Pete might make it to third base tonight. Eight more beats, and he was leading her off to the side.

"It's hot." Grif's loud voice jerked me back to where I was. He was lifting the front of his black tank and fanning it out in front of him, giving me a little peak at a nice six-pack. "Want to go down to the water and cool off?"

"Umm…" I scanned the club for Mariska. We had a standing deal never to leave any club without alerting each other. "I need to let my friend know where I am."

He smiled with those perfect teeth. "We won't be gone long. I doubt she'll even miss us."

He was probably right. I nodded, and took the large hand he offered me, following him out the back door and to the patio area. A wide staircase led straight down into the sand, and he caught my hand, leading me toward the water.

We started walking south, away from the club and toward the dim lights of Bayville. I let out a little noise with my exhale. "Whew! That is the most fun I think I've ever had in this town."

I laughed, but Grif was strangely quiet. We kept walking a little ways, listening to the sound of the surf rolling in gently tonight, the dull thud of bass thumping softer behind us. I paused and reached down to remove my black stilettoes. When I did, I noticed a smaller, thin man was following us at a distance. Something about the way he looked made my stomach clench, but I tried to cover.

"So you're a salesman? What do you sell?" They were the only words I got out before he grabbed me by the shoulders and shoved me against the sand.

I tried to scream, but his mouth covered it. His hands were moving fast, ripping my skirt up and my panties down. Panic hit me hard, and all I could think to do was pull my knee up as fast as I could right into his groin.

He was late to block me, but I didn't land a disabling strike. Still, it rolled him off long enough for me to pull my body to the side and crawl as fast as I could away from him.

"Let me GO!" I screamed, my voice ragged and hoarse.

He was right behind me, catching the back of my thigh and stopping my escape. I screamed again as loud and as long as I could, but we were too far from the club for anyone to hear me. Even if we were closer, I doubted anyone would notice over the loud thump of the dance music.

"Shut up, you little bitch." He grabbed my mouth as he climbed up my body from behind. "Stop fighting and you just might enjoy yourself."

His mouth was right at my ear, and I tried slamming my head back as hard as I could, going for his nose. He dodged the blow, and I only fell backwards onto his shoulder.

Shoving me forward, his thigh wedged between my legs, and my face jammed in the sand. I screamed again, trying not to inhale the grains that would choke me.

"STOP!" I screamed, but my voice cracked, and I sounded more like a child than a woman.

His fingers were inside me, and I screamed, pulling my knees under me and pushing my ass straight up, hoping to knock him off-balance. It didn't work. He only held my waist against his erection. I could feel it straining to be inside me.

"Yeah, that's right." His voice was a low growl.

I was at the end of my rope. That little candle of happiness so recently lit inside me was crushed out. *How was this happening to me?* I started to cry, flailing my arms any way I could until he pinned them against my sides.

I screamed again, but my voice was almost gone. "You'll be sorry!" I sobbed. "My big brother is military. He'll track you down and rip your throat out. Then he'll shove it up your ass."

I struggled to twist against his arms, but he was too strong. A voice jolted me. It was the thin man who'd been following. "Grif, maybe you should let her go."

He only paused, still holding my back against his chest in a vice grip. "Are fucking kidding me? Get the fuck out of here so I can nail this bitch."

I screamed again, but his large hand covered my mouth. "Stop screaming, pixie. I just want a little of your sugar."

My voice was now a whimper broken by sobs. "Please stop. Please." I'd done everything I knew to do, and I'd lost. He was going to take what he wanted, and there was no way I could stop him.

He jerked my thighs open, and my head dropped forward, eyes closed. Every muscle in my body braced for his invasion. Just then I heard the faint squeak of feet on damp sand. A loud *CRACK!* was right at my ear, and my attacker's grip loosened.

Another *CRACK!* and his fingers roughly jerked my arms as he dropped to the sand, flat on his back. I fell forward on my hands and knees, shaking. It was dark, but I could make out a slim male figure standing over Grif, breathing fast.

I kept crawling until I was several feet away before I turned to look. The thin man was nowhere to be seen, but the new guy was fixed in the spot where he stood. His fists clenched and unclenched, over and over, and a low sound like growling whispered through his lips with each labored breath. It was as if an internal battle was playing out in front of me.

Carefully, I helped myself rise on wobbly legs. My shoes were lost in the darkness along with my panties, and my dress was torn. I took a few, hesitant steps toward the man standing over my attacker. I was only holding on by a thread and ready to run as hard as I could back to Mariska.

"Thank you," I managed, my voice broken.

My words seemed to break the spell, and the guy staggered back. He turned to me, but I could barely see his face between my tears and the dim light.

"Are you okay?" His voice was as shaken as mine.

I nodded, unable to stop trembling. "You… you saved me."

He was taller than me, and he had on knee-length shorts and a white tee that caught the light. He rubbed his stomach and leaned forward slightly. Then he coughed and took a deep breath, digging in his pocket.

"Do you need to call your brother?"

Confusion was my first response. "I don't have a brother." Then I remembered my failed last attempt at escape. "That was a bluff."

He took a careful step toward me. "I need to go. Is there anyone you can call?"

The asshole in the sand groaned. "*Shit*," my savior whispered under his breath. "Can you make it back—"

Just then I heard my name being yelled from the direction of the bar. I looked up to see Mariska in the distance heading our way fast, and behind her was what had to be Pete. Turning to the guy, our eyes met, and I had the strangest urge to rush forward and hide in his arms. I didn't even know who he was, and he was clearly unglued over what had happened here. Maybe I was in shock, but I wished he would touch me, hold me. He saved my life.

"Those are my friends," I said quietly. "I'll be okay now."

He nodded. "Good." His hand went up, palm facing me as he backed away. "Go to them."

"What's your name?" I asked, but my voice was lost in the pounding of the surf and the swirl of the ocean breeze around us as he ran, leaving me there on the shore alone.

Slowly, I turned toward Mariska, but I jumped when I saw the thin man had returned. He was helping a moaning Grif onto his knees and glaring at me.

"Stupid bitch!" he spat. "You set him up, you fuckin' cock tease. I watched you dancing with him, rubbing your ass all over his dick. Was that your boyfriend?"

Shudders racked my chest, and I didn't even answer. *This wasn't my fault!* For a moment, all I could do was blink at him like an idiot. Then I started running away from them, in the direction of Mariska and Pete. *Bastard, horrible fucking bastard.* I just wanted to get away as fast as my legs would carry me.

When I finally reached my friends, I collapsed into Mariska's arms. "Take me home," I cried against her shoulder. "I need to go home."

Her body was tense as she held me, stroking my back. "Kenny! What happened? I couldn't find you!"

Pete was with us then, and I felt his warm hand on my arm. "Are you okay?"

I didn't want to talk about it with anybody. Clearly Grif had planned the whole thing from the start, even down to his witness and alibi. It wouldn't matter what I said, they'd claim I started it all. Now I just wanted to go home and crawl beneath my covers.

"Y-yeah." I said, pulling myself together as hard as I could. "I-I had an accident. I was running, and I... I fell. I tripped on the sand."

Mariska gasped. "Oh! Your dress is torn! Are you bleeding?"

I lifted the ends of my dress. "My heel got caught in it. I had to take my shoes off. I-I think I'll be okay."

My friend's brows pulled together, and I was sure she didn't believe me. "Where's Grif?" She looked over my shoulder down the beach in the direction from which I'd come.

"He met an old friend." My mind was flying, making up a story as fast as bits of information would come to me. "They were talking, catching up, and I heard you calling me. So I left. I really just want to go home now."

Mariska and Pete both stood on the beach staring at me for a moment. A shudder rippled across my shoulders, but I took a slow breath and lifted my chin to look at them. I even managed a smile. "I think I had a little too much to drink tonight. Please take me home now. Please?"

My friend's lips pressed together in a tight line, but she stepped to the side. "Sure. Of course!"

Pete turned and led us slowly back in the direction of the bar. His hands were in his pockets, and his shoulders were hunched. Mariska held my hand, our arms laced together, and I forced myself to walk, not to break down, to be strong for just a little while longer.

We made it to her car, and I waited in the passenger's seat as she stood outside for a few moments talking to Pete. The roaring in my ears drowned out any conversation they might be having. My super-controlled breathing kept my back straight, my body from curling into a ball.

Conversation was minimal as we made the short drive back to my house. "Are you sure you're okay?" Mariska asked softly.

I nodded too rapidly and smiled too big. "I'm great!" I said in a voice I knew was too high.

Her bottom lip pulled between her teeth. "I'm sorry I lost track of you. Pete… wanted to talk."

I couldn't even go there with her. "It's okay." I was hoarse from screaming and fighting, and at this point, I was running on will power alone. We were at my apartment, and I pulled my bag onto my lap.

"Thanks, Mare." I reached for the handle, but she caught my arm.

"I know you're not telling me something. If you want to take off tomorrow, I'll tell Rook you're sick. I can call your clients and reschedule or see if Tammy can take them?"

Blinking rapidly, I nodded. "I might do that. Thanks."

Her grip relaxed on my arm, but I didn't meet her eyes. "Thanks again," I whispered, pulling the handle.

In less than two minutes, I was inside my apartment, dropping all of my things in a path leading from the door to my bedroom. My torn dress was quickly over my head, and I pushed naked between the cool sheets. I pulled my knees tight against my chest, wrapping my arms around them and hugging myself into a tight ball. Tears fell silently as my thoughts blurred, and it wasn't long before shock gave way to sleep.

Chapter 7: "Every breath is a second chance."
Slayde

Monday morning, I'd been back at the club at seven, ready to do it all over again when Rook stopped me at the door.

"That your truck?" He pointed out the glass doors at my rusty old Ford.

"Yeah." I squinted at him, unsure if he were accusing me of carjacking or yanking my chain. I couldn't imagine a guy with his resources caring about the junker I used to get from Point A to Point B.

"Got some supplies stuck in Scranton. It's worth it to me to get them here tomorrow if I can find someone willing to drive out there and load it all up by himself." He looked at me. "Think you can handle a job like that?"

I stepped away, rubbing the back of my neck. "You need me to drive to Scranton?"

He reached into his front pocket and pulled out a thick fold of bills. I watched him unfold one, two, three.

"Here's money to cover your gas, food, hotel room."

For a moment, I stared at the cash in my hand. An itch of warning pricked at the back of my neck. "You want receipts?"

"Nah, keep the change." He slapped me on the back, and my conditioned response kicked in.

"I'll bring you receipts and return the difference."

Rook exhaled loudly. "Can't you just take it and say thanks?"

"I'm no charity case."

"Right." His eyes narrowed. "And you're still on probation here. Use whatever's left to buy a new pair of jeans and eat something. I don't want members thinking I hire vagrants."

I started to reply, but he cut me off. "Do it, or you're fired. And don't leave without cleaning the locker rooms. I expect you on the road by ten."

A quick glance at the clock said I had three hours. I'd be on the road in two.

* * *

My old Ford managed the highway better than I expected. The mechanic who sold it to me was pretty scuzzy, but he guaranteed the engine checked out. Looked like he was honest. I made it to Gym Supply in four hours without any issues other than road fatigue.

The girl at the counter directed me around to the dock. She was a petite redhead in jeans and a maroon tee with Gym Supply across the front in white. "Yeah, we got your order." She flipped pages back and forth on a loaded clipboard.
"This driver's strike has us all fucked up."

"Driver's strike?" I didn't like the sound of that. I wasn't looking to cross any picket lines. *Shit*.

Reading my expression, she quickly added. "It's not our guys, it's a union thing. We're not in the loop, but our drivers are taking off to help where they're striking. Lou won't stop 'em, but it's fucking up everything." Brown eyes flickered across my shoulders. "Looks like you can load it yourself. I'm Paige, by the way."

She checked me out, allowing her eyes to linger as they drifted below my beltline. I couldn't help feeling that white-hot singe of desire. She was a pretty girl with a nice rack, and I hadn't been laid in ages. The heat rose to my chest, the old opportunistic urge. I was sure Paige knew where we could go, unwrap those gorgeous tits, shimmy down those jeans. I'd wrap that red hair around my fist and give her the ride of her life. From the look of her, it wouldn't take much to have her screaming my name.

Clearing my throat, I stepped back. "Yeah, I can handle it."

"Follow me, then." She led the way, and I looked around, distracting my mind from the bounce of her round ass. *Shit.* "Here's the order. If you pull your truck around, you can use the dolly."

She stood waiting, eyebrow cocked at me. The hint of a smile was on her lips. Several cardboard boxes were wrapped together with plastic. I wasn't sure they would all fit, but I hadn't known what to expect.

"You got a canvas or something I can use to cover it? We can send it back with our next delivery."

"Help yourself to whatever you see." She put one hand on her hip, as if that included her.

Holding my eyes away, I nodded. That wasn't me anymore. I'd buried that part of myself along with the guy I used to be. "Thanks. I'll be back to load up in the morning."

This was an overnight delivery trip, not a one-night stand, although I couldn't help glancing back. She stood there on the dock, hand on her hip, that little grin on her mouth. Lust was blazing in her eyes, hitting me straight in the gut.

When I was starving, it was easy to focus on food. Now that I was eating somewhat regularly, that old, primal hunger gnawed at my insides. From the dark recesses of my past, the feel of my cheek against the soft curve of a full breast flashed like lightening. I remembered holding lush handfuls, heavy between my fingers… My mouth clamping down hard on a tight nipple.

With a growl, I shook my head, climbing into the cab and starting the engine. I wasn't doing any of that, and I wasn't fucking up this job. I'd return in the morning to bust my ass hauling boxes, forget these stupid memories, and then head back to Toms River.

* * *

Early Tuesday afternoon I rolled into the Jungle Gym lot. Rook had given me the key, and I went around to unload right at the garage. Moving a load of heavy boxes, driving four hours, and moving them all again had me exhausted and ready to call it a day.

Truck empty, I headed to Wal-Mart to find a pair of jeans. If this money was an advance on my paycheck, I might as well use it to get a few new shirts and a little more to eat.

Dinner was half a rotisserie chicken. I could've eaten the whole buttery, greasy bird, but I wasn't flush yet. I'd save the other half for tomorrow's dinner. In the freezer was a package of pulled pork and some cheap ground beef. A supply of buns, mustard, and cheese, and I'd make it to payday. My one splurge was a burner phone and the cheapest package of minutes—just for emergencies.

Showered and with my belly full, I stretched. My muscles ached in a good way from exertion they hadn't felt in months, and I picked up the giant paperback I'd been reading. Even if it was pretty dry, I'd started to care what would happen next to the French kid.

I read for almost an hour, but my skin itched, and my chest burned. That fucking hunger was back, and none of Doc's mantras made it go away. What I felt was deeper than that. Time for Plan B—a walk on the shore. Hopefully, the wind and the waves and the fresh salt air would clear my head.

At the water's edge, I turned north, moving fast. Longing roiled deep in my stomach, and my pace quickened. Closing my eyes, I was surrounded by a curtain of dark hair, and slim hands kneading the muscles in my shoulders. Soft lips feathered my ear with husky whimpers begging for more, and I stopped walking. I pushed my hands against my head, growling deep, but it didn't stop the faceless memories tormenting me. I remembered warm thighs circling my waist, and the squeeze of a hot, wet opening pulsing around my dick.

"Fuck," I hissed under my breath. I pulled off my shirt and shoved my shorts down, stepping out of them and running straight into the water. It was ice cold as I dropped to my knees, plunging my head under the surface and holding my breath until those tormenting memories drowned in the heat of my wake.

Control came seeping back with the bitter cold making its way to my bones, and I waded to shore. Dripping wet, I went to where I'd left my clothes. I was at a pretty deserted section of beach, although I could see in the distance, maybe a half-mile away, one of those bars that fronted on the ocean. Rubbing my hands fast over my torso, I managed to get most of the water off me before stepping into my shorts. I held my shirt for a few minutes, letting the air dry my body a bit longer.

It was a warm night, even though the water was frigid. My calm restored, I listened to the quiet sounds of evening — broken at once by a scream.

My body went on alert as adrenaline shot through my veins. The scream cut off, but it came from the direction of the bar. Slowly I took a few steps when I heard it again — definitely a female scream.

Jogging toward the noise, I could barely make out the shape of a man behind a smaller form of a woman with long hair. She was pushing and throwing her arms all around, but he caught them, pinning them against her sides.

Another man was approaching them, so I slowed my pace, waiting. I wasn't about to let what seemed to be happening happen, but at the same time, if someone else could intervene and help her, that would be for the best.

"My brother's military," I heard her scream. The sound of her ragged voice fanned the rage building in my torso. "He'll rip your throat out and shove it up your ass."

My jaw was tight, and my fists clenched shut as I waited, hoping the skinny guy could help her. I barely heard him say something that sounded like

"Let her go," but the dick holding her shouted, "Go away so I can fuck her."

She screamed again, and rage flooded my vision. Skinny backed off, but I charged forward. In less than ten paces, my clenched fist made contact with the fucker's jaw and a satisfying *CRACK!* ricocheted down my arm. He flew back, but his hold on the girl's arms kept him upright. A left hook, another satisfying connecting punch, and he fell back, flat on the sand.

Abuser, fucking worthless abuser. It took all of my willpower to control the fury blazing in my chest. I stood over him, envisioning myself beating him repeatedly. My days in the ring were in the front of my mind, and I knew every hit I'd lay on him. High-volume punching. I'd smash him over and over until there was nothing left of his head but bloody pulp.

Breath pumped in and out of me like a bellows, and I fought to stop the red, to find the mantra. Nothing was coming. Until her voice, clear as a bell, cut through the noise.

She said something. I didn't know what it was, but the sound of her turned me. I took a wobbly step away from the body lying on the sand in front of me to her. She was beautiful, broken and pale in the moonlight. Long, dark hair draped over her shoulders, and her dress was torn. She cautiously reached for me, and I wanted to gather her in my arms and hold her.

I couldn't do that. She was hurt, and I didn't even know who she was.

"Are you okay?" My voice shook. That was a close one.

She nodded, shaking as well. "Y-you saved me."

I could see her working hard to pull herself together. She was so small, but I could tell she was strong. I remembered what she'd said, or rather screamed, and I dug for the burner phone in my pocket.

"Do you want to call your brother?"

She seemed confused then I saw her remember. "That was a bluff."

Her shoulders trembled hard, and again, I wanted to ask if I could hold her. I took one step toward her, but the fucker on the ground made a noise. "Shit," I whispered, anger mixed with relief. He was coming around, and I needed to go. "Is there anyone you can call?"

As much as I couldn't be found here, I couldn't leave her by herself. Voices yelled from the direction of the bar, and she looked back over her shoulder.

"Those are my friends." It was all I needed to hear. I told her something like goodbye and took off running back in the direction of my apartment.

She'd be okay. Her friends would take care of her. Halfway back, I realized I never asked her name. I didn't know who she was. A beautiful creature, rescued on the beach, and I'd never see her again. The devastation of that thought broke my run.

Staggering to a walk, I looked back over my shoulder. She'd be gone when I got there if I ran back, and even if she wasn't, an angel as beautiful as that? She deserved so much better than a broken down sinner like me, regardless of what I'd just done on the beach. I had to let her go.

Chapter 8: "Don't be afraid to try again."
Kenny

Thursday morning the fist was back. It clenched hard in my chest, making it difficult to breathe. I needed to hit something.

Yesterday, I hadn't even gotten out of bed. After crying myself into a fitful sleep, I woke up screaming, feeling calloused hands gripping my arms to my sides. I threw my blankets back and went straight to the shower. Standing under the scalding-hot water, I scrubbed until my skin was red and tender. It helped remove the sensations, but it was hours before I could relax again. When I'd opened my eyes, it was after five. Mariska had texted me a few times and left a voicemail once.

Are you coming in? Was her first message, sent around ten. It was followed by *I'm guessing you're not,* around noon.

I rolled onto my side and listened to her voice on my phone. "Hey, I'm worried about you. I wish you'd call or at least text. Rook thinks you caught a stomach bug, and Tammy covered your clients. Just call or text me, okay? Love ya."

Disconnecting, I shot her a quick reply. *Will be in tomorrow. Thanks for covering for me. Don't feel like talking.*

The only vehicle in the lot when I arrived was an old junker Ford someone had abandoned. Pushing through the glass doors, I made a point of taking the lanyard out of my cubby so everyone would know I was here before heading to the small boxing room, ready for my early-morning drill. My hair was up in a ponytail, and I had on my usual black spandex capris and black tank. I didn't have gloves, only the gel hand wraps that came with the equipment.

The closer I got, however, I heard the dull thud of what sounded like gloves hitting a bag. Rounding the corner, I froze in my tracks. His back was to me, shoulders up and chin down, and his feet moved lightly as his fists slammed into the canvass body bag in front of him.

He was shirtless, and he was ripped. Every muscle in his shoulders and back flexed with his strikes. The lines in his stomach deepened along with those on his arms. The gloves inked on his biceps read, *Never stop fighting*. Only, from what I could see, the fight was either keeping him alive or killing him.

Perfect form, fists at eye level, his punches flew straight to the center. Quick, precise, sharp. He moved like a professional. He *was* a professional. My duffel slid from my shoulder, amazement mixing with something else, low in my stomach, as I watched. He was beautiful.

He didn't see me, so he didn't stop. Ice blue eyes focused through his furrowed brow on something invisible. His fists were like cannons. He moved out, then he moved back in, shooting three to four swift hits before moving out again.

Right jab, left jab, left hook, out.
Left jab, right jab, left hook, right jab, out.

My breathing picked up as I understood what he was doing. Tension rippled off him in waves as he fought with something unseen. It was a fight I knew well because it was the same one I'd waged every morning for almost a year.

His intensity increased with each strike, and the wings inked down his back flexed like they were trying to escape whatever held him. I wanted to step forward and lay my palms flat against his skin. I wanted to feel the strength of those swift, strong blows. I wanted to close my eyes and merge our arms and see if I could feel the power of his fists, see if they would unlock my own pain and release it.

His punches increased in speed and ferocity, fists shooting forward so fast, they became almost a blur as he pummeled the bag. His furrowed brow creased, and I heard a low growl rising in his throat.

Jab after jab, punch after punch, I lost count there were so many moving so fast until he let out a loud noise and jerked away toward the cinder block wall, banging the sides of his fists against it just under the rectangular window at the ceiling.

His head rested on his gloved fists a moment, his breath coming in gulps. Sweat traced the lines down his torso stopping at the black shorts he wore, and I couldn't help breathing fast with him.

I wasn't sure if I should speak or leave. I felt like I'd walked in on something incredibly personal, almost like when I caught Rook and Tammy in the shower. My heart was flying in my chest—only in this case, I didn't want to run away. I wanted to stay.

Finally, I found my voice. "I-I um... I'm sorry to interrupt."

He looked back over his shoulder, those blue eyes meeting mine, stopping my heart. In a quick move, he scooped up a maroon tank and dropped it over his head before turning to face me. I could see the tops of letters inked in a half circle right at his collarbones, but I couldn't make out what it said. *Why hadn't I read that?* I'd been too overwhelmed by the intensity of his fight.

"Sorry." His voice was hoarse. "I didn't know anybody came in this early."

Unable to hold his gaze, I tried to smile as my eyes moved from his square jaw, past the line down the center of his chin, to his muscular arms.

"I'm the only one who does." My voice was higher in contrast to his. "I missed a few days, but I try to get my workout in before the members arrive."

He grabbed a towel off another bench, and I noticed a small bottle of cheap, generic water and a bundle of what had to be his clothes. "I'll get the locker room cleaned before you need it. If you're okay?"

In that one phrase, recognition almost knocked me down. I was back on the beach. It was dark and I couldn't stop shaking. Still, in that place of darkness as I struggled not to cry, all I wanted was the man who'd come out of nowhere and saved me to put his arms around me and hold me until my fear subsided.

My eyes flew to his, but he didn't seem to realize. *Did he not know it was me?*

"I-I'm okay," I said, and that's when I saw it flash in his eyes. Now he knew.

My heart beat unbearably fast, but he didn't speak, he only clutched his things and headed towards the locker rooms.

Turning in the direction he'd left, my will to exercise was gone, and now something entirely different tightened my chest. Picking up my bag, I walked slowly toward the front, looking around for him. He was in the supply closet taking out the mop and bucket along with the plastic signs for the floor and door.

"Are you Slayde?" I asked when he came back out.

He paused, but I could tell he wasn't fully committed to speaking to me. "Yes."

"I'm Kenny. One of the trainers here."

He looked up at me then, and my chest squeezed. Emotion sizzled just under my skin, and I had to blink away. Somehow I'd have to learn to meet those amazing blue eyes without forgetting where I was.

"Nice to meet you." His voice was low. "Sorry I interrupted your workout."

"No," I shook my dark-purple ponytail. I didn't want him to apologize. I didn't want him to hold me at a distance. We were legions past that point, even if we were only just now exchanging names. "You didn't interrupt me. I mean, I could still work out. I just... I wanted to speak to you."

He waited, and I couldn't tell if he was impatient or uncomfortable, so I stepped back. "I'll let you do your job."

His lips twitched as if he were about to say something, but instead he started down the hall, through the doors in the direction of the locker rooms. I collapsed against the counter, watching him go, trying to calm the tornado swirling in my chest.

Chapter 9: "Pain is inevitable; suffering is optional."
Slayde

She was here. In the same club where I worked. Boxing for Christ's sake.

I hadn't been able to stop thinking about the angel on the beach for two nights. I didn't want to think about her, but *shit*, I couldn't stop myself.

Chances were great I'd never see her again. Then again, in a town the size of Bayville, she was bound to turn up somewhere. I just never expected it to be here.

All day Wednesday, I'd focused my thoughts on *not* looking for her in every face I passed, trying *not* to remember her fair skin, long dark hair, and large, pale eyes. I didn't even know her name. It was nuts.

Last night, I'd spent an extra few minutes in the shower, head pressed against my forearm, remembering the curve of her neck as I relieved the pressure. Then I felt like an asshole. She'd been hurt, almost raped, and here I was jerking off to her memory like it didn't matter. It did matter. I wanted to kill that guy. Nothing had felt as good as slamming my fist into his skull. Twice. But I'd stopped. I hadn't lost control. That in itself was a miracle.

I cranked the hot water all the way up and scrubbed my face and neck hard under the spray. I got out and shaved, focusing on what I was doing and *not* wondering what she smelled like. When I crawled into bed, I went to sleep, *not* fantasizing about touching her soft skin, fighting with all I had to ignore the emptiness inside.

This morning, I didn't care if I didn't have permission. I'd been working at this gym almost a week, and nobody came in before eight. At seven, I parked the Ford in the back of the lot and let myself in. I quickly changed out of my jeans into the only other pair of shorts I owned and shoved my hands into the gloves I'd borrowed from behind the front desk.

Standing a little more than arm's distance from the bag, I stepped forward and clipped it with a solid left hook. *God, that felt good.* Stepping back I went at it again.

Right jab, left jab, right, right, left hook.
Right jab, left jab, right, right, left hook.

Everything went away when I was boxing. Elbows tight, my gloves were right at my cheekbones, a little brush before each hand shot out like a cannon, hitting with an explosive force I felt through my entire shoulder, down through my torso.

I didn't know how long I'd gone at it before I finally let loose with my signature move, a rapid-fire volley of jabs and hooks. High-volume punching not a single fighter could beat.

It was so good. I was a junkie freebasing the best coke on the planet. All the shit was gone, and it was just the fight and me. I could feel the rumble rising at the base of my throat until I backed away, slamming my fists against the wall, resting my head on my gloves as I came back down. It's why I would've been the champ. I was young, and I was fit, and I could keep that shit up for days.

But in one moment, it all crashed down. Those dreams were gone. I'd never have it again, just like my life would never be the same, just like I'd never find her.

Anger, deep, dark, violent and bitter anger stirred in my chest. It was the heat rising, and I opened my mouth to let out the rage...

That's when I heard her voice, and I turned around.

Teetering on the edge of giving up, of quitting and losing all the ground I'd gained, she spoke to me through the fog of heartbreak. I looked up, and the noise died away.

Since this morning, I hadn't spoken to her or even allowed myself in her proximity, but I hung back and stole glances. I studied her reflection in mirrors I cleaned.

Her hair wasn't black; it was dark purple. She was tiny, maybe only five foot, and she couldn't weigh a hundred pounds. Still, her torso was lined, and I could see small muscles in her arms. She was strong, I was sure of it, and she had a nice little ass.

She had the brightest blue eyes. When she listened to her clients, her expression softened in this way that said she wasn't pretending. She was really hearing them. And then she smiled, and the cutest little dimple pierced her left cheek... *Fuck me.*

I wanted to wrap my arms around her and hold her, lift her, kiss her full mouth. With a growl I shook the image away. I was a fucking creep spying on her. A goddamn fool, too—a fucking janitor working at a gym in a shit town in the middle of nowhere wishing for an angel.

"Can you help me with these weights?" A smoky female voice cut through my self-flagellation.

I stopped wiping the now-exceptionally clean mirror and turned to face a woman smiling at me with an expression I knew too well. She wore tight, black yoga pants and a neon pink sports bra, and nothing more. Her blonde hair was loose down her back, and she waited, smiling an open invitation.

"Sure." I didn't respond. I moved past her over to the bench-press bar, which held what looked like about two hundred and fifty pounds.

"Some people are so inconsiderate." Her laugh turned into what sounded like a purr as I pulled off the heavy plates and stacked them on the rack. "Are you one of the new trainers?"

My eyes met hers, and I noticed her bottom lip was clutched under her top teeth. *Was she seriously biting her lip at me?* "No, but I can get Pete for you. Or Kenny?"

She released it in a smile. "Oh, that's alright. I know them. What do you do here?"

"Maintenance. I'm actually headed to the men's locker room right now."

"Can I tag along?"

She was a hot chick, but my brain was consumed in a purple haze. "Only if you like cleaning urinals. Otherwise, better not."

Her nose curled and she poked out the tip of her tongue. "Let me know if that situation changes."

"Will do." I tipped my chin and headed into the locker room.

I needed to get my head out of the clouds. Kenny was beautiful and kind and smart... and she sure as hell didn't deserve to get mixed up with a loser like me.

* * *

My work was done in an hour, and all dreams of romance were flushed with the shit I scrubbed off the toilets. Forcing myself not to look for her, I put all the supplies back in the closet and pulled my keys to leave.

Rook's sharp voice stopped me at the door. "Slayde! You said you'd bring me receipts. Where are they?"

Already pissed, his tone fanned the heat in my chest even me more, and I almost forgot he was my boss and blasted a string of profanity in his face. Instead, I grabbed the reins.

"Sorry," I said, clearing my throat. "They're back at my apartment. I'll add everything up and give you the difference tomorrow."

"You'll give me the difference tonight, punk." That snapped my head up. Boss or not, nobody talked to me that way. My fists balled involuntarily.

He took one look at my expression and laughed. "There it is. I knew you had a dick in there somewhere. I was wondering what it took for you to whip it out. You want to fight me, boy?"

The gleam in his eye was both amused and taunting, and I wasn't sure that he wouldn't enjoy kicking my ass. He had a good six inches and sixty pounds on me. I might've been a champ once, but he was out of my weight class by a mile.

"No, sir." I looked down, and he pushed a hard breath through his lips.

"Quit that shit, I'm not your master. I'm your fucking boss, and I don't expect any of my employees to kiss my ass."

Out of nowhere, I felt a smile pulling at my lips. Lifting my eyes to his, I called his bluff. "What the fuck do you expect of your employees?"

"That's it," he laughed, clapping me hard on the shoulder. "So the little girls have been gossiping all day about you hitting the bags this morning. I thought you quit the fight?"

My mind paused to consider what he was saying. *Which little girls?* I swallowed the emotions warring in my chest and recited the monologue. "I don't fight anymore. That's in the past."

"What the fuck is this tattoo about then? You a cock sucker?"

Fists clenched, I had to take a step back before I took a pop at this mountain of black steel in front of me. He only laughed louder.

"I like you Slayde Bennett. You want to kick my ass, don't you?"

Swallowing the burn in my throat, I heard Doc's voice telling me to identify the emotion, own it, put it away.

"No." I said, thinking I'd better get out of here now.

Rook caught my shoulder in his enormous hand. "That's some goddamn kickass control you've got there." He let me go with a little push. "You ever trained anybody?"

Rubbing the back of my neck, I focused on what he was saying to me instead of how I felt. "No."

He stepped back into his office. "Come in here and close the door."

I stepped inside, into the same place I'd been just a week before when I'd hoped to be lucky enough to score a job that didn't require references. I was a fool coming to a gym. I was like an alcoholic applying to be a bartender.

Rook went around his desk and pulled a picture from the top drawer. He handed it to me, and I stared at it a moment, recognizing his face in a football uniform looking several years younger.

"You ever heard of The Rookie? Top draft pick of... well, the year's not important." He did a little chuckle, but it didn't register. I'd never kept up with football. Boxing was my game.

"This you?" I cut my eyes from the photo to him.

"Yep. Just starting out, dreaming of mansions in Miami, yachts, a sexy blonde on each arm. One blown knee later, I had nothing. No money, no college degree, no woman. Nothing. It was all over."

My stomach tightened sickly. I didn't need his sob story added to mine. I already felt like shit. "That's tough," was all I said.

"Fuckin right it was tough. I went from the penthouse to the outhouse. I worked as a bouncer, a bodyguard, the whole time killing the pain with blow. Then I met Tammy, and she wouldn't let me kill myself."

Nodding, I was ready to go. I wasn't looking for a woman. Or at least I was trying hard not to look for a particular woman... who worked in this gym. "That's good."

"Its better than good. Know why I call myself Rook? Some racist, sonofabitch redneck nickname?"

I didn't know how to answer that question, so I didn't.

"The Rook is the smartest bird in the whole species," he continued. "They use tools, they can be taught to speak, they recognize music... they're survivors. I'm a survivor. When I was a player, they called me The Rookie, someone who's new, ignorant, inexperienced. I'm not a rookie anymore. I'm a Rook. What are you?"

I glanced down at my hands, thinking about his words, wondering if he knew what was hidden beneath my shirt. It was impossible, but I supposed with a few phone calls he could've found out my story.

"I was Slayer," I said. "Now I'm Slayde."

"Slayde? A malaprop of *slain*. Are you dead?"

I thought about that. *Yes.* When I put down those gloves, my life ended. Only now I wasn't so sure. I had been dead or close to it up until two nights ago. Then something happened, something powerful enough to bring me back.

Rook seemed to understand my internal conflict, and he backed off. "Think about what I said. I like keeping the gym fresh, new blood, new offerings. When you're ready, let me know. In the meantime, keep my shit clean and my stuff put away."

Blinking back to the moment, I nodded and went to the door ready to call it a day. I was finished anyway. Opening it without looking, I stepped into the hallway nearly colliding with Kenny.

My stomach tightened, and everything stopped. She was in a different outfit from the one she'd worn all day with her clients. Her hair was still up, but a bit of it hung long over her shoulder like a dark purple ribbon. I wanted to run my finger under it. That cute dimple appeared, and *Shit!* I wanted her.

"Sorry," she exhaled a little laugh. "I think I ran right into you."

"It was my fault. I didn't look where I was going." She smelled sweet, like sugar. I probably smelled like toilet cleaner.

"Hey, I-I wanted to thank you." Her cheeks flushed a pretty shade of pink, and I felt that surge of desire move from my stomach to a lower region. "You saved me the other night. Then you just disappeared. Are you Batman?"

She released another, softer laugh that hit me hard. I wanted to make her laugh again. I wanted to bury my face in her delicious scent, taste her body, see if it was as good as she smelled, wrap her hair around all five of my fingers.

"Sorry to disappoint you," I managed to say.

She smiled again. Her thick, dark lashes made her blue eyes glow. Or maybe they glowed all the time? "I'm not disappointed. I'm serious. Thank you."

"I just did what any decent person would do. That guy was hurting you, and I..." I didn't say *I wanted to kill him*. But I did.

She leaned against the door and cocked her head to the side. "Would you maybe consider..." she hesitated. "Would you be willing to teach me some of your moves? I mean, your technique?"

My brow lined, and she quickly continued. "I was thinking about it yesterday. If you could show me some punches, maybe some self-defense stuff, I could protect myself."

"Someone your size could never fight off a guy like that." I answered without thinking, and I could see her disappointment. "You could try, but you're better off carrying mace or pepper spray."

Her pale pink lips pressed together, and I wondered if they were as soft as they looked. "Would you still teach me? I could meet you in the mornings, before everyone gets here. Like we did today?"

I wanted that more than anything. "I don't think so. Sorry."

Those lips lifted at the corners, and the sly look in her eye slayed me. Ironic. "Well, I'll be here in the morning doing my regular workout. Maybe I'll see you."

I didn't answer. I could only watch as she pushed through the door and made her way to a shiny new Honda in the parking lot.

As sure as I was standing, I'd be here in the morning.

Chapter 10: "Have the courage to live."
Kenny

Rolling onto my side, I tried to focus on the flickering television, *not* Slayde Bennett. All day I'd done my best to avoid him, but like little rebels, my eyes found his whenever my thoughts drifted. Twice they'd met in the gym, and both times my chest clenched like some silly teenager with a crush.

I would *not* let myself fantasize about him this morning, dripping with sex as he hit the heavy bag like a pro, and I would definitely not let my stubborn brain remember him struggling for control after flattening the asshole who'd attacked me on the beach.

With a shudder, I thanked everything I could think of for helping me escape that costly mistake. The flash of what almost happened to me sent a roll of nausea through my stomach, yet the feeling of Slayde's presence, how he handled all of it, covered me in calming warmth.

I closed my eyes and pictured his slim, muscular body, his clear blue eyes and dark brown hair, the faintest hint of a beard along his square jaw, and that line in the center of his chin. *Too much!*

Flipping onto my stomach, I reached for the remote just as my phone started going off. The picture told me it was Mariska, and I scooped it up hoping for any kind of distraction.

"Did you ask him?" Her voice was breathless with excitement.

Mine by contrast was not. "Yes."

"And?"

"He said no." A brief frown touched my lips as I remembered his refusal to train me.

"What? I don't believe it. I'm telling you, he was checking you out all day."

A tingle moved through my stomach, but I dismissed it. I'd talked to him, after all, and he was not interested in me. "He only looked at me once, and he was frowning."

"That was because Darla tried to seduce him." The sound of Mariska walking through her apartment filled my ear. "She's such a cougar. I'm pretty sure I saw her lick her lips when he unloaded those weights."

"I'm sure she did." Chewing my bottom lip, I told myself I didn't care if a sexy gym member made passes at him. It wasn't my business.

It was a lie.

"I bet she loaded those weights herself just so she could pretend she needed help taking them off."

That made me laugh. "He is amazingly ripped."

"And that ink! What do you think he's hiding under that shirt? A map to buried treasure?"

"Hidden treasure."

"I knew it!" My friend squeal-laughed. "You're into him. Are you going in the morning?"

"Of course. It's my daily routine. I don't plan to change just because he might be there." *If only he might be there.*

I dismissed the stubborn thoughts in my head. While Saturday made me believe I was ready to venture into the dating waters, Tuesday verified I only made bad choices when it came to men. Even if Slayde Bennett had saved me, everything he did demonstrated his still waters hid some seriously deep shit, and it wasn't anything he wanted to share.

When she spoke again, Mariska's voice was serious. "Are you okay... otherwise? Since Tuesday, I mean?"

Inhaling a cleansing breath, I answered truthfully. "I think so." I nodded even though she couldn't see me. "I mean, yesterday was hard. I'm still a little shook up, but I'm okay. I'm not hurt. It was a really close call, and I'm so thankful it wasn't worse. But I'm okay."

"Oh, god, Ken, I'm so sorry I left you alone." She sounded near tears. "Can you ever forgive me?"

Pressing my eyes closed, I pushed back against self-pity. "You didn't leave me alone, you were talking to Pete. I was the dumbass who left the bar with a total stranger. You'd think it was my first time out!"

"He seemed like a nice guy."

Reflecting back, I remembered the signs I'd ignored. "He really wasn't, but I was too drunk to pay attention. Or something."

The one other time I'd been too drunk, I'd been lucky. Patrick was a great guy, and Lane was a surprise gift that I cherished so much. Tuesday, luck wasn't on my side, and the message was I needed to grow up. Now.

"It was amazing Slayde was there, that he saved you like that."

Thinking of him on the beach in the moonlight, that warmth stirred again in my chest. It was immediately replaced by humiliation. "Oh, god, I could die!" Pressing hand over my eyes, I fell back on the couch cringing. "I called him Batman. Then I asked him to show me his *moves*... I'm such an idiot!"

She struggled against her laughter. "You are not! It was sort of dark knight-ish the way he showed up and then ran off, and he does have moves. Hot and sexy ones."

"I won't blame him if he gives his two-weeks' notice tomorrow. Between you doing sign language at him and me gushing all over him, he probably thinks we're all nuts."

She hummed. "I doubt it. You just let me know if anything happens in the morning."

"Don't hold your breath."

We said goodnight, and I dropped the phone. Thinking about what I'd said and talking to Slayde after work, a shy grin pulled at the corners of my mouth. I could feel the pink on my cheeks, and I dropped the remote on the couch cushion, going to the bathroom to clean up and get ready for sleep.

* * *

My shoulders fell when I pulled into the Jungle Gym parking lot at seven. Not a single car or truck was there. I fought against the pout pulling my bottom lip and went inside, snatching my key out of my cubby and heading toward the small boxing room in the back.

He said he wouldn't train me. Why did I doubt his words? Besides, he probably had women lined up all over the place. He'd probably gone home with Darla last night and screwed her brains out.

The thought pissed me off. I jerked the gel gloves over my knuckles and stomped toward the hanging bag. When I got to it, I pulled back and hit it as hard as I could. Letting out a little growl, I hit it again with my other hand. Then I hit it harder. I hopped up and down, but I didn't care about form. I just wanted to hit something. I pulled my fists back and hammered them one after the other against that stupid bag, letting out all the frustration I was feeling.

My long ponytail flipped around with every strike, getting caught in my arms. With another growl I stepped back and planted a roundhouse kick to the bag followed by a hard left jab. Then I did a fast combination.

Jab, cross, hook, front kick.
Jab, cross, hook, front kick.
Stupid hair getting in my way.

I stepped back and jerked a glove off with my teeth. Then I blinked, and my stomach jumped. Slayde was in the doorway, leaning against it, watching me intently.

Catching my breath, I took a step back. "I-I didn't think you were coming."

He shrugged and pushed himself upright. "This is when I normally come in."

Of course it was. He always left early, which clearly meant he came in early. I was a self-centered little twit to think it had anything to do with me.

Still, he took a step in my direction. "Your speed and power are good, but your form is a mess."

"I wasn't really worried about form."

"You should always worry about form." His brow lowered. "How you practice is how you'll fight."

I couldn't help a tiny smile at that. "But I'm not going to fight, remember? I'm going to carry mace or pepper spray."

"And if he takes it from you? What then?" His blue eyes were so intense, I had to blink down.

"Hope for Batman?" My voice was soft, and I noticed his stance change.

He took a few steps toward the bag. "Batman's a myth. I'll show you how to throw a punch, but don't get overconfident. The best defense is to stay alert and make smart choices."

The pink was back on my cheeks, I was sure of it. Dumb choices were the reason I'd been on that beach Tuesday night, and I wasn't about to forget it.

"Okay," I said, taking a step toward him. "What do I do?"

"First, let me see how you hit." He motioned, and I went to where he stood. "Stand in front of me and throw a punch."

The heat of his body was like fire at my back. I tried to hide my rapid breathing, but I was sure he could hear my heartbeat thundering in my chest. It took a minute to remember what I was supposed to be doing.

"A right jab." I moved my arm forward in slow motion.

"First off, you need to back up." He stepped back, and when he touched my waist, I bit my lip to hold in a noise. "You should be more than arm's length away. If you're too close, you don't have any mobility."

"Okay," I said, clearing my throat. *Get a grip, Kenny.*

"You okay?" His voice had changed, and I glanced over my shoulder. Blue eyes hit me like a fist, and I blinked away fast. "Yeah. I was thinking I should've known that."

"It's a common error with beginners. I mean... It's not like you're born knowing these things."

He sounded apologetic for calling me out. Which would be ridiculous—I *was* a beginner. I was also acting like a gooney teenager again.

With a deep breath, I straightened up. I'd show him what I could do. "Okay. So I'm out here, away from the bag. Now what?"

He seemed to relax a bit as well. "Give it a hit."

Shooting my fist out, I hit the bag as hard as I could.

"Okay." His voice was commanding, but gentle. "You want to strike with your first two knuckles. Drop your wrist just a bit so they align with your forearm. That way you won't hurt yourself. Now try it again. Right, left."

I dropped my wrist and punched again, *right-left*, following his direction, doing a little bounce without thinking.

"Good. Perfect." Hearing the smile in his voice sent a flood of... *pride?* through my stomach. *Shake it off.*

"Now the other thing." He touched my elbows, and I jumped. "Sorry." He was quick to back up.

"No," I shook my head. "I'm sorry. I was just—I didn't expect... What were you going to say?"

This time he didn't touch me, and I was sad. "You need to keep your elbows tighter. You're fanning them up, like wings."

"Okay." I clutched my elbows to my ribs.

"And you need to keep your chin tucked, like this." He stepped around so that he was facing me, lowering his chin so his blue eyes lasered into mine from under his furrowed brow. My stomach flipped.

"Like this?" I turned my face so my chin was pressed into the hollow of my shoulder, my eyes almost unbearably clashing with his under my lowered brow.

His throat moved, and it was almost as if *he* looked away this time. "That's right. Now see how it feels to strike that way."

I felt like Frankenstein moving my body stiffly towards the bag, elbows and chin tucked tightly down. Then I shot a fist forward, and he laughed. I'd never heard him laugh before. It sounded so good, low and ringing.

"You've got to loosen up some."

Dropping my hands, I turned to face him, my face relaxing with my smile. "That's a lot to remember all at once."

He looked down, and I so wanted to run the tip of my finger down that line in the center of his chin.

"You're right," he said, those damn sexy dimples peeking out. "You don't have to do it all now. Next time you train, keep it in mind and practice."

"Okay." I pushed my ponytail back over my shoulder. "And I'll braid and loop this so it's out of the way."

His lips parted, and for a moment he hesitated. Then for whatever reason, he said what he was thinking. "I like your hair. It's pretty."

I fought the fire blazing in my cheeks. "Thanks. And thanks for helping me. I know you didn't really want to—"

"It wasn't that." He retreated to the door. I could see the invisible wall going back up, and I hated it. Yet, it was something I understood so well. "I don't mind giving you some tips."

"Well... Whatever you did, it really helped me. Thanks."

He blinked and waved. "I gotta get to work. Take it easy."

With that, he was gone, and the entire room felt empty without him. My arms dropped, and I stared at the space where he'd been. He thought my hair was pretty. I grinned like an idiot and pulled my troublesome ponytail over my shoulder.

"What is your story, Slayde Bennett?" I whispered. "Could you be just as scarred as I am?"

Chapter 11: "We live with the scars we choose."
Slayde

She hit the bags like she was fighting something invisible, like she was beating the shit out of it. She was so beautiful, and I understood that feeling so well.

Her small body moved with controlled grace even if her strikes were out of line and her ribs unprotected. She was passionate, and I loved the little noises she made every time her fists made contact with the heavy bag. I couldn't help wondering if she made those sounds when she fucked.

Made love. This was a making love kind of woman. And that's where *I* was fucked. I had absolutely nothing to offer a making love kind of woman.

Still, I watched her, thinking about the loveliest music I'd ever heard. Her pale, slim neck, her petite fists driving with such force. She stepped back with a cute, frustrated growl, jerking a glove off with her teeth, and that's when she saw me.

I played it off, making up some story like the reason I was there was work. Nothing could have kept me from going to her this morning. I wanted to train her. Then I had to touch her, and it was almost more than I could take.

"Keep your elbows tighter, and your chin tucked into your shoulder." I'd tried to show her the basics without getting lost in her eyes, but it was a fight I wouldn't win.

Once she seemed to understand, I took my one opening to get out of there. I needed to get the ladies' locker room cleaned up anyway. If I wasted any more time, Tammy would hassle me. It was always friendly, but it was still hassling.

Leaving her felt like taking a blunt knife and carving out my insides, but I ignored that shit. What right did I have to feel this way? I had toilets to clean.

* * *

A white envelope taunted me from my mail slot. Payday. Lunch would be more than PB on white bread today, and my mouth watered at the thought. I paid Rook back what I owed him, which turned out to be less than seventy-five bucks. Damn, I was a cheap date. Then I headed down to the waterfront where food trucks were waiting. I ordered up a falafel with hot sauce and went to sit on one of the benches. Pulling out my burner phone, I checked in with Doc. It had been more than a week, and I was sure he was curious.

"Hey, kid!" He laughed, and the sound of his voice eased the mixed-up feelings in my chest. "How was your first week back?"

Swallowing the bite of food, I answered. "Better than expected. I'm sure you're feeling smug right now hearing me say that."

"Not at all." I could almost see his lip-less grin behind the salt and pepper scruff. "I'll be honest, I said a few prayers for you last week."

"What? No mantras? You back to hitting your knees?"

"Sure as shittin' I am," he laughed. "And you'd be smart to do the same every now and then."

Putting my food aside, I leaned forward, rubbing the back of my neck as I thought. "I've considered it."

"What happened?" His tone was serious, just like it always was with me, and damn, I appreciated having a good friend more than I could say in that moment.

"I lucked into a pretty good job. No background checks or references." I took a moment to think about how I wanted to frame Rook. "My boss is a former baller. He knew guys who'd fucked up their lives, he said, and he gave me a chance."

"There are still good people in the world, Slayer."

For a moment, I hesitated. "I'm not going by that name anymore. I'm Slayde now."

"Okay." Doc waited for me to take control of my story.

"I got a shithole of an apartment, but it's on the beach." Looking up, I appreciated the clear view I had of the horizon. "At night I can walk down by the water's edge. I don't know. It's therapeutic."

"That's a proven fact."

"Something happened." I needed to share this with him. I needed him to know. "Three nights ago, I was walking and I heard a girl... a guy was hurting her."

The line was silent, and I knew he was waiting for me to say the worst.

"I wasn't really thinking, I just heard her screaming and I reacted." Everything faded to the memory, and in that moment I was alone, on that bench, telling my story. "It wasn't premeditated, I just had to stop him. So I hit the guy hard. Twice."

Continued silence greeted me on the other end of the line.

"She was okay. She *is* okay." Looking at the back of my hand, I made a fist. "He was okay, too. I heard him making noises before I ran. She got away from him…"

"Sounds like there's more to this story." Cautious optimism was in his voice. "How do you know she got away?"

"She works at the gym with me. She's one of the trainers." I tried to keep all emotion out of my voice, but it didn't make a difference to someone who knew me as well as Doc.

"Must be a special lady."

Coming so close to naming it made me back away. "She's special. For somebody. I'm not looking to start any drama."

A chuckle was in my friend's voice. "Just because drama is all you've ever known doesn't mean it's the normal state of affairs. Remember what I told you."

"One step at a time."

"Right. Now I gotta get back to work." He exhaled lightly. "Take care of my friend Slayer."

"Slayer's nobody's friend." Bitterness tightened my chest. "But Slayde's doing pretty good so far."

"Sounds like it. I'm proud of you."

That was all I needed to hear.

* * *

Saturdays were a modified schedule at the gym, but my body didn't see it as any special day. My eyes popped open at six thirty, and I was in my truck, driving to the gym for seven. Sure enough, a shiny Honda sat in the lot.

A shot of happiness hit me straight to the chest, but I tried to tamp it down. She wanted to learn to box, and I was the only person around here qualified to teach her. That's all it was, nothing more.

Inside, she sat on the bench looking at her phone when I walked into the small room. Her blue eyes seemed to brighten a little when she saw me, or maybe I just wanted them to.

"I wasn't sure if you were coming," she said, lowering the device.

"Did you do what I said when you were practicing?" It had only been a day, but I didn't want her to think I'd forgotten.

She ducked her head with a laugh. "I haven't really had a chance to practice. But I could see if I remember today?"

"Whatever you feel like doing." I shrugged.

She stood and I watched as she reached back to braid her long ponytail. Her slim torso lined as she did it, and I looked straight at my shoes. Damn, she was so sexy. I knew if I kept watching her movements she'd see it all over my face — and possibly somewhere lower.

"My eyes popped open at six just like every day." She laughed as she worked, and I turned my hand over, examining my palm.

"You don't have a boyfriend or something?" *Why the hell did I ask her that?* "I just mean, being home on a Friday night."

121

"No," she said, and I saw she'd lowered her arms in my peripheral vision. "There's only one boy in my life."

Those words burned in my midsection more than I cared to recognize. Still, I seemed to be bent on torturing myself. "Oh, yeah? Where is he?"

"Wilmington." She pulled on the gel gloves, and by the look she was giving me, I could tell she wasn't finished.

"What's he doing there?"

"Living with his daddy." Her smile grew a little wider, as if just talking about him made her happy. "It's hard being apart, but he's getting to do way more there than he ever would with me."

"You've got a son." Everything inside me took a huge shift to the side, derailing my stupid dreams. If she didn't need to be around me, a little kid certainly didn't.

Confusion lined her face. "What? You don't like kids?"

"It's not that." Clearing my throat, I figured it was time for me to head back to the front. "You just practice what I showed you yesterday. The more you work on it, the better you'll get."

She didn't understand, but I didn't owe her an explanation. I'd finish my work as usual, and Sunday was my day off. I was back to one foot in front of the other, the best way to keep it.

Chapter 12: "Life teaches, Love reveals."
Kenny

Slayde Bennett is the most impossible man on the planet. Not that I care, of course, but if I did, I'd probably want to hit him in the head with one of those mops he pushes around all day. How dare he turn tail and run at the mention of Lane? I suppose he doesn't think he was a little boy once? I guess he just arrived here as an adult, fully formed?

And why was I getting all fired up about this again?

Shaking the crazy out of my head, I focused on my practice. He might be a jerk, but he did know boxing. I threw a punch, concentrating on keeping my elbows tight, my chin tucked into my shoulder. *What was the other thing he'd said?* If I weren't so pissed at him, I might ask. As it was, I'd figure it out myself. A best defense was smart choices—I remembered that much. Today's smart choice involved giving him a wide berth.

* * *

Mrs. Clarkson had rescheduled her training session from yesterday to today, and I was kind of glad. She always gave me something to think about, even if it occasionally depressed me. Last time, I'd had a mini-awakening of sorts followed by my girls' night with Elaine and Melissa. Of course, it was all shot to hell on Tuesday.

Mariska would roll in around noon, and I knew she'd be demanding to know if anything happened. I'd avoided her texts yesterday, basking in the afterglow of a full, day-starting conversation with Slayde and not wanting to over-analyze it. Now I just felt stupid. What a waste of my time.

"Something's different about you." Mrs. Clarkson's soft voice wobbled with laughter.

I didn't even know where to begin. "Yeah, you could say that."

"I like it very much."

For a moment, I was lost. "You do?"

"I know you think I'm an old fuddy-duddy, but purple is my favorite color. And this deep violet is very attractive with your skin tone!"

"Oh!" My nose wrinkled. "I forgot! I did it last week right after we worked together. I was testing that theory about change doing a body good."

I helped her get her form right as she curled the small dumbbells. "Did it?"

Twisting my lips, I thought about her question. "It sort of did. Then I had this setback. Then... I don't know. I feel like I'm almost right back to where I started last week."

Lowering the light weights, she patted me. "It is a bit of a wave-pool when you venture back into the water. Don't be discouraged."

Slayde entered the fitness room headed in the direction of the men's lockers. On their own, my eyes flew to his, and when they met, my chest clenched and I looked away.

Mrs. Clarkson didn't miss a bit of it. When I turned back to her, her eyes narrowed. "Interesting," was all she said, and I almost died of embarrassment.

"Sorry. I-uh… that's the new maintenance guy, Slayde."

I led her over to the resistance ball to finish her session with balance moves, but when I turned to face her, a tiny grin was at the corner of her mouth.

My arms were straight out, palms up to meet hers. "Ready?"

She nodded, placing her cool hands in mine. "He's very handsome."

Squatting with her as she sat down, I tried hard not to think about it. I tried instead to focus on the way he turned tail and ran at the mention of my sweet little boy.

"He's not my type." I rose with her and prepared to take her down again.

Her laugh was high. "Oh, honey. A man like that is everybody's type."

Wavering between an eye roll and a growl, I shook my head. "Looks are one thing, but I've talked with him a few times."

She pressed her lips together, but her eyes still danced. "Judging by the look you exchanged, it must've been quite a conversation."

I thought about last week, and how we'd discussed her husband and surviving the pain of loss. She was someone I could trust. I thought about how to ask my question as scientifically as possible.

"In your experience," I started, "do you think men usually like children?"

Her face lined as she considered it. "Children in general or their own?"

I hadn't really thought about it that way. "Umm… in general?"

"I'm not sure I understand why you're asking me this. What was your experience with your friend

Patrick?"

Reflecting on how that played out, I wasn't sure it was a fair comparison. "He sort of freaked out." I remembered Patrick shooting his and my whiskeys the night I told him. "Of course, it had been months since I'd seen him. And he was pretty serious with another woman at the time."

"Hmm." Her lips pressed into a thin line. "That was his reaction to his own child?"

Now who was the clever one? She'd figured out my question before I'd even asked it. "I guess I see your point. It depends on the man?"

"And the situation and his experience with fatherhood, his own father. So many factors come into play with men and children." We were slowly walking toward the juice bar. "What is consistent is the way most all men melt the first time they hold their own baby in their arms. It's a game-changer."

Game changer... As usual, she'd changed my outlook as she walked out the door.

* * *

The rest of the day, my chat with Mrs. Clarkson was on my mind. Mariska had begged for details about Slayde, but I told her the truth. Nothing happened. Then I left and drove myself to the pier where Patrick and I had sat after we told my parents about Lane. It was a special place to me.

The sun was setting over the water, and the sky was turning shades of blue, pink, and orange. It was beautiful, and I needed to bring my canvass down here more often and paint. Just because I took the semester off college didn't mean I'd given up on my art.

Standing, I dusted my black jeans and turned only to stop dead in my tracks. Slayde waited at the end of the pier. His expression was a mixture of surprise and curiosity, and I decided I wasn't angry with him. I wanted to go to him.

"Are you following me?" I teased as I got closer to where he stood.

His chin dropped, and with a slight grin, he cut those stomach-clenching eyes up at me. "I was going to ask you the same thing."

Taking a few steps closer, I stopped when I was right in front of him. "You can't because I asked you first."

Where my show of bravado was coming from, I had no idea. I was doing good to breathe normally this close to him. It was the first time I'd seen him outside the gym — when he wasn't saving my life — and he was so relaxed and casual. Still guarded, but almost happy. And oh, so sexy.

Straightening, he pushed his fists into the pockets of his jeans. "I live right over there." He nodded toward a run-down apartment complex. "It's a shitty place, but this is my living room. Every night I walk on the beach."

Winking one eye, I smiled. "Are you saying this time I interrupted *your* routine?"

"I guess you did." He exhaled a laugh, and he was so handsome with the fading orange light brightening his face. All signs of the troubled guy I'd seen this morning were gone.

"Since I let you box with me, will you let me walk with you?" I'd kicked off my shoes, and we had already taken a few steps together in the soft sand.

He shrugged. "It's a free country."

Laughing, I crossed my arms over my chest. "That's not a very encouraging answer."

Small waves broke along the shoreline as we walked, occasionally covering our bare feet. It was like ice, and I squealed. Slayde laughed, and it was the greatest sound. I caught his arm and traded positions with him, and for a while we only walked, watching the water. It was thrilling, and at the same time so easy being with him.

"What brought you to Bayville of all places?" I asked, stealing a glance at his profile. He was stunning in the twilight with the light breeze blowing his dark hair across his forehead. "There are plenty of better options."

He looked out at the sky and exhaled. "I was looking for a place that was simple. I wanted to be close to the water. I rolled the dice, I guess." He looked at me then, his blue eyes forcing me to blink away. "Why are you here?"

"I grew up here. Left as fast as I could." I took a deep breath. "Then when I got pregnant, it seemed like the thing to do. Come home, be near my parents, regroup."

"But you stayed."

Pressing my lips together, I nodded.

"I guess I found more to stay for coming back than I thought I would."

We walked in silence a few moments. He cleared his throat, his voice more serious now. "Are you doing okay? Since the other night, I mean? Any... problems?"

I pushed my hair away from my face. "None that I've noticed. I haven't been in a similar situation, so I don't know if I'm scarred or anything."

I stopped short of telling him whenever he was with me, I felt incredibly safe. Our eyes met, and he held mine a moment.

"You're kind of in a situation like that now, walking with me here on the beach... Are you afraid?"

Stopping, I put my hands on my hips. "Are you saying you're going to try something?"

His eyes went wide. "I would never hurt you!"

"I was only teasing," I laughed, touching his arm as we resumed walking, feeling bolder somehow. "But I guess you have a point. It is sort of a similar situation." I stopped again, but this time, I took a breath and said it. "I don't think I could ever feel afraid if you're around."

His expression relaxed and that warm smile returned. It was amazing how it made him look so different—approachable, kissable. I felt the side of his hand brush against mine, and I allowed my pinky finger to curl with his. My chest was so tight. I didn't want to do or say anything that might break our connection.

After several paces, he pivoted to face the direction we'd come. "We should probably head back."

The way he stood put him directly in front of me. A few steps more, and I walked right into his arms. Our chests touched, and he lifted his hands to the sides of my face, smoothing back my hair. "We're pretty far from everything."

My body was on fire pressed against his, and his thumbs lightly traced my cheeks. My voice was a soft whisper, my chin lifted. "It's like we're the only people on Earth."

His blue eyes penetrated my gaze, and I parted my lips. Blinking to my mouth, I could almost see the internal struggle waging behind those eyes. I remembered Rook commenting on his kickass control, and all I could think was *Stop fighting*.

A low groan was the last thing I heard before his arms were around me, lips roughly covering mine. He consumed me in a desperate kiss that spun my head. Reaching to hold him, I barely registered him lifting me from the sand. My mouth moved quickly, again and again with his, as a hum of satisfaction ached from my throat.

The noise seemed to enflame him, and I felt his hand scoop under my ass. My legs went around his waist, and I kissed him deeper, as if my life depended on it, as if this moment were the only thing keeping me alive.

Our lips sealed together, bodies touching everywhere, from my hands clutching his neck to his arms around me — everything was united in this incredible kiss. When at last he lowered me again, I held on, not wanting us to part.

He cupped my cheeks and kissed my lips, my chin, my cheek, my nose, my closed eyes, before pulling me tight against him, enveloping me in a hug that was more than warm. It was passionate and protective and so intimate. God, I wanted him so bad it hurt.

Slowly the waves of emotion in my brain subsided. I was acutely aware of us, breathing rapidly, his cheek against my head. "I've wanted to do that for two days."

Lifting my face, I traced a finger down the line in his chin. "I've wanted to do that for two days."

He smiled, revealing straight, white teeth. "That's all you've wanted to do?"

"No." Our eyes joined. "I've wanted to do a lot more."

"A lot more?" His voice turned daring. "I was pretty sure you were mad at me this morning."

All of that seemed miles away now. In this place it was just the two of us, holding each other, breathing each other's breath, no conflict.

"I can't remember this morning."

A low noise rumbled in his throat just before his mouth covered mine again. This kiss was even more intense, and I felt his hands moving from my cheeks to my waist to my back and then lower, cupping my ass. A little whimper came from me as he clutched me against him, and I could feel his erection hard at my stomach. *Yes.* The word ached from deep in my core. My inner muscles clenched, and all I wanted was for him to fill that need in me.

He kissed me again and again before pulling his head back with a deep breath and another groan. "Kenny." He hugged me against his chest, working to calm his body's responses. It was so sexy, I struggled not to tear his shirt off.

"I need to get you back to your car." He grasped my hand firmly in his and started walking the way we'd come. I followed trying to keep his pace, skipping along the sand. Every minute or so, he'd glance back. I could've flown at this point.

Once we were at the boardwalk, he stopped and faced me. The lights were all on now, and they cast shimmering-white circles on the black water. Moths and other bugs flew wildly at the lamps, seduced by their humming glow. I was seduced by him.

Pulling me against his chest, he leaned down and kissed my cheek, the side of my ear, before whispering, "I want you in my bed so badly."

"Okay." I didn't even hesitate, but he did.

He leaned back, holding my cheeks. "God, you're killing me. You know that?"

"Why? What's wrong?" I wanted nothing more than to spend the night wrapped in his arms. "Isn't your place right over there?"

"Yes." His gaze raked over my body and back to my eyes. It was thrilling. He ran his thumbs over my throbbing lips, and I wanted him to kiss me again. "I need to take care of a few things first. I'm not ready for you to see my place."

I put my fingers on his square chin again, running my thumb down that sexy line. "You make it sound like you're hiding something illegal."

"No." Pulling my face to his, he kissed me deeply one more time, sliding his tongue to mine, tracing the rim of my lips before pulling the bottom one between his teeth.

I couldn't help a little whimper. "You're a horrible tease."

"You have no idea how this is killing me."

"You could always come to my place."

He was quiet a moment, thoughtful. "You have a point."

Looking up at my car and then back to me, he grinned. "Give me twenty-four hours."

My brow lined and he kissed it, lowering his hands to my waist. Then his lips moved to my temple, and he took a slow inhale. "You smell so good. I can't wait to have my mouth all over your body, Kendra Woods."

A thrill surged through my core. "I can't wait either, Slayde Bennett."

He pulled my face up and kissed me several more times before stepping back. "Now get out of here before I forget I'm a gentleman."

"Are you a gentleman?" I squinted.

"Not really." A naughty gleam hit his eye, and I was sure I'd have to change panties when I got home. "With you I try to be."

Stepping forward, I caught his cheeks and kissed him hard. "Don't try too hard. I've never been much for gentlemen."

"Go. Now." His voice was almost a growl.

"If you insist." Shaking my head, I skipped away to my car. If he wanted to delay our gratification, I could play that game—as sucky as it was.

Pausing, I looked back one last time. He stood there in his jeans and white tee with his hands in his back pockets. That sexy grin was on his lips, and he was yummy enough to eat—or at least run my tongue all over.

I blew him a kiss, and with that we said goodnight.

Chapter 13: "Take every chance."
Slayde

My head was on fire; my whole body was on fire as I stood there watching her drive away. I couldn't believe I let her go. Everything in me wanted to carry her back to my place and make love to her every way I knew how — on the bed, on the table, in the shower, against the wall... Would she scream when she came? Was she quiet? Did she make that sexy little moan? *Fuck! What was I doing?*

I was being smart. I *had* to let her go. I didn't have condoms for one thing; my apartment was a shithole for another. It might work for me to eat, sleep, and shower here, and call the beach my living room. With Kenny, I wanted something better — clean sheets, for starters. Flowers would be a bonus. Maybe I could grill something for her to eat. Or not. I couldn't tell what her appetite was like.

All I knew was she filled my mind like the most powerful drug. Only boxing felt this good. Lying back on my bed, I stared at the ceiling remembering her mouth. She tasted like sugar and mint, just like she smelled, and she felt like heaven. I was counting the minutes until I'd see her again. I didn't work on Sundays, but I'd be in early for our training session. Pulling out my phone I wished I'd gotten her number.

I needed to buy more minutes.

* * *

Tension ached in my throat the next morning. Would she be different when I saw her again? Would she change her mind? Half the night I'd tossed and turned, reliving the feel of her lips against mine, the amazing sensation of lifting her small body in my arms, her legs wrapped around my waist. She weighed next to nothing, and I could've held her that way for hours exploring that mouth. *Delicious.*

I rounded the corner at the gym and there she was. Her gorgeous blue eyes flickered to mine and then away again like little birds.

"I wasn't sure you'd come in, since it's your day off." She smiled, that dimple appeared, and my tension released.

I walked over to where she sat on the bench, doing my best not to look like I was ready to jump her. "You didn't think I'd miss our workout?"

"But you're not training me, remember?"

"I can make an exception in this case, I guess."

"You guess." She stood in front of me then, facing me with a grin. Those gel gloves were on her hands, and she was so small and fierce. I wanted to sweep her up and kiss her until she couldn't see straight. "What happened to 'I don't fight anymore'?"

Our bodies were so close, I couldn't resist wrapping my finger in the ends of her long purple ponytail, giving it a little tug. "I'm not fighting. I don't fight girls."

Her eyes flashed, and my stomach tightened. Damn she was sexy. "I'll kick your ass, Slayde Bennett."

"Oh, yeah?" I smiled and her eyes darkened.

She punched my shoulder with one of the gel gloves. I barely even felt it. "See that poster? I'm the tiger. *Me!*"

I couldn't help laughing. "That all you got, Tiger?"

She punched me harder, still bouncing. "How bout that?" Then she did it again, *right, left, right.* I caught her around the arms and lifted her, pinning those little fists against her chest.

"Put me down!" She struggled for a second before her chin lifted. Our mouths were a breath apart, and if this was a test, I didn't give a shit about passing it.

"Fuck it." I lowered her and caught her face, covering her mouth with mine. All the frustration from last night flowed into that single act, and she let out that sexy little moan as her arms wrapped around my neck.

Mint and sugar were on my tongue, and I moved my hands to her waist lifting her again as our tongues curled together. I wanted to consume that smart mouth.

She gasped and broke away, turning her face. I took that opportunity to touch her neck with the tip of my tongue before closing my lips against her skin.

"Oh, god," she gasped, before catching my face again and pressing her lips to mine. Our kisses were fast and desperate, almost as if our mouths were chasing each other's.

My hands fumbled with the edge of her tank until I found her bare skin and slid my palms across it, cupping her lower back and drawing her close to me. From there, my hands moved lower, scooping her up by that fine little ass as her legs went around my waist. She moved against me in a way that I knew was getting her off. Another little whimper, and it was like gasoline on a fire already raging in my chest.

I wanted her so bad, but we were at the gym… We were the *only* people at the gym. I caught her lip between my teeth wondering what she would say if I—

"Nobody else is here." She gasped, holding my neck with her gloved hands, pressing her lips against my skin. "Nobody would know."

She read my mind. Glancing around, we weren't too far from the men's locker room. Holding her in my arms, I carried her straight to the metal doors as her lips moved to my ear.

"I dreamed of you inside me last night," she whispered against my skin.

"Shit, girl, I hope you liked it fast and hard." I pulled the door open, and we were inside.

Her hands gripped the edge of my tank, helping me whip it over my head. I barely registered the gasp hissing through her lips, and she lightly touched the ink around my neck. I knew what she was seeing, but I didn't care. Slayer was alive and well, and I was a fool to think he wasn't.

My hands were under her tank at her sports bra, shoving it up and off. Small, beautiful breasts, a beaded nipple was in my mouth, and she dropped her head back with a moan. "Oh, god, Slayde."

Her hands threaded into the sides of my hair pulling me closer, and I pushed a hand inside her yoga pants. Her hips fell open as my two fingers slid inside. Another little noise, and I almost shot. *Fuck me.* She was dripping and clenching on my fingers.

"These pants need to be off. Now." My voice was a low command, and she immediately moved to obey when a loud voice cut through our moment.

"What is this? Fucking Karma?" Rook was right behind us, and Kenny squealed, pressing her body against my chest.

Straightening, I held her to me, using my arms to cover her.

"Shit," she whispered, her head tucked under my chin.

"Get the —" My voice broke off as I stopped my instinctive response. I was pissed and ready to shout at him to get the fuck out of here. Only, I remembered the pecking order, and it was very possible I was about to be fired.

"You're supposed to be on your day off." Rook stood there frowning with his arms crossed. "If you're going to be up here, it'd better be because you're thinking about what we discussed."

All I was thinking about at this moment was the small woman in my arms, her soft breasts pressed against my chest, my straining dick, and how bad I wanted to be inside her. Kenny's head moved against my skin, and I glanced down at her. I didn't want to be fired. I wanted to be here, seeing her every day.

Clearing my throat, I managed to calm my voice. "I thought about it. I'm going to train Kenny."

"And what exactly are you training Kenny to do?"

She lifted her chin to face him. "If you wouldn't mind giving us a minute. I'd like to put my clothes back on."

He paused a beat longer then lowered his arms. "No fucking in my men's room. Got it?" I nodded, and with that, he turned and headed out the door.

We both released our breath, and I distinctly heard her mutter *hypocrite*.

She was still in my arms and I looked down. She lifted her chin, so I could see those eyes. "Damn," I whispered. "You are so beautiful."

Her cheeks blushed a delicate shade of pink, and I couldn't resist leaning down and kissing her one more time. Her mouth opened, and her hand touched my cheek. My hand moved up to her small breast, rolling a still-tight nipple between my thumb and forefinger.

"Mmm," her moan had an edge of frustration in it.

It was one of the hardest things I'd ever done, but I managed to pull back. "We better hit the bags."

* * *

We didn't have much time left to train, and to be honest, it was hard to think about much past what we'd almost done in the men's room.

She stopped punching the bag and stared at me as if reading my mind. "How am I doing?"

I blinked the X-rated images out of my brain. "Elbows are tight and chin tucked, but you're still too close." I touched her waist, and a little surge moved between us. It was crazy how bad I wanted to finish what we'd started. "Start a little more than arm's length out."

Glancing back over her shoulder, she smiled. "Will you suit up and practice with me?"

"You want me to?" Her dark purple ponytail bounced with a nod, and I thought about it. "I could hold the pads while you work. Maybe do some practice sparring."

"It's probably a bad idea. I'll just want to hang on you the whole time."

That made me laugh. "I've never been in the ring with someone I only wanted to hold." She threw two jabs followed by a left cross. "That's good. Your form is really good."

At that she turned her back to the bag, eyes shining. She really got off on me complimenting her. "I just saw the time. I've got to hit the showers. You staying?"

I thought about my own plans. "Nah, I've got a few errands to run before tonight."

The corner of her mouth curled up. "Meet at the pier?"

"That would be perfect."

She left the room, and I gathered up my stuff. Only a few hours and we'd be together again.

Chapter 14: "Drop every fear."
Kenny

Mariska was bouncing with excitement when I finished with my last client. As soon as I'd said goodbye, she almost jumped over the bar. "You are so bad. Tell me everything, you naughty girl!"

I ducked under the counter, going behind the bar. "I have no idea what you're talking about."

"Liar. You know exactly what I'm talking about. And it starts with an *S* and ends with a *T*."

"Wait... what? I thought you were going to say—"

"Slayde Bennett." Her grin was smug, and I felt my cheeks get hot.

"What do you know? Or think you know."

"I know what I heard Rook telling Tammy on the phone. Somebody was steaming up the men's locker room this morning, and it wasn't in the showers!"

Pulling her close, I pinched her arm. "Keep your voice down."

"Ow!" She screamed. "You're so damn violent. No wonder you're into him. Anyway, I think it's awesome. About time Rook got a dose of his own medicine."

"It wasn't like that." Lifting the key lanyard over my head, I shoved it into my cubby. "Slayde was showing me some pointers, and it just sort of... escalated."

"I'll say! Are you meeting him tonight?"

Chewing my bottom lip, I wasn't sure how much I wanted to share. It was all so new and tentative, and I wasn't certain how he felt. Exactly.

"Oh my god, you are!" she shrieked.

"Shh!" I pinched her arm again, and again she squealed. "We're meeting at the pier, and I don't know. It's possible something might happen."

"Why are you lying to me?" She leaned back and crossed her arms, trying to act pouty even though she was bubbling over with excitement. "Your aura is burning red."

"Would you be cool? Please?"

She swept her long, curly brown hair behind her shoulder, causing her bronze crescent-shaped necklace to shimmer. "I am *always* cool. Just because you can't appreciate my gift of perception doesn't mean I'm uncool."

Crossing the small space, I wrapped my arms around her waist and rested my cheek on her thin shoulder. "I'm sorry. You're fantastic, and I love you. But Slayde is… delicate."

"He is so far from delicate it's hard to even quantify—"

"Okay, delicate is the wrong word." Closing my eyes, I tried to picture what I meant. "He's very… guarded."

"Yes. That is the truth." She nodded, holding my arm with her many-ringed fingers. "It took a week before he would even answer when I spoke to him."

"So you understand, then." I lifted my head and caught her pretty hazel eyes. "I'm trying to take it slow and not let him think too much about it. I don't want him to run away."

Her lips broke into a broad, white smile. I couldn't help smiling back. Mariska was so pretty. "Are you saying you don't see how crazy he is about you?"

Blinking down, I hated how my stupid cheeks blushed at the drop of a hat. "It's not always like that when we're together. He was very reluctant to get close."

"Umm, not," she laughed. "He told you no, what? One afternoon? And then less than twelve hours later, he was right here, exactly where you said you'd be."

"It was a little more than twelve hours." I stepped over to the blender. Her recipe book lay open, and I slid my fingers over her curly handwriting.

"Thirteen hours? That's very lucky."

It was impossible not to grin. "My point is, don't be too vocal about it all yet. Give him a little space."

Crossing her arms over the white tank she wore, her eyes narrowed. "You're majorly serious about this guy."

I couldn't look up because I couldn't argue. She'd see straight through my lie. Still, it all felt so fast. Then I remembered what Patrick had said about being open.

"More like I'm curious. He makes me feel things…" I didn't want to finish that sentence. "I want to see what happens."

She dropped her arms and stepped forward, catching my hands in hers. "I have an incredibly great feeling about this, and I'll be as indifferent and apathetic as you need me to be."

My brow relaxed, and I hopped forward to kiss her cheek. "Love you, girl."

"I want so much good for you, hon. You deserve it."

* * *

Shaving my legs for the third time, I sat on the edge of the tub and thought about my clothing options for the night. It was such a cliché, but I always felt more confident in my stilettos. I bought the cutest pair of brown leather ones with red patent-leather Mary Jane straps across the ankles last year.

My red chiffon dress had been begging to be worn since the day I bought it on sale at American Eagle with Mariska. She, by contrast, had picked out a circle-skirt in an amazing southwest-Indian print and worn it a dozen times already. Mine had been hanging in my closet untouched. It was short, flirty, and perfect.

Glancing at the clock, it was two hours until seven. Why hadn't we set a time? I didn't know what to do, so I decided to play with my hair. Sectioning it off into quarters, I took the top portion and teased it into an Amy Winehouse-style beehive. Okay, it wasn't *that* big—more like one of those lumps Patrick would say were in Lane's oatmeal. Still I felt a little of my edge restored with my bombshell hair, a small dose of confidence.

With a sigh, I saw it was still an hour until seven. Pulling out the curling iron, I sat on the sink and made loops in the length hanging down my back. After I had a nice cascade of curls, I put it aside and pulled out my black eyeliner. My knees were practically at my ears as I leaned forward and drew a dramatic line over my eyes. A little tweak at the corners, and I sat back. My blue eyes shone like crazy with all the drama, but it was too much. I reached down and pulled out my brush. A few swipes and the bulk of my mini-beehive was gone. My eyes were still drama, but I looked less like a hooker and more like a vixen.

It was seven. I didn't know if that was the right time or not, but clearly I couldn't stay in this apartment anymore. No telling what I'd look like when I met him.

Swinging my feet out of the sink and into my shoes, I leaned down and buckled the straps then I headed for the door. I hadn't thought to slurp down a glass of wine in all my preparations—why hadn't I done that? Now I was all nerves.

I was heading out into the night, moments away from facing the most gorgeous guy I'd ever seen possibly ever... okay, Patrick was pretty damn hot, but that was doomed from the start. This situation, on the other hand...

My insides were quaking when I pulled up to the pier. I couldn't get out like this. I put the car in drive and headed to the nearest gas station. It was too well-lit, and a few tweens were hanging out on the curb holding skateboards and acting like punks. God, that used to be me.

Charging inside, I went straight to the refrigerated area and pulled out a four-pack of Woodbridge. It was fast and dirty, and I paid the cashier and charged back to my car. Not having a set meeting time, I felt slightly better about parking near the pier and twisting the top off a little bottle.

Trembling, I lifted it and slugged the whole thing at once. It was enough—I didn't want to be juiced when I met up with him. I didn't feel it just yet, but I hopped out, hit the automatic lock and threw my keys in my bag.

With every step, my limbs felt a little warmer, a little looser. He wasn't at the pier, but at least I wasn't shaking now. The pier posts extended above the wooden planks, and I leaned my cheek against one thinking about what had brought me here. All the events leading up to this moment, from my drive to Wilmington to my disastrous night with Mariska to meeting Slayde in the gym to last night to this morning...

"Hey." His low voice snapped me out of my reflections. I turned and stood straight to face him, energy surging through my stomach.

He exhaled a low, "Wow."

Suddenly self-conscious, I looked down, taking in the filmy red dress, my tall shoes. I was pretty fancy compared to him in the same faded jeans and a navy tee.

"I've been waiting for a reason to wear this," I said, apologetically. "It's been hanging in my closet forever."

He was barefoot in the sand, but he stepped up onto the pier and quickly took both my hands. His eyes shone, and I could hardly look at them.

"Why do you do that?" He caught my chin and turned my face back to his. I could've gazed all night at his dark hair moving in the constant breeze, his square jaw shaded by the faint scruff of a beard, and that sexy line down his chin—if it hadn't been for those ice-blue eyes.

My voice was quiet. "People always say I have beautiful eyes."

"You do." His answer was quick.

"But so do you. I look in them, and I feel like I can't breathe."

He stepped forward and cupped my cheek in one hand before closing his lips against mine. It was a gentle kiss. No tongue, but full of warmth. I felt his breath whisper across my cheek when he leaned back and looked straight into my soul.

"I'm so glad this dress was hanging in your closet forever. You're beautiful."

"You keep saying that," I laughed, turning my face to the side. "You're the beautiful one."

"Come with me." He pulled, and I stumbled after him. At the edge of the pier he stopped. "Sit."

I followed orders, and his large, warm hands circled my ankles. "I love these shoes." He turned my foot side to side. "God, I hate to do this." In one quick motion, he slid the ankle strap down, and it was off. Then he did the same with the other. "Walk on the beach with me, but hang onto those. We might put them back on later."

A little charge raced through my core at the prospect of how that might go. I didn't have time to dwell on it because he pulled me to his side, and his muscled arm wrapped around me, holding me close as we walked north along the shoreline.

He looked forward into the breeze. "How is it possible I came here thinking I'd fade away, and I found you?"

Entranced by the sight of him holding me so close, I was sure he felt my heartbeat, and I found myself being utterly truthful. "I was so messed up.

Everything about me was wrong until you appeared."

"I don't believe it." A laugh was in his breath. He was so amazing, confident, determined, impenetrable, and yet vulnerable at the most unexpected times.

He stopped walking, and for the space of two heartbeats, I stood there, wrapped in his arms, his fingers laced with mine at my back, our mouths a breath apart. Then the breath was gone. He kissed me with so much emotion, my legs grew weak. Lips parted, tongues curled together, I struggled to get my hands out of his.

At first he wouldn't release them, and feeling his strength, the sense of being trapped by him was intensely erotic. His grip loosened, and I pushed my arms around his neck. I loved the way he lifted me, holding my waist, our mouths never parting, only moving in time—open, closed, tasting—until he pulled back with a start.

"Shit! We've got to get back!" He lowered me quickly to the sand.

It was so unexpected I had to laugh. "What?"

"Come on." He held my hand and took off fast in the direction we'd come.

"Slayde!" I couldn't breathe as he picked up the pace. His legs were a bit longer than mine, and I was gasping before we were even halfway there.

He stopped abruptly, and I ran into him. "Oh!" I cried.

Catching my face, he kissed me fast on the mouth. "Hop on my back."

He turned so his back was to me. Lifting my hand, I placed it on his corded shoulder. "I can honestly say I never expected this to happen."

150

"Hurry, our dinner is on the line."

With a little hop, I was on his back, shoes in one hand, both gripping him hard across the chest. He reached around and held me as he jogged up the shoreline in the direction we'd come.

My voice was bouncy and breathless, as I strained to hold on. "You're so fit. We should make this part of our training regimen."

Once we were within sight of his apartment, he lowered me and grabbed my hand again. We dashed over the boardwalk, across the parking lot to a dingy white door labeled 24-A. It wasn't even locked.

"Welcome to my place." He didn't look back, running across an unbelievably small room with a curtain hanging around one corner, out a small back door.

While I waited, I looked around the space. The finish on the ancient wood floors was dull. An efficiency kitchen was in the corner opposite the curtain, and a two-seater table with two chairs was in front of it. On the table was a short, glass vase holding two red daisies and three big white lilies. *Interesting.*

Down from the kitchen was a door that led to what I assumed was the bathroom, since I didn't see one anywhere else. The space where I stood must've been the living room — wait. Correction — he'd said the beach was his living room. I could see why.

Curious about the curtain, I stepped toward it and had only pulled it back a fraction when he was back inside.

"Checking out my crib?" I dropped my hand, and he laughed. "It's not much, but at least it's clean."

I smiled and went to where he stood by the door. "It's everything you need in one compact space."

"I read in New York some micro-apartments are two hundred square feet. Total."

"See? You're practically in a mansion!" I laughed, and he wiped his forehead.

"I'm a sweaty mess." He looked down as he wiped his palm on the back of his jeans. "And I only saved one of the steaks."

The white tee he wore clung to his lined chest where the sweat dampened it, and I wanted to be back against that hard body so badly.

"We could go for a swim in your living room."

He glanced around the studio. "I'm not following—"

"You said the beach was your living room."

His eyes traveled quickly down my dress to my bare feet. My shoes were at the door. "Did you bring a swimsuit?"

"No." The change in his expression made my pulse tick a little higher. "I could borrow one of your shirts, I guess."

"My only clean ones are white."

Stepping to him, I fluttered my fingers over his stomach, catching the edge of the shirt he wore. "That's okay."

"I'd better put our last steak in the microwave."

* * *

The moon shone round and full over the water, touching the tips of the breakers in silver light. It was a gorgeous night, and the disappearance of the sun hadn't caused the temperature to drop too much. Still, it was fall and the water was cold. I'd danced around the edge for several minutes before Slayde hoisted me over his shoulder and charged straight into the black waters, me laughing and squealing the whole way.

Now we drifted on the waves, my arms around his shoulders and his around my waist. The water was chilly, but I was warm against his skin in the too-big white tee that drifted up like a dress. My legs wrapped around his, and I tried to remember why I hadn't removed my panties. Oh, because he hadn't given me a chance. I laughed through my nose.

"What are you thinking about?" He smiled and leaned forward to kiss my neck, right at my ear. His touch made me shiver.

"All of this is so crazy and unexpected."

His arms tightened around my waist, and his lips moved to my eyebrow. "You've made everything unexpected for me."

Resting my palms flat on his shoulders, I looked into his blue eyes, clear in the moonlight. "You've made everything easy for me. Before it was all confusing and frustrating."

"Why frustrating?" His eyes traveled over my face.

Thinking about my answer, I focused on his mouth. "I needed to change how I was living, but I was afraid. I didn't know if it would be too hard or if I'd make another mistake... so I didn't do anything. Until you."

"Stand up," he whispered. He'd been walking toward the shore, and I hadn't noticed until I lowered my legs, and my feet touched sand.

The white shirt I wore was like a transparent second skin on my naked body, and I saw his eyes darken as I stood facing him. Lust trembled in my chest as his warm hands cupped my hips then trailed up past my waist, higher to my ribcage. His eyes burned into mine as his thumbs followed a line toward my heart, stopping when they reached my hardened nipples. My brow collapsed as he circled them, teasing me, flooding my already wet panties with heat.

The muscle in his jaw moved, and his voice was a throaty whisper. "Being with you is incredibly easy. Whether it's a mistake, I guess we have to wait and see. I'd like to think it's not."

My body swayed with the movement of his thumbs over my breasts. "I want you to kiss me."

In one swift movement, his mouth covered mine. An ache of longing moaned from my throat into his, and he pulled my bottom lip between his teeth. Wrapped in his arms, tight against his firm chest, heat shimmered under my skin.

He whispered over my lashes as he pressed his lips to my forehead, the scruff of his beard roughing my skin. "I've dreamed of holding you this way since that first night. I hated myself for it because you'd been hurt—"

"You kept me from being hurt." My voice was breathless with desire.

His lips moved back to my cheek, down to my jaw. "You're so beautiful standing here in the moonlight."

Dropping to his knees, cool air flooded where the warmth of his body had been. Strong hands moved to my waist, one holding my side, the other flat against my lower back as full lips kissed my stomach through the damp shirt. His mouth moved to my hip, and I felt my legs start to tremble.

"Slayde," I whispered, barely staying on my feet. It had been so long since I'd been touched this way, I wasn't sure how much I could bear.

So fast I hardly noticed, he hooked his fingers in the side of my panties and pulled down. They were off as a deep groan left his throat. The hand on my lower back held me steady as he kissed the skin just above my clit.

"Oh, god," I gasped, threading my fingers into the sides of his hair as his tongue slid between my folds. My whole body shook as he kissed me intimately, his tongue moving full and slow, the scuff of his beard teasing my skin.

"I don't think I can stand," I panted, but he didn't stop.

My toes curled in the sand as he passed over and over my sensitive bud. Unbearable heat coursed through my thighs. My mouth was open and my eyes closed as tiny sparks fired through the arches of my feet. A high-pitched moan filled my ears, and I realized I was making the sound.

Rising on my tiptoes, I almost lifted off when two thick digits roughly invaded my core. Twisting and curling, he massaged the building ache inside me, until all at once, every muscle in my body squeezed unbearably tight and then... exploded.

"Slayde!" I cried, riding the orgasm out on his hand. "Oh, god, don't stop!"

He didn't stop. His mouth flooded me with pleasure as his fingers worked me until I couldn't bear it any more. "Oh! Stop now," I laughed, pushing his shoulders and dropping my head forward.

Smiling eyes blinked up at me, and with a grin, his warm lips traveled to the crease in my legs, licking the soft skin there, shooting another tickling aftershock straight to my core. My palms were flat against his cheeks, and he kissed his way back up my belly, pausing to circle his tongue around my tight nipple, until he was back to standing.

Weak from my incredible high, I held his arms. His eyes were on my breasts, and once again his palms rose to cup them, thumbs circling my tight nipples.

"I haven't even gotten to these yet." A ravenous tone was in his voice, sending shimmers of pleasure down my body.

"I haven't gotten to any of you." After that sample, I was aching to welcome the hard rod now pressing against my stomach.

He moved one hand up to my face, holding my chin against his palm, his long fingers wrapping around my neck and beside my ear. Tilting my face upward, his eyes traveled from my parted lips, up along the line of my hair before stopping at my eyes. It was such an intensely possessive gesture, and strangely, it didn't bother me at all. I liked him claiming me.

"Are you hungry?" My mind flew through a thousand ways to answer that question, but he didn't wait. "Let me take you back to my apartment and feed you."

Nodding, I held his shoulders. "Okay."

He scooped up my panties and shoved them in his pocket, still holding my hands. His shirt hung to the tops of my thighs, so technically, I was covered. But every step massaged my lower lips, and I ached with longing for him to fill me completely.

Back in his small apartment, he left me standing in the middle of the space while he stepped through the door that was a bathroom. Emerging, he had a thick, white towel in his hand. "I only have one, but it's really large. Wrap it around yourself."

I reached down and lifted the wet shirt off my body, so I stood completely nude before him.

The towel dropped from his hands as he hissed in a breath. "Damn, Kenny."

I moved two steps so I could unfasten the button on his tented shorts. His eyes rolled shut as my hand slid down the length of his cock. It was thick and long, and I shivered with wanting it inside me. Dropping to my knees, I licked my tongue over the mushroom-tip, tracing a line around the edge before pulling it into my mouth.

"Fuck." He groaned, lightly touching my cheek with his fingertips. My head bobbed quickly as I massaged the base, sucking and drawing him to the edge.

His voice was a ragged whisper. "Fuck, fuck, stop!"

He caught me under the arms and swept me to my feet, guiding me to the curtain and past it, onto the bed. A crinkle of foil and he was back over me, shoving my thighs apart and driving himself deep into me.

"Oh, god!" I gasped, the sound mixing with his muttered swear.

More than two years had passed since I'd been here, and the sensation of fullness, of his hard length rocking into me over and over awakened a hunger I didn't even know existed. I'd been starving.

Strong arms were on either side of my face, and my wrists were above my head in his tight grip. I struggled to free them, but he didn't release me. He used them to leverage his ripped body just above me as his hips slammed into me repeatedly, shooting wave upon wave of burning pleasure down my legs and into my torso. The sensation of being trapped heightened all my responses. I wanted to hold him, but I could only do it with my thighs. Wrapping my legs around his waist, I arched my back and bucked my hips, meeting his thrusts, driving him deeper into my core. The sensation was mind-blowing.

My orgasm broke, shaking through me violently. I cried out, and a low growl rumbled at the base of his throat. I recognized it as the noise he'd made that day at the gym when he'd unleashed the nonstop volley of punches, only this time it was his hips rocking into mine.

"Kenny, oh fuck," The sexy groan shook from his throat. He flexed, and I felt him jerk inside me as he came. Another groan and his grip on my wrists tightened. He thrust two more times before holding the last, dropping his head against my collarbone.

We were both breathing so fast, and my entire body was weak. He still held my wrists firmly in his fists above my head on the mattress. I wanted to touch him, to hold him, and I struggled, pulling down before he seemed to realize.

"Sorry," he breathed, releasing me. At once, my arms were around him, pulling his face to mine as I consumed that sexy mouth in a ravenous kiss. He kissed me back, equally hungry, equally spent, breaking away to kiss my ear as he panted into my hair.

"I'm sorry I wasn't more gentle. It's been a while."

Smoothing my palms down his lined back, I inhaled deeply. "Don't tell me that or I might play hard to get." His body rippled with a laugh, and I softly added. "It's been a while for me, too."

His lips pressed against my neck, trailing a line up to my jaw before he lifted up and found my eyes. "Stay right here, and I'll bring you what's left of dinner."

Rising quickly, he turned his back so fast, I barely had time to check out the ink on the front of his torso. On the back were those dramatic wings pointing down to a perfectly tight ass. He disposed of the condom and pulled on dark boxer briefs and a thin wife-beater before heading out to his small kitchen.

"I hope you like your steak well-done," he called, and I heard the sound of plates clanking.

I shifted up in the bed, fluffing the pillows and raking my fingers through my crazy hair. My stomach let out a low rumble, and I smiled. "I'm pretty sure I'll like anything right now."

The noise of drawers opening and closing met my ears and then I heard his footsteps on the squeaky wood floor heading back in my direction. "Good, because I nearly burned up both of them."

When he came around the curtain, I couldn't help a sharp intake of breath. His dark hair was messy from the beach, and those blue eyes glowed. His lips were slightly parted, revealing his straight, white teeth, and his square chin with the little line down the middle almost killed me. Top it all off, he was holding a plate with a steak and two mountains of vegetables in one hand, and a bottle of wine and two cheap glasses in the other.

"I'm trying to think of anything more sexy right now," I sighed.

He laughed. "You're hungry."

Placing everything on the side table, he climbed onto the bed, and I sat up with the sheet clutched under my arms. Glancing at my predicament, he hopped up again. "Not that I'm happy about this or anything, but I have one clean shirt left you can wear."

Biting my bottom lip, I smiled as he returned with another white tank. Taking it from him, I slipped it over my head, letting the sheet fall to my lap in the process.

He breathed an *Mmm*, at the brief glimpse I knew he got of my naked torso, and a little thrill moved through my stomach.

"You are the model of traveling light," I said, teasing him.

"If you ever lose everything, which I don't recommend, you'll find there's very little you actually need."

Curiosity gnawed at me. I had so many questions for him. I wanted to know everything about him.

"Mariska would be very pleased with your 'mental maturity' as she likes to call it." He cut a small square of steak and held it on the fork in front of my lips. I quickly leaned forward and ate it. The savory velvety texture of good steak filled my mouth, and I let out a little groan. "Delicious."

He smiled, looking back to the plate and cutting another piece. "I like Mariska. She's funny."

"She says you're a biter."

His brow creased. "Biting's illegal. You can lose your license for that."

"I'm pretty sure she meant outside the ring."

"In that case, it depends on the bitee. You're pretty tasty."

Covering my mouth, I laughed. "She's also my best friend."

On the plate were asparagus spears and mixed vegetables. He stabbed a large forkful of them and shoved it in his mouth. Watching his square jaw move, I couldn't help wanting to touch it.

Leaning forward, he poured us each a glass of red wine. "How'd you two meet? At the gym?"

"Actually…" I started before pausing to eat the new bite of steak he held out to me. "We met in art class. At Ocean County College."

His eyebrows rose briefly before he shoved another large forkful of vegetables into his mouth.

I couldn't take it any more. "Are you a vegetarian? Vegan?"

"Why would you think that?" His brow lined, and I realized what he was doing. He was giving me all of the steak.

Another giant wave of emotion hit me, but I tried to cover, grabbing the fork from his hand.

"Stop hogging the vegetables! The rest are mine. You eat the steak."

His eyes caught, and I knew he understood. I'd busted him. I also wondered how much he had spent on this special dinner we'd almost ruined making out on the beach.

I shoved a huge forkful of vegetables into my mouth before continuing. "Those flowers on the table are so beautiful. I almost wish we were eating out there."

"Thought you'd like those," he said, taking a big bite of steak off the fork I now held to his lips.

"You were wrong. I love them."

We were at the end of dinner, and I scraped the last of the vegetables together with the last bite of steak and held it to his mouth.

"You have it," he said with a smile.

"No way!" I cried. "I don't have half the muscle mass you do. I'll look like a pig on Monday."

He breathed a laugh and took the bite. My nose wrinkled as I leaned forward to kiss his full mouth.

"Have dinner with me tomorrow night," I said. "My place. I want to cook for you now."

That gorgeous smile softened his expression, and he nodded. "Okay."

Chapter 15: "The sun sets to rise again."
Slayde

How was it possible she was so amazing? I lay awake, staring at the ceiling, Kenny's soft body draped over me as she breathed quietly against my chest.

Lifting a long strand of dark violet hair, I slid it around my finger before holding it to my nose, inhaling the scent of the ocean. Everything in me wanted to pursue this. Hell, there was no way I could stop pursuing it... But how would she feel if she knew my whole story? How would she feel about Slayer?

At the same time, it was possible I was expecting too much. She could just be in this for fun, a few dinners, a roll in the sack, and back to friends.

No, I knew that wasn't the case. It went against all the signals she'd been sending.

Allowing my mind to travel back, I thought of how she looked when I first saw her tonight. The red dress she wore hung on her slim body in a way that drove me crazy. I wanted to slide those spaghetti straps off her shoulders, lift that filmy skirt and explore everything underneath. Topping it all off, she had on these insanely sexy shoes. I was seriously bummed about taking those off her feet.

She was so tiny without them. Her funny old-fashioned hairstyle was like something a former beauty queen would wear, a little lump with gentle curls spilling down her back to her waist. That's not right. A beauty queen would be all platinum and pink, and Kenny was jet-violet and red. Damn I loved her boldness.

It activated that possessiveness in me that I'd tried to curb. I wanted to pull her hair back and claim that mouth. I wanted to claim every inch of her, but I knew from my experience to take it easy.

Only a few times I wavered, lost control. She seemed turned on by it. When I took her like a fucking animal our first time, she cried and twisted, wrapping her legs around me and pumping her hips against mine. It was so hot. I was fucking the shit out of her, and her body was begging for more.

The memory provoked a semi under the sheets, but *damn*. I could've only been surer if she'd told me, yet she seemed as bewildered as I was by our intense connection. I was a self-centered prick, but I loved the idea that she hadn't been with anyone in a while. It made me imagine her waiting for me—as much as I'd been waiting for her.

"Hmm... Slayde?" She turned her head, and my heart stopped. Was she calling for me in her sleep?

Lifting her head, she blinked a few times, but I couldn't tell if she was awake.

"What's wrong, baby?" My voice was so tender, I almost hoped she was asleep. If not, my feelings would've been far too evident.

She took a deep breath and bent her elbow. Eyes still closed, a slender hand moved to her forehead, and she pushed a dark lock away. "Is it okay if I spend the night?"

Chuckling, I wasn't sure if it was possible for me to feel more for her until this very moment.

"Yes. I'm not letting you go anywhere tonight."

She sniffed and cuddled closer against me on the bed. She was off of me now, but her head was tucked into my ribs against the white tank I wore.

Glancing over her shoulder, I could see the length of her long, pale back, so elegant and beautiful. I traced my finger from the base of her skull all the way down the line to the top of her ass. A tiny shiver moved through her, and I remembered the way she'd shook when she came for me tonight.

"Goodnight, beautiful," I whispered before kissing her head and closing my eyes.

CHAPTER 16: "EVERY JOURNEY BEGINS WITH THE FIRST STEP."
KENNY

Slayde would be at my apartment in less than an hour, and I was totally not ready. After realizing he'd spent most of his small paycheck on our date last night, there was no way I was letting him off without a meal on me. Maybe two or three. Hell, I was ready to suggest he have dinner with me every night. For that matter, he could spend the night with me every night... Laughing, I shook my head as I leaned forward to check the meatloaf in the oven. Talk about going way too fast!

I didn't know how to cook much, but my mom had taught me to make savory meatloaf and a macaroni and cheese casserole that even I drooled over. Parmesan was crumbled across the top to form a crispy, cheesy crust, and I couldn't wait for him to taste it.

Chopping the small, English cucumbers I'd bought into slices, I dumped them into a bowl with sliced celery, onion, carrots, and walnuts and threw the entire concoction into the fridge before dashing to the bathroom.

I already had on the beige slip-dress I planned to wear tonight. It was thigh-length with thin straps over my shoulders, so I didn't wear a bra. My eyes were somewhat done, but I had to powder my nose and finish my hair.

I was bouncing off the walls, and it was only Monday. Mariska had teased me all day, fishing for details, but it was all so new. I wanted to keep us close for now, like my precious secret.

This morning, I woke with a start in his bed at nine a.m. His apartment was empty, but a note was on his pillow. I picked it up, tracing his neat, block handwriting with my fingertip.

Had to go in to work, but not before I watched you sleep for several minutes. God, you're so beautiful. Thanks for spending the night. See you soon. –S.

The idea of him watching me sleep filled my stomach with the happiest flutter. It probably helped that he kept saying I was beautiful. It was such a lie compared to him. He was the most beautiful man I'd ever seen. The best part was I truly wanted him. Oh, god, I wanted him too fucking much.

All day at work, I'd been slammed with clients, and he'd been busy with his tasks—cleaning up everybody's crap, helping Rook with deliveries, unloading and loading. Carrying heavy boxes to the juice bar for Mariska, although I was pretty sure she scouted out heavy objects for him to carry just so she could watch his muscles flex.

She'd fan her face and pretend to faint when his back was turned, and I'd burst out laughing in the middle of helping a client. The last time, I was working with a very proper older woman, and her stern response said she wasn't amused. I almost laughed more.

As soon as my last client had left, Mariska practically pushed me out the door.

"Go! Make sexy food with lots of cayenne and capsaicin. Peppers are good for the heart and the libido — it's a win-win!"

"You just love spicy food." I shoved my key in the cubby before charging out to start the dinner I'd been planning since the night before, when I realized he was feeding me at the cost of what might be his meals for a week.

Emotion burned in my chest. I couldn't believe how strong my feelings were for him. That moment last night when he'd held my face, when I'd wanted him to claim me, it was when I knew. However this ended, he was leaving a permanent mark on my heart. Nothing could stop me charging full-speed into this.

* * *

He stood on my doorstep, in a dark green tee and the same jeans he'd worn last night. In one hand was a tiny bouquet of five flowers — again daisies and lilies — the other was shoved in his pocket. Shit, he looked good enough to eat.

He peeked past me at my comparatively large apartment. "Smells really good."

"I made meatloaf." Then I started to laugh.

How much more old school could I get? I didn't care, I wanted to stuff him full of cheesy starches and meat and cover his mouth with kisses.

"Whatever you made, it smells delicious."

I loved the twinkle in his eye. Grabbing his arm, I pulled him into my apartment. "Give me those," I said, taking the flowers out of his hand. "Where do you keep finding them?"

"At the market. They have this disc... this bin."

My cheeks rose with my smile. I didn't care if they were day-old flowers, they were beautiful. "Come over here and talk to me."

I went to the bar, where I pulled out a small glass vase and a pair of heavy scissors. First, I dumped in the white flower mixture then I filled it with water. Next, I stood by the bar and snipped off the tips of each stem before sliding them into a neat arrangement. It was pretty and perfect.

"I'm not such a great cook," I confessed. "My mom taught me to cook a mac and cheese casserole in case I ever had to do one for a funeral or whatever…"

"You're making me funeral food? Shit, that sucks."

I burst out laughing, holding my palm against my forehead. "No—it's just the only fancy thing I know how to make."

"I'm not fancy."

In that moment, I wanted to feel that smile against my skin again, the scuff of that light beard. Last night he'd been all around me, inside me, everywhere. It was amazing, and I wanted to go there again. But first, we'd eat.

"You're my guest! Now come with me."

Reaching for his arm, he paused to unlace his heavy boots.

"Your place is really ridiculous," he said, looking around. "You have a whole extra room. Wasteful."

I snorted a laugh. I'd only been able to get in here with Patrick's help. Once Rook promoted me to trainer, I could finally cover all my own bills. "Yes. I'm the Queen, so you'd better act right or I'll summon my goons and have them throw you out."

Boots off, he straightened right in front of me. His mouth was a breath from mine, and it was almost unbearable. "You call those goons. I might like a good fight before I climb your walls and claim you for my own."

I clasped my hands on his cheeks and kissed him then. He didn't pull away. In fact, he scooped an arm around my waist and lifted me, kissing me deeper.

My fingers slid down, grazing the line of his jaw, before holding his neck as he released me.

Looking straight in my eyes, he grinned. "Where's this meatloaf?"

* * *

We sat at my table laughing over plates of meatloaf, mac and cheese, and glasses of white wine. I took another sip from mine and noticed his hadn't moved since I'd poured it.

"You don't drink," I finally said. It had been the same the night before. His red wine glass was full when he carried everything back to his small kitchen.

"Busted," he laughed, pushing the glass to the side. "I quit a few years back."

Chewing my lip, I was dying to know more. "Are you in AA?"

"No." His eyes seemed to glow when they met mine again. "I respect their program, but I've never been an addict."

Unsure what that meant, I smiled and forked a big bite of mac and cheese casserole. "You can sleep here tonight if you want."

"Oh, queenie, I plan to do so much more than sleep."

No denying, my stomach did a full 360-degree flip then.

* * *

Dinner finished, dishes washed, we walked outside on my side porch. It was uncovered, and we leaned against the low brick wall that formed my balcony, watching the stars blanketing the sky. Occasionally, we'd see a white streak low in the west.

"Can you believe some people have never seen a shooting star?" I asked, turning to meet his gaze.

He'd been so controlled and quiet the whole night, I wasn't sure what to make of it. At the club today, we'd been friendly, flirty even. Tonight it was different, more formal, as if he was holding back.

"Some people live all their lives in the bright lights of the city." His voice was quiet. "They have no idea what they're missing, and yet they think they're the center of the universe."

"It sounds like you have experience with that."

He exhaled and wrapped an arm over my shoulder. "I have some experience, but none of it compares with getting to know you."

Allowing my eyes to travel over his face, I took in his expression — tense forehead, chin not quite tucked, but ready.

"So let's get to know each other. What's the earliest thing you remember?"

He relaxed but shook his head. "My childhood was pretty shitty. What's the earliest thing you remember?"

"My parents were really normal. I thought they were so square. They took me to the state park every fall for cranberries, church every Sunday. For no real reason, all I ever wanted to do was be different from them."

His eyes flickered around my face. "I bet you succeeded in that."

Blinking down, I nodded. "More than you know."

"What was your favorite hobby? Swimming? Riding bikes?"

I laughed and blinked down. "Finger painting."

"What?" he laughed.

"My dad and I always butted heads, but my mom found that she and I could relate through art. She wasn't an artist, but she had a great eye."

"So you went to galleries?"

"We lived right here in Bayville, so no. We finger painted together." Smiling, I studied my hands in my lap. "She'd check out books from the library on the works of famous painters, and we'd recreate them with finger paint."

I could see him considering what I'd said. "Sounds—"

"Silly? It was silly, but we enjoyed spending the time together. Then I decided to go to art school, and the rest is history."

Turning to face me, he reached out and slid his palm over my cheek. "I was going to say *neat*. I think it sounds really neat," he said. "I'm a little jealous."

Sitting straighter, I examined his face. "Would you let me sketch you?"

"I—"

"Don't overthink it, just say yes!" I laughed, trying not to gush. "It's really not hard."

"Do I have to be naked?"

"Of course!" I cried. Then I laughed more. "But not your first time."

That gorgeous smile broke across his face, and I was so happy he was giving in. "What do I do?"

"Sit here. I'll be right back." I hopped up and ran inside, snatching my large sketchpad off the couch and a charcoal art pencil. I returned in a flash, pausing to study him looking out at the horizon. "That's just how I want you to stay."

He glanced back and I walked over to him, positioning his arm so his elbow was bent and his fist at his forehead.

"You're the modified Thinker."

"How long do I have to hold this?" Blue eyes slid to mine, nudging that little butterfly in my stomach.

"Just til I get the basic sketch. Hold still, and I'll be quick."

Starting at the top of his head, I quickly drew an oval, shading a bit along his jawline before going back and placing guide dots where his eye and nose would go.

"Drop your chin," I said, glancing up quickly and then back to the paper. My hands were flying— I wanted to get a good outline of him. His bicep peaked, and I knew he was getting tired.

"Just a little bit more," I whispered, quickly adding the angle of his elbow, the circle of his fist against his head. The rest I could fill in from memory. "Okay, you can relax now."

His arm went down, and he quickly scooted over to look at the pad. "Hmm…"

I couldn't help laughing. All I had done was the outline of him. "I'll fill in the rest later from memory."

His eyes traveled up to my face, studying me intently. "You can remember me that well?"

"You're pretty unforgettable."

He reached forward and placed his palm against my cheek in that way again. His fingers threaded into my hair at the base of my skull, and his thumb slid lightly over my mouth.

"I'd only seen you once, and I couldn't get you out of my mind." His thumb tugged at my bottom lip, and I was pretty sure I'd implode if he didn't kiss me soon. "Only, it was so dark, I thought your hair was black. But I knew your eyes were blue."

I couldn't tell if I moved or if he pulled me, and it didn't matter. Warm lips covered mine, and my mouth quickly opened to allow his tongue to curl inside. Dropping my sketchpad, I shifted forward so I was on his lap in a straddle. My knees were bent, and his hands spanned my back, holding me tight against his firm chest. Our kiss was ravenous and intense, and I loved the feel of his large hands traveling up my skin. One rose to the top of my dress and into my hair. The other traveled down, under my skirt, cupping my ass through my panties.

The memory of last night was so sharp in my mind, I couldn't help a little moan when he touched me. It was all he needed before his fingers were threading into my underwear, slipping into my wet opening.

"Kenny," he groaned, breaking our kiss and dropping his head against my collarbone. "I want you so much."

"I want you." My fingers threaded into the sides of his hair, and his hand that was at my neck, moved around to unfasten the tiny buttons at my chest.

One by one, they popped open, revealing my bare skin underneath. A little hum, and he reached around to grab the center of my back, lifting me slightly before he pulled a tight nipple into his mouth.

"Oh, god," I gasped, leaning back so he could have better access to my body. My change in position rocked my hips over his erection, and I couldn't resist doing it again.

That caused his chin to rise, releasing my breast with a light sucking sound before he kissed the bottom of my chin, lifting me entirely from his waist so we could stand. He led me inside and paused only a moment.

"Down the hall to the right," I said in a voice almost desperate.

In a moment, we were in my bedroom, and he laid me back against the mattress. My dress was open to my waist, revealing my breasts, and he grasped my waist in his large hands, running his tongue up the centerline of my torso before closing his lips over my skin.

"You taste so sweet," he said.

"It's this… organic lotion," I sighed over the need aching in my core. "Edible." Another sharp breath as his tongue touched my skin.

"It's good." He stood briefly to discard his jeans.

His shirt was still on, but I wasn't in the mood to fuss over details.

We were both ready, and I licked my lips as he rolled on the condom. Eyes darkened at my gesture, and in one swift motion, he was on the bed, sliding between my thighs.

"Oh, yes," I hissed, lifting my hips as he filled me, stretching every part of me like before.

His mouth moved from my shoulder, up my collarbone, to my neck as his hips rocked slowly into me. I wanted him to fuck me hard like he had the night before, but he seemed to be pacing himself, going slower this time.

"I want to taste all of you," he groaned, moving a little faster. "Your skin is like sugar."

"Oh, god," I moaned. The rocking of his hips was hitting my clit, causing sparks to radiate down my legs with every thrust. "Just don't stop."

That seemed to make him move faster, and the building sensation was making me crazy with desire. It was tingling and sparkling, and if he dared stop, I was sure I'd die. He didn't, in fact his forcefulness was back. His head lifted, our eyes locked, and the burning lust I saw there pushed me over the edge.

My back arched as the orgasm shook through my thighs. I cried out his name. His mouth covered mine, and I felt his groan rumble against my chest as he continued hitting me hard and fast. It was amazing and unbearable, and I didn't want him to stop.

"Shit, Kenny." His mouth broke away, and he slammed into me two more times before holding inside me, jerking with his orgasm. "Fuck," he whispered through a ragged breath. A few smaller thrusts, and I felt his heart pounding in his chest against mine.

He relaxed in my arms, and I only wanted to hold him. He was buried deep inside me with my legs wrapped around his waist. His forehead was pressed against my neck, and in the afterglow it felt like our bodies melted together.

Lips moved against my skin. He kissed my neck softly before lifting his head to look into my eyes. "You made yourself for dessert?"

I laughed, breathing through my nose, as my fingers trailed a line from his forehead to his neck and shoulders.

"I actually bought angel food cake with fresh berries and whipped cream."

"Mmm," he leaned down to kiss the side of my jaw, slipping his tongue out and tasting me again. A ripple of shimmering aftershocks flowed through my shoulders. "That sounds good, but you're more delicious."

He rolled to the side, sliding out of me, and I sat up. "Give me two minutes."

I scooped up the thin white tank he'd loaned me the night before, and in as short a time as possible, I was back, cleaned up and carrying a large slice of cake covered in mixed blueberries, strawberries, and raspberries. A generous dollop of whipped cream was on top.

Slayde had straightened the bed and sat with his back against the pillows. His green tee was still on, but with the sheet across his lap, I could tell he was nude from the waist down. His eyes traveled from what I carried down my body as I entered, and a spark simmered low in my stomach.

"Why so modest?" I teased, climbing on the bed beside him. Crossing to him on my knees, I forked a bite of cake and held it to his mouth.

He opened and took it. "I don't understand."

"The shirt." I took a bite of cake. "I saw all of you last night, you know."

"Mmm," he looked down. "It was darker then. We were in the moonlight."

"So I only get to see you in the moonlight? That doesn't seem fair. Are you a shifter or something?"

He laughed. "Wrong nickname."

My mind swirled around his words until finally it became clear *Slayer*. "You don't have to hide your ink from me. I think it's cool."

His lips tightened and he looked down. "It's not who I am anymore. Or who I want to be."

Setting the cake on the nightstand, I turned back to him. His eyes rose to mine, and I tried to fill my gaze with warmth. "If you want to tell me, I'd like to listen. If not, I understand."

He reached past me to the nightstand, dipping his finger in the whipped cream. "It can wait."

Tracing his finger over my lips, he left a trail of cream on my mouth. His eyes darkened as he watched before leaning forward to lick the sweetness away. It was intensely erotic, and my lips parted allowing my tongue to meet his.

Finding the edge of my tank, he lifted it over my head, returning his hands to cup my breasts, rolling my nipples between his fingers. I moaned into his mouth as I reached for his shirt. I needed to feel his skin against mine again.

He allowed me to lift his shirt, but as soon as it was off, he turned me so my back was against his chest. One hand moved from my breast downward between my legs, and I moaned, dropping my head back against his shoulder. Sensations flooded my brain. His fingers circled my clit, and as he kissed a line from my neck to the center of my shoulders, the light scruff of his beard sent chills flying through my torso.

"Oh, god," I felt like I was vibrating in his hands. They left me briefly to apply the condom, and then he was back, leaning me forward, his body never losing contact with mine.

My ass was lifted as he slid into me like a knife through butter. One of my arms was bent behind my back, and he grasped it as he thrust, bracing my hips with his forearm, his fingers still circling between my thighs.

He hit me deeper than he'd ever gone, and I knew it wouldn't be long before I saw stars. They were already shooting through my body making me tremble with desire.

"So beautiful," I heard him murmur, and in that moment, the tightness burst through my limbs.

"Oh, Slayde… Slayde…" I moaned, fisting the sheets in one hand. My other was still pinned behind me as he used it to drive himself deeper into my clenching insides.

I came so hard, my eyes squeezed shut, and in two more swift moves, he fell over me, a ragged moan rippling from his chest. Gasping, he released my arm, circling my waist, holding me tight against his chest.

His heart beat at my back, and I heard his breathless whisper. "So fucking good."

We lay that way, still connected, pulsing for several moments longer. I was snug against his body, eyes still closed, and his mouth was pressed to the back of my shoulder. I wanted to kiss him, so I moved forward before turning in the bed to face him.

Blue eyes smiled down on me as I touched his cheek. "I love the sound you make when you come," I whispered, stretching my chin up to kiss his lips.

They parted and he licked inside, smooth and hungry. "You make me crazy. You're so small, and yet so…"

"Responsive?" My nose wrinkled with my laugh, and he smiled back.

"I was going to say open."

"Same thing."

Resting my head on my hand, I traced a finger along the letters inked at the top of his chest. From the corner of my eye, I noticed his lips tighten, but I asked anyway. "What does it mean?"

He rose onto his forearm and reached for the white tank he'd taken off me. It was over his head and covering his torso faster than I could see anything lower.

"It was my fighter name," he said, turning his back to dispose of the condom before lifting the bottle of water I'd left on my nightstand. I watched him almost drain it before leaning back against the headboard again. I pulled myself up beside him.

"It's nothing to be ashamed of. You had a career as a fighter. Lots of guys do that."

His eyes dropped, and he looked at his hand, opened then clenched into a fist. "That name reminds me of what I was. It keeps me from going back there again."

My voice was quiet. "What happened? Did you have an accident?"

He expression was so pained in that moment I almost couldn't bear it.

"Nevermind," I said fast. "You don't have to tell me. I'm sorry for asking."

He met my eyes, brow clutched. "I used to be pretty messed up. It took a lot of work, but I learned to be a different person, to control it. Now I'm trying to start over and live a better life. A saner life."

Smiling, I lay my palm flat against his cheek. "I hope you'll let me help you."

"You already have. More than you know."

Chapter 17: "Though she be little, she is fierce."
Slayde

I didn't spend the night with Kenny. I wanted to. Everything in me wanted to sleep with her all around me, make love to her again and again, the way we had the night before. But I had to get away and think about what was happening here. I had to think about the questions she was asking and how I wanted to answer them.

With disappointment heavy in my chest, I told her goodnight, claiming I needed to get an early start the next morning. I left her standing in her doorway, beautiful in my dark green tee, after kissing her soft lips once more.

Everything about her called to me. For the first time in years, I wished my life were different and I could approach her like a regular guy. Not like a broken-down has-been with more baggage than a trans-Atlantic flight.

She deserved better, yet she wanted me. She touched my face and asked me to let her see inside my darkest places. Now I had to decide if I was brave enough to say yes, to risk losing her by granting her request.

* * *

We hadn't met for an early morning workout in a few days. Yesterday, she'd been sleeping so well, curled like a kitten in my bed, I'd left a note and went in without disturbing her. This morning, she was there, waiting for me when I arrived.

"Ready to train?" She smiled as I entered the boxing room.

My brow relaxed at the sight of her in tight black exercise pants and a dark purple sports bra. Her hair was wrapped in a messy bun on her head, and I was certain I'd never seen anything more adorable.

"You bet," I said, and she skipped over to kiss me. A little groan breathed from my throat. "Mmm, unless you keep doing that."

"I missed you last night." Her eyes sparkled with her smile, and she held her hand up. "Help me with my other glove."

The thin black gloves she wore were fingerless and had gel cushions over the knuckles. They strapped around her wrists and were meant to stabilize and protect her joints against the impact. She'd already pulled on one, so I held the other at the center of my chest. Lifting her hand, palm facing me, she opened her fingers to push them into the slots.

That's when I saw it—a tiny black teardrop inked in the center of her palm. A cool flush washed through my insides but I held my expression steady. I knew what that symbol meant, any tattoo artist would know what it meant, and for the first time since I met her, I considered the possibility that she might have secrets of her own she didn't want to share.

She didn't seem to notice my change as she lifted her now-gloved hand to eye-level at her cheekbone. "Ready when you are!"

Her smile was so genuinely flirty and cute. It didn't make sense to me how a girl like her could be hiding a secret that big. Maybe to her I didn't make sense either, but one thing was for sure—we had more talking to do.

"Show me what you got."

We trained, me giving her pointers, correcting her form, until the clock told us both we had to call it quits. The group classes would be arriving, and I'd be stuck here late, waiting to clean the ladies' locker room.

"You go ahead," she said, using her teeth to pull the gloves off. I hadn't even noticed the small tattoo before, yet now it was all I saw. "I'll have my breakfast smoothie and let you finish."

"I'll have to work fast."

Stepping back to kiss her brow, I took off toward the front.

CHAPTER 18: "SURRENDER TO WHAT IS."
KENNY

Mariska waited with a matcha-tea smoothie for me when my last client of the day finally left.

"Smoothie on me." She slid it across the counter.

"Thanks," I said, noticing Slayde's key was back in his slot. He'd left for the day without telling me, and I couldn't stop a frown.

My best friend didn't miss a thing. "What's the latest on you and Batman?"

"Oh," I tried to laugh it off, dropping my chin. "He... umm... had something to do this afternoon." I couldn't tell her the truth. I had no idea what was going on.

"It looked like things were getting pretty hot and heavy on Sunday."

The smoothie she'd made me was good — tea with mint and a little sweetness. I took another long sip before answering. "Monday, too."

"Well, it's only Tuesday!" She laughed. "Why do you look like your favorite stiletto lost a heel?"

I stabbed my drink, wishing it were something stronger to numb this growing pain in my chest. "I'm afraid I might be pushing him too fast. That he'll pull away all of a sudden."

Her brow lined, and she stepped over to lean beside me against the counter. "I'm sure you're not." Reaching up, she slid a ringed finger down one of my long purple locks. "But I swear, the way he looks at you. He might be moving himself too fast."

"Maybe." I looked down, remembering last night in bed. I didn't want to talk about it anymore. Two days ago, the center of my chest felt like it was expanding with joy. Now all that extra space was collapsing in on itself.

Mariska continued wrapping my hair around her fingers, watching my expression. "I want to have you both over for dinner and Turkish coffee Friday."

Smiling, I blinked up at her. "I'm sure he'd like that. He told me he thinks you're funny."

"Then we'll put it on the calendar in pencil." Pulling me into a hug, she spoke against my ear. "Hang in there. Men get spooked when you touch them deeply, but he's not going anywhere."

I couldn't tell her I'd been the one touched deeply. The speed of it all had my mind reeling, and I probably needed a little break to sort it out myself.

Squeezing her arm, I straightened up and pushed my hair behind my shoulder. "No matter what happens, I'll be there Friday night. I can't make my plans worrying about what some guy's doing."

"That's the spirit. Friday it is — in pen."

* * *

Lying on my couch, I pulled out my sketchpad and charcoal pencil. The drawing I'd started of Slayde had only partly come to life. I'd finished his eyes last night, shading them slightly oval, darker at the edges and clear in the center. I'd worked on them after he left, while they were still fresh in my mind. Tonight they made my stomach hurt they were so beautiful. I started on his jaw, shading and blending until I had the bone structure and texture of his light beard just right. That brought me to his perfect chin, and I exhaled a painful sigh as I finished it. Why didn't he tell me goodbye? He hadn't called or anything, and I didn't know how to get in touch with him.

I dropped my head back on the couch cushion. I'd been happily alone for so long... well, somewhat happily. Then all of a sudden, he came along in a blast of intensely erotic and unexpectedly sweet companionship. Now I was even worse off than I'd been before. The tightness in my chest, that inability to breathe was almost unbearable.

Lying on my side, I ran my finger down the line of his square jaw on my large pad. I traced the side of my thumb down the center of his chin. Closing my eyes, I could still feel the brush of his lips over mine. The memory of his beard scratching the sensitive skin behind my neck made me shiver. I remembered him holding my breasts, pulling them into his mouth, and...

"*Dammit!*" I shouted, standing up fast and kicking the side of the couch as hard as I could.

"Ouch!" I screamed, dropping back again. "Shit shit *shit*!!!"

Pulling my foot up, I jerked off my sock. My toe wasn't broken but it was already dark red. "Shit!" I hissed, standing and limping to the bathroom. "Fuck you, Slayde Bennett." I growled, turning on the water. "You are fucking not going to make me feel this way. You can kiss my ass."

I jerked my hair up into a messy bun and stepped into the tub. I'd shower and I'd brush my teeth. Then I'd get in my bed and read a good book, and I would not be jerked around by a guy. Not ever again.

* * *

Just like clockwork, my eyes popped open at six a.m. I threw the covers back and stood quickly, then sat back down again with a hiss. "Dammit!"

My toe was swollen today, and I could barely walk. It only made me angrier. A good night's sleep had not made me feel better. I was ready to beat the shit out of something. Limping over to my drawers, I pulled out my exercise clothes and jerked them on. I'd be at the gym in thirty minutes.

The sound of gloves slamming against canvass met my ears before I'd even rounded the corner of the small boxing room. I paused for a moment, taking several deep breaths, trying to decide how I felt as I watched him move. His muscles flexed with every stroke, breaking into deep lines and taut ripples, causing my fingers to burn with desire to touch him. God, he was gorgeous.

It didn't matter. I felt fine. That was how I felt. *Fine*. Lifting my chin, I limped confidently to the bench, dropping my bag beside it like always and pulling on my first glove. Slayde didn't stop punching. He didn't even pause. I didn't even care. I pushed my hand into one of the gloves and struggled to get on the other. I'd always been able to get both gloves on before. No reason why I couldn't do it now.

Fumbling with the second glove, I hadn't noticed the punching stop. I was distracted and mad when I felt his hand on my elbow.

"Need me to help you?" I hated the way his voice made my insides squeeze.

"No, thank you," I said without even looking up.

He ignored my response and took the glove out of my hand, holding it at the center of his chest just like yesterday.

"I said I could do it." I cut my eyes at him before pushing my hand into the glove. Taking my hand back, I waited, unsure what to do next. "Are you almost finished?"

He looked down at his shoes as if he were trying to find the correct answer.

"It's a simple yes or no question, Slayde."

"Kenny..." he exhaled deeply before pressing his lips together. "You can have this. I'll work on the speed bag."

Angry or not, I couldn't help watching him go to the small bag hanging from the ceiling. I'd always wanted to master that little bastard, ever since it knocked me in the head. Now he was walking over to it just as confident as I knew he'd be.

Waiting, I watched as he lifted his arms, elbows high and began the bicycle movement, knocking it quickly in a rhythm as his biceps and shoulders flexed.

Right, tat tat
Left, tat-tat
Right, tat-tat
Left, tat-tat

191

He kept going and going, a ripped statue of boxing gorgeousness, just like nothing had happened. Turning to the heavy bag, I decided if he didn't care, neither did I. Holding out my fist, I stepped a little more than arm's length away. Proper stance, elbows tight at my ribs, shoulders up, I tucked my chin and threw a series of punches.

Right, left, right, right, left hook
Left, right, left, left, right hook
Right, left, right, left, right, left
Left, right, left, right, left, right

Faster and faster I hit it, chasing after the release of that tension in my chest. The warm hand on my shoulder caused me to let out a little yell. I jumped forward, holding the bag as if it were my opponent.

"I'm sorry." Slayde's glove was off, and the dark green 21 was plainly visible on the hand touching me. "I didn't mean to startle you."

"What do you want?"

His eyes hadn't met mine. His brow was furrowed like it always was before, and he focused on my gloved hands.

"I'm sorry I left yesterday without a word. It wasn't until I got home that I remembered I don't have your number."

My back was to the bag, and I only waited. So he didn't have my number. Bayville wasn't that big, and he knew where I lived. His eyes met mine then, and I hated that my stomach tingled in response.

"Last night I thought it might be better if we took a little break, make sure we're not moving too fast."

Pressing my lips together, I nodded. "Okay." I started to turn and resume my workout, but he stopped me.

"Can I have your number?"

"Sure," I said with a shrug. I wasn't about to let him know how much this was killing me inside. "Where's your phone?"

He pulled out a small burner phone, and I typed in my digits.

"Thanks," he said, saving it.

"Don't share it with anyone." I turned and started hitting the bag again. As he left I heard him quietly answer.

"Don't worry."

* * *

Wednesday at the gym was absolutely miserable. I hated trying to act so perky and happy with my clients when I felt like my heart was breaking. Which was ridiculous! So what if I'd had the best sex of my life two glorious nights in a row? Who cared if he kept passing through the weight room taunting me with his sexy presence? I was a grown, professional woman. I did not need a man to make me happy. Much less a flaky one who ran at the first sign things might get serious.

"Thanks so much, Kenny." My new-mother client gave me a squeeze before leaving the weight room, and I went straight to the juice bar ready to grab my things and get out of here.

"I hope I never piss you off as long as I live." Mariska leaned forward on the bar grinning, her voice lowered. "You're doing a kick-ass job freezing his nuts off."

Shoving my key into my cubby, I picked up the matcha-tea smoothie she pushed toward me again. "Thanks. Hand me my bag, would ya?"

She reached down and picked up my purse from under the bar. "Your phone's been going off all hour."

That made me forget everything. "Mariska! Jesus! You've got to tell me when that happens. It could be Patrick!"

"Oh my god." My friend looked like she might cry. "I didn't even think of that, I'm so sorry!"

Digging out my phone, I didn't recognize the number associated with the four texts I'd received. "No, it's all good." I reached across and squeezed her forearm. "It must be spam or something. I don't know this number. It's okay."

Opening my text program, I silently read the first one: *You have no idea how hard it was to leave you Monday night.*

Then the next one: *You have no idea how hard it was to leave without telling you goodbye yesterday.*

My jaw dropped as I read the third: *You have no idea how hard it was not to touch you this morning.*

The last one sealed it: *You have no idea how much it's killing me that you won't look at me right now. I'll call you tonight.*

"Oh my *GOD!*" Mariska cried. "What the hell are you reading? Is he sexting you?"

Blinking rapidly, I tried to curb the smile threatening to break my face. Being cool was very hard when my sex-god trainer-with-benefits or whatever he was sent me texts like this.

"I guess this is his way of apologizing."

"I knew it!" She cried, practically jumping up and down.

"I'm putting his name next to yours *in pen* for Friday."

"Not so fast," I said, raising an eyebrow. "He still has some explaining to do."

"Oh, fuck that." She rested her cheek on her hand, giving me a dreamy look. "When your face looks that happy, I know exactly what it means."

"What does it mean?" My eyes were narrowed, but she had me figured out.

"It means this guy's got some serious baby-daddy potential."

"I have no intention of making a baby with anyone." I threw my bags over my shoulder and grabbed my car keys. "At least not any time soon."

* * *

Showered, fed, and snug on my sofa, I pulled out my large sketchpad and resumed work on Slayde's portrait. His nose was small and perfect. I had it finished in no time. Then I moved to his full lips. Those done, I started on his dark hair. It wasn't too long, but it was long enough to get messy in the ocean breeze around his forehead and ears. Not curly, but just the slightest bend. It was thick and soft and oh, so sexy to tangle my fingers in.

I was just finishing when my phone started buzzing at my side. I let it ring a few times before picking it up.

"Hello?" I did my best to act like I hadn't been waiting for him to call.

"Kenny, hey. It's me, Slayde. I hope you got my texts."

"I did." I tried to think of how I wanted to frame them. "They were informative."

He breathed a laugh, and an involuntary shiver moved across my shoulders. I remembered so well how it felt to have his breath on my skin.

"I guess I have some explaining to do." His voice was low, and I couldn't help wondering if Mariska had tipped him off.

Putting down my charcoal pencil, I rubbed my forehead with my fingers. "I don't like games, Slayde. If there's something you want to say to me, please do. If not, just leave me alone, okay?"

"Okay," his voice was quiet. "I want to see you again. Bad. But there are things you should know about me first."

A charge raced through my stomach at his admission. I traced my thumb over his lips in the sketch I held. "Are you trying to warn me away from you?"

I heard him exhale. "I guess. I mean, no? God, Ken, I never expected to be in this position, and now you're here, so beautiful and amazing…"

We were both quiet on the line.

"I finished my sketch of you. It's pretty good if I say so myself."

"I'm sure it is."

"You can't be sure it is," I laughed. "You've never seen any of my work."

"You're right, but if you pursue your art the way you do everything else, you're probably a master."

"Hmm, flattery will get you everywhere." He laughed, and I continued. "It's very lifelike. I'm tracing my finger along that sexy line in your chin. Feel it?"

"Yes."

Lightening flashed outside my window, but it was nothing like the flash that went off between my legs at that single word.

I rolled onto my side, putting the sketch on my coffee table. "It's going to be stormy tonight."

"It's already storming here. You'll probably be getting it in the next five minutes."

"Mariska wants us to go to her place Friday night." Closing my eyes, I imagined him beside me. "She's actually a really good cook, and she makes the most amazing Turkish coffee."

"Sounds great. Let's do it." The smile in his voice made me smile.

"I'm sorry I pushed you too fast."

He was quiet a beat. "I'm sorry I left you alone."

"See you tomorrow?"

"Of course."

With a goodnight, we disconnected, and I slid my phone on the coffee table next to his sketch. Tracing my finger down the line of his jaw, I closed my eyes, feeling him with me through the night.

* * *

When I arrived in the small boxing room the next morning, he wasn't there. I was confused, but I started my workout, pulling on my gloves and doing my drills. I was twenty minutes in when I felt his touch on my arm.

Stopping, I dropped my fists, wanting to charge straight into his arms, but I didn't.

"Now I'm the sweaty mess," I said, looking down at my body.

He smiled. "Too bad we can't go for a swim in my living room."

Frowning, I looked up at him. "Where were you?"

"I thought I'd do the ladies' locker room before I met you. I think it was the wrong decision."

That made me laugh. "Because now I need to use it?"

"No way." He pulled me into a hug. "Because now I smell like toilet cleaner." He pressed his face against my neck. "You smell like good, clean sweat."

"Oh!" I tried to pull away, but his arms tightened around my waist.

"I've wanted to hold you like this for two days."

I stopped struggling and wrapped my arms around his neck. It was crazy. We hadn't really fought. In reality, we'd just had a misunderstanding. Still, being apart for forty-eight hours had felt like forty-eight years. I leaned back and placed my palms on his cheeks.

"I want you to kiss me."

That sexy grin flashed across his lips just before they covered mine, parting them, his tongue finding mine. In a sweep, I was off my feet and we were right back where we'd left off.

Chapter 19: "Find what you love and let it kill you."

Slayde

Being apart from Kenny was the most acute, self-inflicted torture I'd ever experienced. In a period of just a few weeks, she'd become the light in my otherwise bleak existence. If the ocean were my living room, she was my sun and moon.

Tuesday, she'd been confused. Wednesday, she was pissed. I was in the pit of hell.

She was completely justified, and it only made me want her even more. If I thought distancing myself from her would give me clarity, I was an idiot. It only clouded my mind and made me think of nothing but having her back in my arms.

I'd close my eyes, and I'd see her deep violet hair. I'd throw an arm over my head, and I'd feel the curve of her breast against my mouth. I'd shove my head under the pillow, and I could see her ass, small and round, her hips perked and waiting for me to slide inside as she made those little noises begging for more.

FUCK! Yes. Torture.

This morning when she asked me to kiss her in the gym, the floodgates opened and satisfaction filled every crack in my broken insides. I consumed those lips, tasting her sweet mint flavor, dying a little bit because I knew I'd have to tell her everything at some point, and God only knew how that would end.

At the same time, after what I'd seen in her hand, maybe there was hope for me? If she were carrying a secret that big, maybe nothing I might say would send her running? It was impossible to know until we talked.

Last night I was back in heaven, wrapped in her arms. In only three days, I'd missed her like snow in the wintertime or flowers in spring. I sought out every part of her body to cover with my mouth as she twisted in the sheets and laughed, catching my cheeks and kissing me every chance she got. Finally, we slept, happy and satiated.

Tonight we were headed to Mariska's for dinner. For a moment, I sat in the old rusted-out Ford in front of Kenny's apartment. Her place was also small, but it was a hundred times nicer than my piece of shit studio, beach living room notwithstanding.

I'd looked at her door and thought about her inside getting ready. Occasionally, she'd hum some song while she did her hair. She was like a little bird..., which stirred old feelings of guilt. I wanted none of that tonight.

Hopping out, I went quickly to the door, but she had it open before I even knocked.

"I thought that was you." She flew out in a swirl of black and violet.

I caught her in my arms and pulled her close against my chest, covering her small mouth with mine and sweeping my tongue in to find hers. Damn, I could keep her here all night.

Her hair was up in a high ponytail, but the ends hung down to the center of her back. She wore a black leotard-looking top with a deep blue patterned skirt that hung to the ground. I knew she had on some of those giant shoes underneath because her eyes were just at kissing level on me. When she was barefoot, her head rested perfectly in the center of my chest. I couldn't decide which height I loved more.

"You are very exotic." I let her twirl under my arm before coming to rest against me. Her skirt swirled and landed around us.

"Thanks," she laughed, stretching her chin up and kissing my neck. I caught it in my hand, steadying her as I kissed her full on the mouth.

"Umm..." she sighed once I released her. "We'd better go. Mariska hates when I'm late."

She followed me to the truck, but I stopped before we got in. "We can take your car if you prefer—"

"What! No way—I love your old truck." She scooted closer under my arm. "It has character."

"We should give it a name."

"You're right!" She bobbed her head, and her hair danced around her shoulders. I couldn't help a smile. "Henry."

"Henry Ford?"

"It's not very original is it." Her perky nose wrinkled, and I laughed.

"Works for me."

* * *

Mariska met us at the door dressed similarly to Kenny. "Welcome! Come in!"

The two hugged and as Kenny went inside, her friend leaned forward, whispering. "I'm reading your future tonight, Mr. Batman."

"I don't think Batman uses Mister."

201

She laughed, "You're not really him anyway, so who cares?"

It was true, and I couldn't help a laugh. She'd been razzing me since the first day she'd tried using sign language on me.

"What's for dinner?" Kenny called from the kitchen.

"Oh, it's an old family recipe," Mariska said, skipping past me into the kitchen. "Sarmale, which is basically stuffed cabbage with pork and sauerkraut and tomatoes."

Lifting the lid off a Dutch oven, Kenny took a deep breath. Even I caught the savory aroma from where I stood. "It smells delicious."

"Mmm," she winked, giving it a stir. "Wait til you taste it!"

Leading us back into her elaborate sitting room, she made us all pull up huge pillows around a small table where a strange-looking copper pot sat. Three water glasses were placed beside three tiny cups on saucers.

"First, the fun part." Our hostess was clearly excited. "Fortunes!"

"Oh, you know I don't believe all of that." Kenny flopped back against the couch.

Mariska's place was exactly what I'd expected. It was small like Kenny's apartment, but she had elephants as lamps and all sorts of paraphernalia on the shelves in front of her mountains of books. The books were the only things that outnumbered the trinkets.

I was pretty curious about these fortunes. "How does it work?"

Her eyes sparkled as she hopped forward on her cushion across from me. "First you have your coffee." She lifted the copper pot and poured the black beverage into each of our cups. "Give it just a few minutes so the grounds settle to the bottom."

While we waited, Kenny took a bright yellow, candy square off a dish by her cup. It was covered in powdered sugar. "I thought coffee was for after dinner."

"Don't be so technical." Mariska fussed, picking up an orange square and holding it out to me. "Turkish delight?"

"Really?" I took it from her and looked at it closely. I'd only heard about this stuff in a children's book. It didn't look at all how I expected.

"Your coffee's ready," she said, and I lowered the candy.

Lifting the small cup, I took a hesitant sip. Thick and rich, it was smoky and earthy and had the faintest taste of mushrooms. I'd never had anything like it.

"Mmm," Mariska said as her eyes slid closed and she licked her lips.

"It's good," I agreed, taking another sip.

Kenny ate another candied square before sipping hers. "I need more sugar. It's too bitter."

"Baby!" Her friend laughed before finishing off her cup. I followed suit, but she stopped me.

"Remember not to drain the cup. It has a lot of grounds at the bottom."

"That's how she's going to tell your future," Kenny said, leaning into my arm.

I lowered the small cup that was decorated with purple brush strokes and what looked like a blue egg with a black yolk, sunny side up. "What's that?"

"The Evil Eye," Kenny whispered ominously.

"It's a *nazar*." Mariska held out her hands. "Protects against the evil eye. Hand it over."

Taking my cup from me, she removed the saucer from underneath and placed it on top. Then she flipped the entire thing and rubbed her palms against the upside down coffee cup. "Let's see what we have here."

She was clearly turned on by the spectacle of the entire thing. She removed my small cup and studied the black mess of grounds now sitting on the saucer.

"Hmm..." she stared into the mound. "Interesting."

I couldn't help laughing. "What does my future look like Madame Mariska?"

"It appears you are going to take a long sea voyage." She turned the saucer a few times. "But you have to finish the journey to find what you desire."

Her green eyes lifted to mine, and she was all mysterious. Resting my elbow on the table, I nodded pretending to be serious. "Wow. That's some trick."

She bounced on her pillow grinning widely. "You think so? My grandma taught me how to do it."

"The only problem is I'd never get on a boat. I don't know how to swim."

"What!" Kenny sat up fast. "Slayde! What about the other night in the ocean?"

"I'm not afraid of water, and I'm fine if I can stand in it."

"Why can't you swim?" Mariska looked straight into my eyes. She was still being mysterious.

204

"My mother drowned when I was a little boy." The silence that fell over the room made me shift uncomfortably. "My dad never took me near water after that."

"Yet here you are, living by the ocean." Mariska was still searching.

Kenny slid her small hand into mine. "I'm so sorry." Her beautiful blue eyes were full of concern.

"Wasn't trying to be a buzz kill." I pulled the back of her hand to my lips. "It was a long, long time ago. I've had plenty of time to get over it."

Her smile was tinged with concern. "Still…"

"Your turn!" Mariska called, picking up Kenny's cup.

She repeated the entire routine again, and then studied her grounds. "Humph. Not what I expected."

Kenny's brow clutched together. "That's not what you want to hear from your fortune-telling bestie!"

Mariska laughed. "No, it just says you'll have a change… or a discovery that will change your life. It could be anything!"

Kenny was thoughtful a moment. I noticed her glance move to my hand still holding hers and the smallest smile lift her cheek. Before anybody could speak, she hopped up and headed to the kitchen. "Let's eat. I want some of that stuffed cabbage!"

We spent the rest of the evening talking about work, Rook and Tammy, Pete, who apparently was in love with Mariska. I'd missed that altogether. With stomachs full, we said goodnight and headed back to the truck. I wanted nothing more than to take Kenny home and spend the rest of the night with our bodies tangled together.

"Can you believe those fortunes? Sea voyages, discoveries..."

She was in my arms, and I pulled her up, kissing her head. "I'll trade you my sea voyage for your discovery."

Her arms rose to circle my neck. "I've already had my discovery. Take me with you on your sea voyage."

I couldn't think of anything I liked better. "Deal."

Exercising regularly had made Slayde's physique even more defined. Tonight, after our dinner at Mariska's, it took all the control I could muster not to beg him to remove the thin wife-beater he still wore. I wanted to see everything.

Sitting on my bed facing each other, he'd already removed my skirt and bodysuit. I sat in front of him in my black bra and panties while he ran his fingers up the lines of my stomach. I shivered, touching his stomach through the transparent white tank.

"You have a butterfly," he said, lightly outlining the insect Carl had inked for me at the top of my ribs.

"I got it after my husband died," I said quietly. "For a long time I didn't even get out of bed, and then when I did, I thought of butterflies. How they practically die in the pupa before transforming into something completely different."

As I spoke, I watched concern fill his beautiful blue eyes, only to be chased away by warmth.

"You never told me you were married." His voice was soft as his hands moved to the tops of my shoulders and down my arms. "You must've been young."

"I was nineteen," I said. Then I lifted my hand and ran my finger along the letters showing around the neck of his undershirt. *S-L-A-Y-E-R*. I didn't read it aloud. Instead, I asked, "The wings on your back are very dramatic. Are they symbolic?"

His eyes grew stormy and dropped to his lap. "It's more of my shitty childhood."

I was quiet a few moments. The last time we'd gone here, he'd pulled away for two days. I wasn't sure I could take that again. And yet...

Sliding forward on the bed, I put my head against his shoulder, holding him around the waist. "I want to know, but more than anything, I want to be with you."

His lips pressed against my neck, moving down to my shoulder. My eyes were closed, and I floated my hands under the bottom of his tank, spreading my palms over the lines of his stomach. I could feel the bumps and ridges, and oh, how I wanted to see them, to run my tongue over them.

"Lay back," he whispered against my hair. I immediately complied, and he hooked his fingers in my thong, quickly removing it and wrapping my legs around his forearms. His mouth was quick to cover me, and energy flooded my core with each pass of his tongue. He was making out between my legs, and the sensation of his soft pulls mixed with the scruff of his beard against my thigh, drove me crazy.

I threaded my fingers in his hair, moving my hips in time with his luscious mouth. "Oh, god, baby," I hissed, as the pressure started to build. "Oh my god, I need you inside me now."

His arms quickly unwrapped from my thighs, but his tongue didn't leave my clit. Each flick sent a shimmery jerk through me, and I was so close to coming, I couldn't move.

A tear of foil, and in seconds, he was up, sliding that gorgeous body along mine, plunging his thick length deep inside me. It was the most incredible sensation, tingling and full. I'd never get enough.

Rocking me hard until I was crying out his name, he kept moving, building toward his own orgasm. He sat back on his feet, lifting me onto his lap in a straddle, and with every rise of my hips, I flexed around him inside.

"Oh, fuck me," he hissed, his forehead pressed against my breast. "Fuck me, Kenny."

I did just that, pressing against the mattress with my legs, rising and dropping until I heard his labored groans and his fingers gripped my ass hard. All at once, I was on my back again, never losing contact as he caught my knee, bringing it up and pushing several more times deeper. The final time he held onto me. I held onto him, eyes closed, gasping through the intense sensation of our bodies becoming one.

We slowly came down, and he released my leg. I straightened it, twining it with his as his arms moved around my body. We held on, savoring the blissful moments of afterglow.

"That just gets better and better." He breathed in my ear before kissing my skin.

I shivered at the sensation and exhaled a laugh. "You are one sexy man, Slayde Bennett."

His mouth covered mine again in a long, gentle kiss, his tongue caressing waves of happiness all the way to my toes. One more kiss, and he pulled away briefly, turning to dispose of the condom and then back, pulling me against his chest, spooning.

"You're one cunning temptress, Kendra Woods." His palms spread flat against my stomach, and he pulled me closer.

That made me laugh. "Cunning temptress?"

"You had me in your clutches during coffee."

"So early in the evening? I should've taken you to the bathroom and had my way with you."

"I would have had no problem with that."

We both laughed, and I threaded my fingers with his. We were quiet, and I thought about what he'd revealed. "I'm really sorry about your mom."

He was quiet a moment. "It was the event that changed my childhood."

Cautiously optimistic, I continued, hoping he'd open up to me. "It sounds like it wasn't a good change."

He released our embrace and rolled onto his back. I was quick to roll into him, placing my cheek on his chest and listening to his heartbeat.

"That's when everything went to hell. All the goodness left with her."

We lay in silence a few moments, our breath swirling in and out. I wasn't sure if he'd tell me more until he did.

"I was pretty broken by my mom's death, but my dad took it the worst. He started drinking and pretty much didn't quit."

My arm tightened across his waist, and I tried not to let myself envision a dark-haired little boy with light blue eyes, orphaned with a dad who had checked out.

"It got to where I wanted to be invisible. I tried to stay out of his way as much as possible, because as soon as he saw me, he'd remember something I'd done wrong."

"How old were you?"

"Seven." I felt the rage tighten in his stomach. "He'd decide I was being too loud and grab his belt. Or I'd left my Legos out and he stepped on one. He'd grab the belt."

Catching my bottom lip between my teeth, I did my best not to cry.

"He'd hit me pretty hard, but usually I could take it." He paused, quiet again. "Until this one time... somebody gave me a puppy. I don't know if it was a teacher or a friend... Anyway, it was a little beige, shaggy-haired dog. It had these big brown eyes and was happy and cuddly. It was this one bright thing, and I wanted to keep it so much. I don't know what the fuck made me think I could do that. I guess I thought I could hide it from him."

He paused, and I could feel this was hard for him by the way his breathing changed. His entire body was tense. The pause, the waiting was painful, but I wouldn't rush him. I couldn't.

"That damn dog peed all over the house. I was just a kid, but I did my best to follow it around and wipe up every mess as fast as it happened. My old man was out cold for the most part, but of course, he woke up and found some shit before I did. He tore off that belt and beat me with it. I was screaming and crying, and that damned puppy was jumping all around, whining and not understanding."

My heart beat so hard. I didn't want to hear the rest of this story. It hurt in my chest, and my stomach was tight.

"He snatched that dog up and beat it." Slayde's voice broke off a moment, but he kept going. "His belt was like a long, black whip... I'll never forget the sound of that puppy crying. It was so loud, and my old man wouldn't stop. It was like he was possessed. He beat that dog again and again until it didn't make another sound."

He stopped talking, and I turned my face into his skin, pressing close to his chest. My stomach hurt, and I couldn't stop my tears. I clung to him, holding him and wishing I could go back and comfort the little boy he used to be.

"I cried over that dog for a week. Until that sick bastard got tired of hearing me cry and out came the fucking belt. He beat me until I never cried again."

Sliding up his body, I placed my palms gently against his face. "I'm so sorry that happened to you." Tears covered my cheeks, and I kissed him softly. "I want to give that asshole a dose of his own medicine."

Slayde's eyes were somber in the dim light of the lamp. "You asked me about the wings on my back. When I was about twelve, I made this net out of string. I draped it around tree limbs and shrubs — just to see what I'd catch. I got mostly moths and butterflies. Once I caught a bird in it. It was an accident, and I couldn't get it loose. It kept struggling and struggling. It wouldn't be still. It would peck at me, and the more it struggled the worse the net tangled. It was getting tighter, and I got so frustrated. I clamped my hands over that little bird and squeezed it... until it didn't struggle anymore."

The room was quiet several moments. He didn't say more, so I carefully prompted. "I don't understand. You —"

212

"I killed it." His voice was flat. "That's when I realized I was no better than my old man. I killed innocent things just like he did for no good reason. Because they wouldn't do what I wanted."

"No!" I jumped forward to cover his lips with my fingers. "That is completely different."

"Is it?" He lifted my fingers. "When I was older, I got the wings on my back because I'd taken that life. It was the only way I knew to memorialize it. Then when I started boxing they called me Slayer, the death angel."

I pressed my lips against his skin and wrapped my arms around him. "You're not that. You're not cruel or violent. You saved my life when I was in danger, and you've only been kind and gentle with me. If you're any sort of angel, it's the guardian kind."

"It was true for a while. I had a lot of demons to fight out. I would drink until I was numb, and I'd fight until I lost control—just like him—until they pulled me off my opponent. Before it went too far, before I..." He cleared his throat. "It was great in the ring, when other people could control me."

It was hard to hear him saying these things, but I was beginning to understand why he pulled away. I thought about everything we'd done, about all the things Rook had said, about his kickass control.

"But you're not like that anymore."

His hand rubbed up and down my arm, smoothing my skin. "I've done my best to change. The question is whether that erases the past."

Closing my eyes, I thought about his question. "I don't think you can live in the past, dragging it forward with you all the time. I think what matters is what you do once you realize you're wrong."

Strong arms tightened around me, and I held him tightly in response. "I hope so," was all he said.

Chapter 21: "I am fearless because I've been afraid."
Slayde

Carefully, I'd lifted the veil, and she'd listened without fear. I'd told her the worst story from my childhood. I'd told her the worst part of myself when I was a boxer, and she'd covered it all with forgiveness and understanding. I still wasn't sure I deserved it.

Today, she'd gone to visit her little boy in Wilmington. She'd spend the night, and I'd be alone until Sunday.

"I guess this is it," I said, holding her as she stood on the side of her car. Her arms were around my neck, and her brow creased. "You're leaving me for the only boy who'll ever have your heart."

A gorgeous smile broke across her face, and she leaned into my ear. "He's my boy, but that doesn't mean I don't have room for a man."

I'd kissed her long and hard, covering her soft mouth with mine. Her hair was up in a high ponytail again, and the ends grazed her shoulders in soft bends. It made her look younger than she was, and I spanned her lower back with my hand as I traced a curl off her shoulder, not really wanting her to go. "Drive safe, okay?"

"I'm sorry to leave like this. I don't want you to think I'm running away after last night."

"I hadn't thought of that," I teased, loving her worried face.

"Now, that's exactly what I'm thinking."

"Slayde!" She pinched my arm, and I laughed an *Ow!* "I've been thinking about what you said. With the bird."

Her eyes fluttered down, and I remembered the time I'd thought they were like little birds. I only wanted to shelter her, keep her safe.

"I don't think you should carry that guilt anymore," she continued. "You were just a kid. You panicked."

Lifting my hands, I held her cheeks, forcing her to look at me. "Such a mom, finding a reason why the bad things I've done aren't really as bad as they feel in my mind."

She shook her head, breaking free of my grasp. "I'm not saying it wasn't bad, but it was a long time ago. You were sorry then, and you're sorry now. I think you can set yourself free from that one."

Her lips were close to my face, and I couldn't resist gliding my thumb over them. "I'll miss you while you're gone. Have fun with Lane."

She smiled and kissed my thumb. "I'll see you tomorrow afternoon."

* * *

Now I was back at the gym, finishing up my cleaning duties, thinking about what she said. Maybe she was right, and I could be absolved of that one crime. But that was only one.

"You done for the day?" Rook stuck his head out of his office and nodded for me to come there. "I need to talk to you about the next several weeks."

Walking into the now-familiar office, I took a seat. "Yeah? What's up?"

"I've got a deal with one of the cargo-ship captains. It's a trans-Atlantic line. They dock here once or twice a year. The crew gets free memberships when they're in port, and they ship stuff for me when I need them to."

My eyebrows rose. "Okay. Why are you telling me this?"

"Every time they come back, more and more of their guys show up wanting to work out. It's a fucking zoo for a week—longer if they get held up in port."

"Goes with the motto, yes? Where the wild things are?" I grinned, but he wasn't laughing.

"Don't be a smartass. It'll affect your job, too. These guys mean more cleanups, longer hours… I'm telling you because I need you to be a trainer while they're here."

That caused me to sit back. "I've never trained anybody."

"You've been training Kenny. It's basically the same thing. Watching form, making sure they're lifting correctly, doing full sets, not lounging on the equipment, putting shit back when they finish."

"Sounds like a few extra tasks in there besides training."

"It is, and for ten days, with a bunch of seamen who barely speak the language and don't know gym etiquette, it matters. I'll work with you tomorrow then you'll know what to do. You also get a raise. Trainers make a lot more an hour than janitors."

Shrugging, I stood. "Sounds like an offer I can't refuse."

* * *

My work was done, and I was sitting on the shore by early afternoon, thinking about Kenny. Not so long ago I'd spent every night alone. Now, it had been a while since I'd picked up my enormous paperback and checked in with the French kid. It had also been a while since I'd checked in with Doc.

I wanted to do both of those, but first, I called her.

"How's it going with your son?" I asked when her soft voice filled the other end of the line.

"Oh, Slayde, he's breaking my heart." I was pretty sure she was kidding, but the sound of her in distress cramped my stomach. It had since that very first night.

"What's going on?" I asked.

"He's growing up so fast!" She sighed. "I convinced Patrick and Elaine to take a date night, so it's just me and him. He can count to ten! He knows more colors... He keeps patting my head and saying *purple...*"

"How old is he again?"

"Two!" She cried, and even though she was upset, I couldn't help a laugh.

"Isn't that still considered a baby?"

"He's a toddler. And I remember so clearly the day he was born."

The image of her caring for a little guy made me smile. "It sounds like you're one of the best moms."

The line was quiet a few moments, and her voice was hesitant when she spoke again. "Thank you. For telling me that story last night."

My stomach tightened. "It was a shit story. I'm sorry I told you."

"I'm glad you did." Her voice was more forceful. "It helps me understand you better."

"How about next time we just stick to your stories. They're a little easier." I looked at the *21* on my hand, thinking about her one bit of ink we hadn't discussed, a potentially difficult Kenny story.

"Okay." I could hear the smile in her voice. "But I wanted to thank you for trusting me."

A fist unclenched in my chest, and I knew what I wanted to say. I wanted to tell her how I felt, the possessiveness expanding and opening out to surround her. Instead, I stuck to the basics.

"I don't want you to think I'm holding you out. There are just some things I'd rather not relive."

"I understand that." Her voice was quiet. With my eyes closed, I could see her mouth, and everything in me wanted to taste it.

"I wish you were here."

"I'll be there this time tomorrow." She was smiling again. "I miss you, too."

* * *

Rook was waiting in his office when I arrived at the gym Sunday afternoon. "You wouldn't happen to be licensed in CPR, would you?"

"No," my brow lined as I watched him write on a blue card.

"Didn't think so. I can't officially certify you until you are, but I can make it pending that. It'll cover us so long as Kenny or Pete is in the building."

"I'm not interested in being certified—"

"Like I said, I'll have to increase your pay. How does an extra five bucks an hour sound?"

"Fuckin' good." I might actually be able to buy a few more groceries. Take Kenny to a restaurant instead of my crap apartment for dinner.

"Let's get started."

Learning to be a trainer wasn't much different from being trained. Basically, it was shit my own trainer had taught me when I was boxing—monitoring form, encouraging clients to push themselves.

"You're stronger than you look," Rook said, as I finished a set, bench-pressing three hundred.

Sitting up with a loud exhale, I shrugged. "You've had me moving some heavy shit around here."

He laughed and clapped me hard on the shoulder. "That's enough for today. You know more than most trainers starting out."

I followed him back to the front ready to head back to my place. A quick look at the clock told me Kenny would be arriving soon, and I had a surprise in mind for her.

"The crews won't be in port for another week or two. When they come, most of them won't want a trainer. You'll just make sure they don't wreck the place." We stopped at the juice bar, and Mariska slid over a white cup.

"Try that out and tell me what you think. No charge." I glanced at her, and she winked. "It's a new recipe. Supposed to build muscle mass. I need to know if guys will like it."

It was a ruse, but I smiled and took it. Soon I wouldn't be such a fucking charity case.

Rook continued. "You'll need to hang around the gym more than you do now. Kenny and Pete's schedules are pretty full with our regular members. You'll pick up any overflow."

"Got it." I said, nodding as I took a big gulp of the protein shake. It was good—thick and not too sweet.

"Tammy will make you a timecard, and you'll punch in and out. No more Sundays off."

"I knew that was too good to last."

He smiled and held out a hand. It was the first time he'd offered to shake, and I couldn't help feeling honored. I gripped his large palm, and he finished.

"No more probationary period." He held on a beat longer, and I was about to make a crack about not being his girlfriend when he blew me away. "You're a good man, Slayde Bennett. Keep up the good work."

His words hit me so hard. I had to clear my throat before I answered. "Thanks."

"Oh!" Mariska cried, clasping her hands under her chin. "Where's my damn camera when I need it?"

"Don't spoil it." Rook deadpanned, and I laughed. He released me, and I looked at my palm. Then I headed out. I had to make a quick stop before I was ready for tonight.

Chapter 22: "Live in the sunshine, swim in the sea, drink the wild air."
Kenny

Patrick was dressed to go out when I arrived in Wilmington. Jeans and a polo were his standard going out attire, and his dark green shirt made his hazel eyes glow... as he narrowed them on me.

"What's different?"

"You're so suspicious!" I dropped my bags on the floor. "Nothing's different."

"Liar. This is not the pensive, angst-ridden Kenny who visited us last time."

Rolling my eyes, I stopped at the refrigerator to grab a bottle of water. "You're so full of shit. That's a total exaggeration."

"You're full of shit."

Elaine entered the room carrying Lane, who only wore a diaper and a towel. "Baby here—no more swearing," she called. "He just had his bath, and I barely got a diaper on him when he heard your voice."

Laughing, I scooped his wiggling, grinning body from her arms. "How's my big boy?" I kissed his chubby neck and took a deep breath of Baby Magic. "I'm sorry I was gone too long this time."

He struggled in my arms, and I loosened them. Putting his hands on my cheeks, his blue eyes grew round. "Two mommies."

Behind me I heard Patrick snort, and I cut my eyes at him. Back to the baby, I held my expression neutral. "Yes. Lane has two mommies who love Lane very much."

"Ah, now you're making it sweet." Patrick pretended to complain.

Elaine breezed into the kitchen at that remark. "What's sweet?"

"Lane has two mommies." I said, and she paused.

Her hand went to her hip, and her expression grew thoughtful. "I guess we never really talked about that. Should we make out now or wait until later tonight?"

Patrick almost choked on a laugh, drinking from my water bottle, but I hugged Lane closer. "Do you think it's confusing? I mean, should we call me... something else?"

She walked over to us, rubbing Lane's little back. He reached out and stuck his fingers in her silky hair. "Two mommies."

Her voice was gentle. "You *are* mommy —"

"No way, you're mommy," I argued. "You're doing all the work."

For a moment we only stood there, the two of us looking at the small human tying us together. My stomach twisted, and I couldn't help wondering if she'd ever be able to think of me as anything more than a problem. Her annoying cross to bear.

Elaine was still rubbing Lane's little back. "I love this guy." The warmth in her voice gave me hope.

"Me too," I said softly.

Our eyes met then, and she sighed, a small smile peeking on her lips. "Sounds like Lane has two mommies."

Patrick put the water bottle down and walked over to where we were. "Daddy is very lucky. Two mommies is hot."

Elaine punched him in the arm, and I snorted. Lane's little face frowned. "No hit. Bad."

"Daddy likes when Lainey hits him." I kissed his little nose. "What else are you learning at preschool?"

"Not enough cleanup." Elaine scooped an oversized racecar and a handful of stray Duplos off the floor, tossing them into a square bin in the living room. Then she was back, purse on her shoulder. The black dress she wore had geometric beige panels down the sides, making it look like a halter.

"I love that dress!" I sat in a chair by the table still holding Lane.

"If you were taller, I'd give it to you." She kissed my head briefly before giving the baby a longer kiss on his chubby cheek. It was unexpected, and I liked the gesture. "We won't be out too late."

"Stay as late as you want! We'll have dinner and then snuggle up with a few books until we fall asleep."

She smiled and headed to the door as Patrick stepped forward to hug me and kiss his son.

"Tell teacher Lane's mommies kiss each other."

"Patrick!" Elaine scolded from the door, but that made me laugh.

"Good one," I chuckled, as he pecked my cheek.

"Tomorrow I want to hear all about this new guy."

I tried to frown, but it came off as more of a distorted grin.

"I have no idea what you're talking about!"

"Exactly." He winked and followed Elaine out. I carried Lane to the living room, ready to relax and spend the evening with my boy.

* * *

The next morning, when I emerged from Lane's room, Patrick's going out clothes were replaced with jeans and a white tee. He held a mug of coffee. I held my overnight bag on one arm and my sleepy little son on the other.

"Did you two catch up?" he asked, handing me the mug.

"Yes!" I was refreshed after spending an easy evening watching airplane and video-game movies then going to bed at ten snuggled up with my baby. "I think we read every new book he got since my last visit. Holy crap!"

"Preschool had a book fair." He grinned, rubbing Lane's back.

"I figured it was something like that."

Lane reached for him, and I passed the little guy over. He tucked his blond head into his daddy's neck.

"Take care of your mini me." I sipped my coffee watching Lane's chubby fingers moving up and down on Patrick's shoulder. "You two are too cute."

"So tell me about this guy." Patrick sipped his usual morning OJ, and Lane's head popped up.

I smiled watching the two of them—Patrick held his glass while Lane took a drink. When they were done, I shrugged. "Just one of the new guys at the gym. He's working with me on my boxing."

Patrick's eyebrow rose. "He's a boxer?"

"Ex." I took another sip. "Ex boxer."

"Is he from Bayville? Somebody you knew before?"

"No," I looked down, chewing my lip. "I'm not sure where he's from originally. He just moved to the area."

Patrick's brow lined, and my chest felt squirmy. "What's his name? What do you know about him?"

"Slayde Bennett? He's my age, so he must've been just getting started when he had to quit. Boxing, I mean."

"Why'd he have to quit?" Patrick was studying me too closely.

These were all valid questions, and I hated not having answers for him. At the same time, I knew Slayde. He didn't.

"I don't know," I finally admitted.

Patrick's lips pressed into a thin line. "Those guys can be violent sometimes."

"He's not violent." My mind traveled to the night on the beach when he'd rescued me. There was no way in hell I could tell Patrick about that. He'd lose it.

"Sounds like there's a 'but' in there."

"There isn't!" I shook my head, meeting his eyes. "I was thinking of how to describe him. He's more into meditation and stuff. He has a system. He's very controlled."

Inwardly I cringed. It was all coming out wrong, but thankfully Patrick didn't jump on that. Instead, he exhaled deeply.

"You're a grown woman—"

"Thank you!" I said a little too loudly.

"And I was about to say I trust you." He held my gaze, and my little boy did as well, watching me from where his head lay on his daddy's shoulder. "But it's like you women are always saying about my Harley—you've got other people who need you now, too. Remember that."

"Oh, Patrick." I stepped toward them both. "I could never forget that. I love you guys."

"Mommy purple." Lane pulled a long strand of my hair into his little hand. I caught it and kissed his baby knuckles.

He leaned down, and I took him from Patrick, hugging him close and kissing his neck. A lump ached in my throat. It was so hard to leave him, but that was what true love meant—sacrifice, making unselfish choices for the good of your loved one.

"Mommy will be back very soon," I whispered. "Be a good boy for Mommy."

Patrick took him, and it was like my heart stayed with that little body. I rubbed Lane's back a moment longer. "Tell Elaine I said thanks. I'll be back soon."

"Take care of yourself, okay?"

Nodding, I grabbed my bag and headed out.

* * *

Driving back to Bayville, I thought about how Slayde withdrew when I first mentioned Lane. It was so common for children of abuse to think they shouldn't be parents or have any contact with children. I tried to imagine what kind of a little boy he must've been to survive the abuse he'd suffered.

He fought all his life, and then he became a boxer. I hoped one day he might trust me enough to tell me why he walked away from his career. Perhaps it was something as simple as he didn't want to fight anymore.

All of his thoughtful gestures filled my mind, from the flowers to his attempts to feed me instead of himself, and when I pulled into my parking garage, all I wanted to do was throw everything in my house, shower quickly and head right back out to see him.

Just then my phone buzzed with a text. *Come to my place before you go home. I have something to show you.*

It was Slayde, and I smiled, looking through my windshield a moment before turning the key and backing out of the garage again.

Henry was sitting in the parking lot when I arrived at the crummy apartment building he called home. I tried to imagine what in the world he could want to show me as I studied the sun glowing deep orange as it made its way lower in the sky. It was a beautiful evening.

My phone went off again. *Text me when you get here.*

I smiled. *Just pulled in.*

From the corner of my eye, I saw his door open, and he stepped out wearing dark jeans and a white tank. The sight of him made my chest swell with happiness. He was so gorgeous with that light scruff on his cheeks, his muscled arms bent with his hands on his hips. A smile touched his lips, making him look even sexier, and I wanted to run across the parking lot and jump into his embrace. Instead, I opened the door and walked to him.

"Hey," I said.

He still had that sexy grin on his lips, and he reached for me, tracing a line from my forehead down my cheek to my neck. Energy buzzed through my entire body.

"You were only gone twenty-four hours," he said quietly. "It felt like you were gone a week."

Reaching forward, I held his neck as I rose on my tiptoes to kiss him. He quickly wrapped his arms around my waist, scooping me against him in a kiss so full of emotion it stole my breath. His lips moved to my cheek then up to my eyebrow, and I tried to calm my breathing.

Leaning back, I traced my thumbs over his cheeks. "What did you do while I was gone?"

"Worked yesterday. Today Rook made me an official trainer and gave me a raise."

"Hey!" I laughed. "Sounds like I need to go out of town more often."

"No way. I'd rather have you here." He smiled before leaning forward to kiss me again, right at the base of my ear.

"What did you want to show me?"

With one more squeeze, he released me. "Come on."

Instead of going into his apartment, he led me in the direction of the pier. I didn't understand, but I followed him until he stopped abruptly causing me to bump into him.

He laughed. "Sorry." Catching my cheeks, he kissed me quickly again, and happiness filled my chest. Leaning down, he caught my ankle, slipping off my shoes as I held his shoulders. Then he stood up again. "Close your eyes."

I wrinkled my nose, and he took one of my hands, lifting it to my eyes. "Close them."

I did as instructed, and he led me slowly over the sand to the wooden boardwalk. A light breeze blew off the water, and I was glad I'd worn a cardigan for our impromptu beach stroll. Only we didn't go to the beach. As I followed him, I recognized the sounds. We were walking on the pier.

"You're going to stop before we get to the end, right?" I teased.

"Stopping... now." He pulled my hand away from my eyes, and I blinked, looking all around. "Look down."

My eyes went to the wooden planks in front of us where two large pads were arranged with three small plates holding red, blue, and yellow paint.

"I... I don't understand."

"It's finger paint." He stepped carefully across the setup still holding my hands. "Sit. We don't have a lot of daylight left, but you can show me how it works."

My mouth dropped open, and I sat slowly across from him with the two large, empty sheets between us, slipping my arms out of my sweater.

"I don't have any fine art books, but I figured nature is a pretty good substitute."

It was all so unexpected and amazing and sweet. "Yes, I mean, definitely nature is the best subject."

"Except naked women, of course." He gave me a sly grin, and I laughed.

"I'm pretty sure we'd get arrested out here."

"Too bad." He sat forward, and in the light tank he wore, he might as well have been shirtless. "Blue and yellow make green, right?" He held up a white plastic bottle, tilting it side to side.

"I have white here, but I ran out of plates."

"What do you want to start with? The ocean?" Leaning forward, I dipped three fingers in the dark blue paint and slid them across the paper in a wavy motion.

He'd flattened his whole hand in the yellow and sat back. "Wow. You really know what you're doing."

"I've finger-painted a time or two. Watch it! You're dripping!"

He looked down at the paint trickling down his forearm and quickly put it down at the top right corner of his page. "The sun."

"Nice. I might've missed it if you hadn't told me."

"Don't be a snob." He grinned and moved back to dip his index finger in the red. "I have a better idea for a subject."

I watched as he started making lines.

"Keep in mind your medium," I said, lifting the white and pouring a drop on my fingertips, blending it under the wavy blue lines I'd made, creating a lighter blue. "You can't be very precise with this type of painting. Go for more broad strokes."

Slayde didn't even look up. Wrinkling my nose, I studied what looked like a big red triangle.

"Mondrian liked to use large fields of color in his art," I added, hoping to be encouraging.

"Which guy just threw paint everywhere?"

"Jackson Pollock?" I squinted up.

"Yeah, I'd like to try his technique sometime."

"Yves Klein covered nude models in ultramarine blue and then had them roll around on the canvass."

Slayde's eyes flashed to me. "Why the hell did I set all this up out here? We need to take this back to my place. You've given me a great idea."

"Oh, yeah?" I grinned, leaning across the canvasses. He met my lips halfway, and I put my painted hand on his cheek.

Pulling away a fraction, he laughed. "You're going to get it now." I felt his yellow-covered hand sliding down the neck of my floral sundress.

"Slayde! My dress…"

"It's washable. Look." He held up the bottle, and sure enough, *Washable* was printed on it.

"I guess that means the gloves are off."

"You're speaking my language now." He sat back quickly, plunging both hands into the plates. "Get over here."

Jumping up, I snatched the blue before taking off running down the boardwalk. He was right behind me, one hand dripping red the other bright yellow.

"Slayde!" I screamed, but he caught me, hands sliding up my thighs to my bare stomach beneath my dress.

"Where would be the most unexpected place I can get paint?"

The blue was open now, and I poured it on my hands. Too much gushed out, and it ran down my arms, but I spun around, pushing my hands under his tank. It was up and off, his torso, which was now covered in dark blue.

"All you need is a canvas," I laughed.

In a sweep, I was over his shoulder, and he charged straight into the surf. The water was like ice. I screamed again, but he held me tight against his body, warming me with his heat. We were panting and laughing, my arms around his neck, our noses almost touching.

"It's all washing off in the salt water." I made a sad face, looking around us at the rainbow.

"It's also non-toxic, so the fish are safe."

"You thought of everything." I grinned before kissing him hard on the mouth.

His hand moved behind my head to hold me still while he kissed me slower, parting my lips so he could find my tongue. Heat blazed between my thighs, and I shifted my body so my legs wrapped around his waist.

A small groan rumbled in his throat, and he turned us in the water so he was facing the shore. "Looks like nobody else is out here."

My lips moved to his ear, and I nibbled his earlobe. "Aren't you worried about our artwork?"

"No." His voice was a raspy whisper as his hands slid up my thighs. Jerking aside my panties, his fingers sank deep into my core.

"Oh!" Flexing, I lifted up against him.

"I want to roll you in blue paint and make love to you on a canvas." His mouth moved along my jaw, kissing and pulling small bits of skin between his teeth. I shivered with every little nip, his words sending desire straight to where his fingers were massaging me.

"Yes, please," I moaned, my hips moving with his hand.

"But I'd like to be inside you here first." His mouth moved to mine and a splash of salt water went with it. As he moved me around, the ocean mixed with the minty flavor of him.

"Mmm," I moaned, feeling his hands working at his waist. His erection was at my thigh, and in one swift motion he sank deep inside me, teasing me to the next level of pleasure as the waves lifted our bodies together.

"You feel so good," he whispered in my ear. "Nothing's like being inside you."

The salt water mingled with his words, intensifying his thumb still circling, his teeth nibbling at my jawline. The light hairs across his chest teased my nipples, and my head swam with all the sensations. It wasn't long before I was hitting the edge.

"Oohh!" My inner muscles tightened so hard, and tremors broke through my legs as the orgasm spasmed in my core. I cried out again, lifting up, holding his shoulder as I rocked my hips faster against him.

His muscles were tense, and I knew he was fighting to hold back. I couldn't hold back. Waves of pleasure racked my body, and I moaned through the intense sensations.

"Finish, baby," he breathed in my ear, his free hand trailing lightly over my ass under the water.

That tingling move sparked another, harder aftershock in my core. "Oh, my god, Slayde." I gasped, riding it again until with a low groan, he quickly lifted me off of him, pulling out.

Fumbling my hand down, I quickly found his rigid shaft beside my thigh and pumped my hand up and down him quickly.

"Fuck," he groaned, and I felt him jerk, coming in the waves that rocked us. His hips flexed as he thrust into my fist several more times. His eyes were pressed closed, and I kissed him against the temple, down his jaw, as his movements slowed.

He whispered something inaudible against my hair, and I hugged myself closer, pressing my lips to his. He consumed me roughly in that kiss, like he'd been held back from me and was finally released. He held me against his chest, and the emotions moving through me with every heartbeat were almost painful.

We were both breathing hard, melting into each other as the waves continued rocking. Now they were like a lullaby, easing us to calm.

His chin moved, and he kissed my cheek, still holding me firmly against his body. "I could do that a lot." I breathed a laugh, and he continued. "I'm sorry I had to pull out on you like that."

Leaning back, I held his neck. "I started the pill Friday, so we'll have backup in a few days."

He looked deep into my eyes. "I'll get tested so you don't have to worry about anything. I mean, you don't have to worry now, but just so you're confident."

Nodding, I traced my fingertip over his brow. "I trust you."

"Until then, we'll be safe."

Looking up, I noticed the sun setting. I thought about the fact that he was holding me here, shirtless in the water, and I wondered if that meant he was ready to reveal everything.

"Why don't you head up to my place and get dry. The door's unlocked. I'll clean up the paints and meet you there."

Chewing my lip, I understood he wasn't quite ready. I nodded. "Are you sure you can get them yourself? We kind-of got paint everywhere."

"Yeah," he grinned, kissing my jawline. "I still want to try that sex on canvass technique."

"That can be our next finger-painting date."

We were slowly making our way out of the surf. My sundress was soaked and sticking to me, and he scooped up his paint-covered tank, holding it against the front of his body. SLAYER was clearly visible at his neck, but whatever he was hiding was further down, on his ribs, where the white tank was pressed securely under his arm.

"See you in a minute." I caught his chin and kissed him, determined to show him how safe he was with me. "If you need any help just leave it. I'll only be a second."

Chapter 23: "Let Be be finale of Seem."
Slayer

I watched her walk up the shore, the red floral sundress she wore clinging to her wet body and her long violet hair swaying in beachy waves down her back. Damn, if I didn't get a semi just watching her walk.

Last night, while she was gone, I'd returned to my old routine of cold meat and white bread for dinner followed by a walk to the shore with that behemoth book. I wasn't even really keeping track of the story so much anymore as consuming the words to pass the time.

When it got too dark to see the text, I lowered it and looked out at the water, wondering what I'd be doing if I hadn't been out here, running away from my demons that night. She said I'd saved her, but the reality was she was the angel who saved me. Now I was trying to hold onto her — as if I could be that lucky.

Walking slowly toward the boardwalk, I savored the memory of being inside her for the first time with no barriers, just her and me. Glancing around, I adjusted myself, glad I didn't have an audience. I looked down at the painting she'd done. It was a skilled artistic rendering even if it was finger paint. She'd swept waves across a blank sheet of paper that rivaled the ones behind me hitting the shore.

I stacked the paint-filled plates on top of one another and collected the four bottles. It wasn't much to carry, and she was rubbing a towel in her hair when I walked through the door.

"I was just coming to help you!" She lowered the towel and looked a little sad.

"I told you I could get it all. Here." I held out my painting to her. At the top of the red triangle was a yellow circle and from there, several purple lines hung down.

"Is this me?" she exclaimed as if it were the *Mona Lisa*.

I grinned. "How did you guess?"

"You have hidden talent, Mr. Bennett. I think you should be promoted to the advanced class."

Shaking my head, I held up her ten-second masterpiece. "This is really good. You shouldn't be taking a break from college. You need to keep this going."

Her eyes warmed, and she looked down. "Maybe next semester I'll get it going again. I had just sort of… lost interest."

"I'll be glad to help you find it again."

"You already have."

Putting the paint-filled plates in the sink, I touched her cheek briefly… and left a spot of paint. "I'd better get cleaned up before you're covered in paint again."

Stepping into the closet-bathroom, I switched on the water. In time it took me to shower and wash my hair, she'd cleaned the dishes and put everything away. I smiled watching her move through my tiny space in her bare feet and my oversized tee.

"I hope you like sausage pizza," she called when I stepped around the curtain hiding my bed to put on a fresh shirt. "It should be here any minute."

I returned to her, buttoning my jeans. "I thought I might cook—"

"Nope! I'm treating you to pizza." She skipped over and kissed my lips. I reached for her shoulders when a loud knock on the door broke us apart.

Scooping up her purse, she ran to the door before I could say anything, taking the large, brown box from the teen guy standing there and passing him a bill. "Keep the change," she called before turning and carrying our dinner into the living room.

Every time she did something like this, I felt another chink in my walls being removed. It was a scary feeling, but at the same time, nothing was as great as being with her.

We ate our dinner, and she told me about her little boy, complete with pictures on her phone. "He's got your eyes," I said, checking out the blue-eyed towhead. "He's really cute."

Her eyes glowed when she described how he knew his numbers and colors and even could recognize words in his picture books.

"It's because Elaine's a teacher," she said, leaning back against the couch. "I mean, Patrick and I are smart, but she's probably sounding out words with him and all that stuff."

I hated the way I felt when she mentioned this guy, Patrick. It was sick of me to feel jealous, but fuck, I couldn't help it. "How long were you married?"

Her expression changed, and she seemed surprised by my question. "Umm... almost three years. Why?"

Now I felt like an ass. "You just have such a good relationship. That's probably a rare situation."

"Oh, no!" she laughed shaking her head. "Patrick and I were never married. God, no. It was... well," worried eyes rose to mine. "He and I kind of had this random fling. I was such an idiot, I got pregnant. It was totally my fault."

She was so cute being embarrassed in front of me, as if I hadn't done worse things. "You know, it takes two people to make a baby."

"I know." She nodded, pushing her hands into the sides of her hair. It was a gesture I'd learned meant she was flustered. "But I told him I was on the pill. I'd been sick and taking antibiotics, and... We were so drunk and stupid. I was such an idiot."

The room went quiet, and I tried to think of something to say. Her face was hot pink, and I still couldn't get over how she would blush. Her, in all her purple hair and bold personality. The blushing killed me.

"You probably think I'm a complete flake now." Her voice was quiet, and I almost laughed.

"I don't think that at all."

"I would. I'd think I was some kind of psycho."

Scooting forward, I scooped her onto my lap.

Her legs straddled my waist, and she looked down, not meeting my eyes.

"Hey," my voice was soft. "Look at me." She didn't, so I said it with a little more force. "Look. At. Me."

Those little blue birds fluttered to meet my gaze, and fuck, if she didn't take another little chink. "Everybody does stupid shit they regret. I'm the world champ at it."

Her mouth pressed into a little sideways grin. "You keep saying that, but I'm still not convinced."

The lightness in my mood disappeared. I caught her chin and made her look at me. "Trust me. I'm the champ."

Her brow fell, and I hated that I'd been so forceful with her. Pushing back, she sat on the floor in front of me, looking at her palm. "I've made more stupid decisions than anyone I know."

It was more of an opening than I'd ever expect to get, so I took it. "What's that about?" I nudged her hand. "Why do you have that there?"

She didn't lift her head. Her voice was a quiet monotone as she spoke. "When my husband died, I kind of lost it. Everyone hated him—my parents in particular—which is probably why I loved him all the more. He left out of here like a bat out of hell, and I chased right after him. Then he died."

An ache moved in my chest at her words. I hated thinking of her going through that kind of pain alone. "I'm sorry. "

"He had a best friend Max... Max's older brother felt sorry for me, so he gave me a job." She grinned up at me. "I worked as a tattoo artist for a little over a year."

I smiled back. "That's pretty cool."

"Yeah, only I didn't know anything about the culture or anything. What things meant." She looked back at her palm. "I'd seen a few guys with teardrop tattoos, and I thought about how much I'd cried after my husband died. So I put a tear in my hand, like for all the tears I'd held wishing he were still alive."

She didn't say more, and I couldn't think of a good response. When she looked up at me again, she seemed to read my mind, and we both exhaled a laugh. She rolled her eyes and leaned forward against my chest, her shoulders shaking with her laugh. "I'm such a dumbass."

Wrapping my arms around her, I kissed the top of her head. "It's actually a pretty good gag. You really had me going at the gym."

She sat up fast then, catching my eye. "Oh my god, you thought I was a murderer?" She shook her head. "And you were still brave enough to sleep with me?"

"You're pretty small. I'm pretty confident I could take you."

"Don't make me kick your ass again." She narrowed those beautiful blue eyes at me. I caught her chin to kiss her roughly.

"You know where that leads." A white-hot image of us so close to making it in the men's room flitted across my brain, prompting a response below my belt.

"Hmm…" Her wicked grin only made me harder. "I remember liking where that led."

Lifting her easily, I carried her straight to my bed. Laying her back against the pillows, I slid forward, holding my torso up with my forearms. Our mouths were only a breath apart, but I waited. I wanted to look into her blue eyes a little longer. She was so strong and she had that edge, yet at the same time, she was still innocent. *God, what was I doing?*

My heart wouldn't let me think about it. It was a damn, stubborn taskmaster, and it wanted one thing — this gorgeous creature in my arms. I might be so tough and controlled outside this bed, but laying here, with her small body in my arms, her legs slipping around my waist and her fingers threading into the sides of my hair, I was powerless.

It didn't scare me at all, which was why I should've known to be afraid.

CHAPTER 24: "YOU'RE FREE WITH ME."
KENNY

Nothing was keeping Slayde and me apart now. If I wasn't at his place, he was spending the night at mine. He still left early each morning to be at the gym, cleaning the locker rooms and getting ready for the day, but now that Rook had made him a trainer, he was with me more all the other times.

Slayde never said how many years he'd been a fighter before he quit, but he was so skilled at everything, it had to have been a while. Even Pete asked him for pointers on lifts and moves.

He'd already left for the day when I was hanging out with Mariska that Wednesday afternoon, dishing about my super sexy boyfriend. She was dressed as always in her Boho-Goth style. Deep emerald bodysuit with a long, rayon skirt wrapped around her slim hips. Her long, wavy brown hair was pinned back on the sides and silver skull earrings were in both her ears.

"Is he really rough?" She leaned forward, hazel eyes sparkling.

"Like when you're doing it, does he hold you down and shit?"

"No," I laughed. "That's such a freakin' stereotype." My knee-jerk response I'm sure was a result of Patrick's intense line of questioning the last time I'd talked to him. *Shit*! Had that been two weeks ago? I needed to plan a trip to Wilmington now.

Mariska's eyes narrowed. "I don't believe it. He has those wicked-sexy eyes, like he likes to strangle you."

Leaning forward, I scanned the bar to be sure we were alone. "I've always wanted to try that," I whispered. My friend squealed, and I kicked her. "Shut the fuck up," I hissed. "That's why I can't tell you anything at work."

"So does he do it? Do you come really hard?" She was leaning forward on the bar again, and I was about to tell her we'd never tried it when a man pushed through the glass doors.

He strode toward the counter, and we both snapped to attention. He was gorgeous, tall and slim but built, and the way he carried himself, I could tell he was used to giving orders — and being obeyed. He was military, I'd bet my life on it.

As I looked at him, something was so familiar, from the light brown hair with caramel highlights to the intense hazel eyes that were almost green. The more I studied him, the more he reminded me of...

"Can I help you?" Mariska's voice cut through my thoughts with a force that caused me to step back.

"I'm looking for Kendra Woods. She goes by Kenny."

The handsome man surveyed the gym behind us. Blinking up at him, I straightened. "I'm Kenny."

Stern eyes moved to my face, and he hesitated. "I expected someone... older."

Embarrassment mixed with anger. *Was he insulting me?* "I'm twenty-six, and you are...?"

"Stuart Knight. You know my brother Patrick."

My mouth dropped open, but I quickly closed it. The few times Patrick had mentioned his older brother Stuart, it had always been to say what a hardass he was or to note how much they didn't get along. I could see where he was coming from, but I wasn't about to be intimidated on my own turf.

"I know Patrick. What do you want?"

"May I speak with you in private? It's about your son, my nephew." He never once lost his imposing posture, but he reached up and rubbed the back of his neck, revealing the slightest crack in the armor along with some pretty impressive ink hiding under his long sleeve.

I took a breath and exchanged a glance with Mariska. Patrick's brother or not, I wasn't comfortable being alone with this guy. "Mariska's my friend. We can talk here."

He glanced at her, and for a moment, his eyes got caught. It was like he saw her for the first time, and even I could feel the unexpected charge that passed in the air between them.

His voice changed, sternness gone. "Hello."

Mariska's cheeks warmed along with her voice. "Hi—it's Stuart? Would you like a smoothie? I make them myself... right over there." She pointed across the bar. "It'll give you a little privacy. While you talk."

Watching the two of them, I almost suggested I make the smoothie and leave them alone together, but he grabbed the reins.

"Thank you," he said, breaking their moment. Still, his gaze drifted to her ass when my friend sashayed across the bar. I resisted rolling my eyes at her obvious hip swish.

The deep voice was back on me, sternness restored. "I didn't mean to frighten you. I have something for Lane. I'd like you to keep it for him until he's old enough to have it."

I watched him dig in his pocket and pull out a small bundle wrapped in a black cloth. It fit in his palm, and as he unwrapped it, I ducked under the counter to stand in front of him. "What is it?"

Opening his hand, light glinted off the shiny bronze. It was a medal on a navy ribbon with red stripes. "It's my father's distinguished service award. It was given to me when he died. I need you to give it to Lane as the first grandson when he's older."

Concern flooded my chest. "Why are you giving this to me now? You can give it to him yourself. Later."

He was quiet, his eyes fixed on the memento in his hand as if he saw something more than just a piece of metal. "That might not be possible, and I need to pass it down. It's important I do this."

Flying through the millions of possibilities, I studied his face. "Are you ill? Do you want me to call Patrick?"

That broke whatever reverie he was in. "No," he ordered. "This is just between us. I don't want my brother involved."

"But he has Lane…"

Stuart nodded. "That's why I'm asking you for this favor."

I shook my head. None of it made sense. Heirlooms were handed down when someone died. Stuart appeared healthy, shit he appeared freakin' hot as hell, but I could tell something was off with him. Chewing my lip, I wondered if I should press the issue.

I was about to speak, but Mariska slid the smoothie she'd just made across the counter to him. "On the house. It's full of lavender and blueberry. It'll help you relax."

He looked at her, and that charge was back. Perhaps it was because physically he was so much like his brother, I felt like I could read his body language. Their eyes met and mingled, and Mariska's cheeks flushed. Still, he resisted.

"I have to go." His voice was quiet—as if he were speaking only to her.

My friend wasn't the least bit discouraged. She reached forward, touching his hand. "Where are you going?"

Even though I could tell he wanted to pull away, he seemed hypnotized her. "My uncle has a place out west where… where I can breathe. Maybe I can find some peace."

The muscle in his jaw moved, and he stepped away from the counter, away from her. He'd done what he came to do, and I could tell Mariska was more than he expected from this errand.

"Please," I stepped toward him. "Let me call Patrick. I'm sure he'd want to know—"

"No." His eyes flashed, and a charge of fear radiated in my chest. Clearly, Stuart Knight was not someone to cross.

"Do not call my brother. I don't want to see him."

He turned and headed for the door, but Mariska grabbed the smoothie he'd left behind and ducked under the counter. Stuart might scare me, but she wasn't letting whatever had passed between them get away so easily.

"Wait! You forgot something!" She caught his hand, and he paused. He turned back to her, and his expression softened.

For a moment, he stood there. She held his hand as well as his gaze. "Thanks," he said, taking the beverage she held. Their eyes met again, but he let her go, pushing through the glass doors.

I went back inside the bar, shoving the bundle in my bag and fishing around for my phone. Badass or not, something was seriously wrong, and I needed to call Patrick. His brother was proud and clearly strong, but the guy who just handed me his father's medal of honor was contemplating some serious shit.

"Oh my god, Kenny." Mariska collapsed against the bar. "I'm in love."

My lips pressed together as I touched my recent calls and then Patrick's number. "I saw that. What the hell was going on with you two?"

"That mountain of honey brown, hazelnut deliciousness just left here with my heart."

I moved around the small space, waiting for the call to connect. "Gorgeous genes clearly run in their family."

Patrick's phone kept ringing until finally it went to voicemail. Hearing his greeting, I thought about it. I wasn't exactly sure what to say—and even if I were, it probably wasn't the type of thing to leave in a message. I hit disconnect and shoved my phone in my purse.

Mariska was still leaning against the wall, one hand on her heart, when she turned back to me. "What are you doing?"

"I'm calling Patrick, what does it look like? That mountain of hazelnut... whatever you called him is not in a good place, and he just gave me their father's heirloom."

"You can't call Patrick!" She stood up quickly. "He asked you not to. Twice!"

"Stuart Knight is in a dark place. I've got to tell Patrick."

"He said he needs to breathe. Don't break his trust."

"And what if... what if he hurts himself?" I hated to imply something like that, but all the signs were there.

She looked back at the glass doors, her voice growing softer. "He won't. My soul called out to his, and I felt him calling back. He needs space to sort this out."

"I'm pretty sure that was your ovaries calling out for his babies." My jaw tightened as conflict swirled in my chest. "Did he say he was going to stay with their uncle? That could be good..."

"He said their uncle had a place out west." She was still dreamy.

I took a deep breath, uncertainty making my head hurt. "Make me one of those blueberry-lavender things."

She ducked under the bar and started adding ingredients to the blender. We were quiet a few seconds then her nose wrinkled, and she laughed.

"I totally want to sleep with him. Is that nuts or what?"

"No. He's sexy as hell." I waited as she finished my supposedly relaxing concoction. "If Stuart's anything like Patrick in the sack..."

"Don't be cruel." She cut her eyes at me. "The chances I'll see that gorgeous thing again are slim to none."

"But I thought your souls were calling to each other or whatever."

"Doesn't mean he'll listen." Her voice was a little sad, and my eye caught the other hot guy in her life, working with an elderly client in the weight room.

"What's wrong with Pete? He's totally smitten with you."

She sighed, leaning against the bar. "He just doesn't do it for me. I don't know why. I'm not blind—he's a great looking guy. It's just not there. And believe me. I've tried. Several times."

"Well, I'm headed out." Kissing her cheek, I picked up my drink. "Thanks for this. I'll give the elder Mr. Knight a few days, but it's against my better judgment. I think Patrick needs to know now."

She smiled and looked down. "That was the most amazing experience I've ever had. I'm sure I'll see him again. Don't worry."

Walking out, I shook my head thinking how much I adored that nutty girl.

* * *

Stuart Knight's unexpected visit was forgotten when I opened my door. The delicious smell of grilled steak met my nose, and I quickly moved through my apartment, dropping all my bags, to find the gorgeous man who had my heart on the patio looking out at the horizon. The small, charcoal grill at his feet apparently held our dinner.

"Hey," I said, sliding the glass door open. The way his brow relaxed when he saw me sent a happy tingle through my middle. "Are you making me steak?"

"You're not going to believe what I found in your freezer." He walked to where I leaned on the doorjamb.

"Have I ever told you I could watch that sexy swagger all day long?"

"Do I swagger?" He laughed, seeming surprised.

"Yes. Now kiss me."

He leaned down and covered my lips with his. I released the glass doors and slid my fingers into his dark hair. He lifted me like always—and I loved it like always—kissing him harder as I held him in my hands.

Pulling back, I kissed the corner of his mouth before asking. "What did you find in my freezer?"

He lowered me slowly before sliding a purple lock off my cheek. "You had six steaks in there. What's that about?"

My brow lined as I thought. "Oh, shit. I think Patrick did that!"

"Patrick again." His mouth made that tight line, and while I knew he had absolutely zero reason to be jealous, something wicked inside me loved that he was.

"He used to hassle me about being too thin all the time." I rubbed my hands up Slayde's lined arms. "Strike that. He still hassles me about being too thin all the time. But he actually used to send me meat every month. Can you believe?"

Slayde couldn't stop the sexy grin crossing his lips, but he looked up and over my shoulder.

"You are pretty thin, but I know you eat."

"He's such a pain. Remember when I said he was my big brother?" Slayde looked back down at me. "It was the closest thing I could get to saying he's like my dad without being gross."

"Because of the whole having a baby together thing?"

"Exactly, but damn is he a pain in my ass sometimes." I exhaled going back to the kitchen. "Do you mind if I have a glass of wine?"

"Of course not." He went back to check the grill before joining me in the kitchen. "You still care about him. No matter what you say."

"Oh, sure." I said, going over to hold his hand. I turned it over and traced my finger over the bold green *21* inked above his thumb. I noticed him flinch, but I played it off. "We're like family now, I guess. You know I can fix tattoos?"

I wasn't sure why I said it. Probably because it was how Patrick and I met—with me changing one of his least-favorite tattoos into something he could live with.

"Did you have something in mind?" he smiled, sliding my hair off my cheek. I looked up and scooted around the bar, catching his sexy jawline.

"As a matter of fact, I do." Pulling him gently, he readily leaned forward to catch my lips with his. "It's a surprise."

* * *

The owner of the White Lotus tattoo shop in Toms River was a new client, Wren. She was a tall woman with short black hair and sleeves of ink down both her arms. One was a green-and-red rose vine with enormous thorns and the words *Love Hurts*. The other was several blue-and-green Hokusai-style waves with the words *Love Heals*.

As I'd helped her with form and increasing her strength, I'd admired the artistry, which led to talk about my past experience. I told her I wished I had access to a gun to touch up some of my own ink, and she only asked me to bring my license. She was more than happy to let me use her equipment—once I'd completed the necessary paperwork, of course.

After I finished my touch-up at Wren's, I went to the small gift shop off the boardwalk. I'd seen a trinket weeks ago I'd forgotten until last night. I was kissing Slayde's back, tracing my fingertips down the lines of the wings inked there, when the memory floated through my brain.

The cashier was kind enough to wrap it for me, and I headed home, stopping off to grab some take-out Thai food before driving to his studio apartment.

"You're killing me with all the takeout," he said, meeting me at the door with a kiss.

"It's impossible to remember what you say when you kiss me like that," I teased.

The bandage on my hand couldn't be hidden, and he lifted my wrist before I'd finished unloading the bags.

"What happened?" He pulled it toward his chest, carefully lifting the gauze from my palm. When he saw what was underneath, he didn't speak. His face grew unbearably serious as he studied my palm. I felt like my chest was about to burst open.

"Please say something."

He blinked up at me, his clear blue eyes fathomless. "What have you done?"

Feeling self-conscious, I tried to explain. "Tattoos are supposed to commemorate things, right?" Taking a quick breath, I continued. "When my husband died, I put the tear in my hand for all the tears I cried. Because I believed I'd never love again, and I didn't want to forget."

Blinking up at him, he watched me, that intense expression sending shimmers through my chest. "You've shown me that part of me isn't dead."

I waited, unsure if I was ready to say it. Inhaling a deep breath, I swallowed my nerves and just told him. "I know I can love again, because of you. I know… because I love you."

He held my hand and when I said the last words, I felt his grip tighten ever so slightly. Blinking up at him, he stared at my palm with an expression I'd never seen before. It was something like wonder.

Then he lifted my palm to his lips and kissed it.

He studied it a moment longer before speaking. "Kenny," he stopped and seemed so torn. I felt guilty for showing him. It was like I was rushing him again, pushing him into something he wasn't ready for.

He caught my cheeks, and lifted my face. "Kenny," his voice was barely above a whisper. "I love you so much."

My insides melted at his words. "Slayde…" I couldn't finish.

It didn't matter because he wasn't finished. "All this time, I fought. I fought myself wanting you. I fought myself believing I was good enough for you. I'm not. I'm not any of those things. I don't deserve you. But dammit, Kenny, I love you."

I was laughing and holding his face. Kissing him, and smiling. His hands were finding their way under my shirt, and I remembered his gift.

"Oh, wait! Hold that thought." I danced around the bar to the brown bag I'd left on the counter. My shirt was loose and open, and I saw his darkened eyes watching me. "I got you something."

Reaching into the bag, I pulled out the small box. He took it from me with a confused face.

"Don't buy me any more gifts." His voice was stern, but I just leaned forward and kissed his cheek.

"Don't be like that. I buy you gifts because I love you."

His eyes blinked to mine then back to the box. After a brief pause, he lifted the lid and immediately, he lowered it. His brow lined and he stared at me so hard.

"What will I do with you?" So much emotion was in that whispered question.

I caught his cheeks and kissed him. "Make love to me again and again."

That made him smile, and he lifted the gift out of the box. It was a small copper bird, weathered and vintage, and in the center was etched the word *Free*.

"You're free from the pain you try to hold onto." I took the necklace from him and put it over his head. It fell down to the center of his chest, just above his heart, and it seemed right to me. "Be free, my love."

CHAPTER 25: "NOTHING IS PROMISED."
SLAYDE

I couldn't calm the tornado of emotions wracking my insides. The last time I'd experienced such an onslaught, it had been heartbreak, destruction, the end of me. Now Kenny was holding my hands and saying she loved me, giving me a bird with the word *Free* engraved in the center.

She was at my apartment bringing me food. I was complaining about takeout, telling her not to give me gifts like a fucking asshole, and she blew it all away. Holding her face in my hands, I could only look into her eyes. I was lost in them. I didn't deserve this.

"Kenny..." I tried, but all I could do was kiss her.

I could only take her sweet lips with mine, find her tongue with mine, slide my worthless hands down her beautiful body in a prayer of thanks to all of the gods who might give a shit about a loser like me. Second-chance gods who believed a killer could be worth saving. How could they send this amazing creature into my life?

In her hand, the teardrop tattoo was transformed. She'd added another teardrop inverted, making it a heart.

What she couldn't know was the heart in her hand was mine.

She'd hold it forever. I never wanted it back.

* * *

The next day at lunch, I made an excuse and slipped away down to the boardwalk. Pulling out my cheap phone, I dialed the familiar number. The voice on the other end told me to wait, and I sat, holding the copper charm in my hand, reading it again.

"Doc here." I couldn't help but smile at the familiar voice.

"It's me Slayde."

"Slayde! It's been a long time. What's going on?"

"Not much. Too much." Looking down at my hands, I thought about what I wanted to say. He didn't have a lot of time, I knew. "I guess I need your advice. Again."

"You know I'm here for you, kid." He waited, but I could hear voices in the background. I had to make this quick.

"Remember that girl?"

"The one you saved on the beach? The one you were working with?"

"I'm still working with her." My brow lined as I thought. "She asked me to teach her boxing. Show her some moves, self-defense."

A smile was in his voice. "You started training her? In boxing?"

"Yeah, and she's really good, a fast learner." A knot was in my throat, and I knew I had to stop beating around the bush. "I've been seeing her away from the gym. She's really kind and beautiful."

"That's great news." Doc's voice was cheerful. "So what's the problem?"

"She doesn't know about me, about my past." Pressing my fingers against my closed eyes, I rubbed my eyelids. "I know I need to tell her. I can't seem to find a way. I wondered... would it be wrong if I didn't? No—I know I have to tell her everything."

"It sounds like you know the answer here. What are you asking from me?"

Taking a deep breath, I sat back on the bench. "I'm not asking for anything, I guess. I just needed to hear a friendly voice."

"You got this, my friend. If she's the woman you believe she is, she'll be strong enough for your past."

"I love her, Doc." An ache of dread moved through my chest. "I didn't know I'd never been in love until I met her."

It was all I was able to say, but he knew the rest. "True love destroys fear. It covers sins. It's stronger than any human emotion."

"How do you know that?"

"It's in the Bible." A voice spoke to him, and the raking sound of his hand over the receiver filled my ear. "I've got to go, but listen to me. I know you, and I know your heart. If you love this girl, she has to be something pretty special. Tell her your truth. She'll love you through it."

"Thanks, Doc."

"Talk to you soon."

I switched off my phone and stared at it a little while. Then I got up and walked slowly to my truck. I would tell her. I'd take a day, collect my thoughts, and I'd tell her my story. If I loved her, I had to believe she was strong enough to hear it.

Chapter 26: "I am Fortune's fool."
Kenny

The days flowed by like keys on a piano, each one a beautiful note of music. We spent every night together, either at his place or at mine, and every day at the gym, we exchanged glances from across the room, occasionally passing in the halls to steal a kiss, which naturally led to him copping a feel. I understood Rook and Tammy's problem with keeping it in their pants now. When you loved someone this much, it was hard to stop at just a kiss, but we did. Slayde respected Rook's rules.

We passed each night in each other's arms, making love every way possible. I'd have to revise my answer to Mariska, because he did occasionally hold me down and fuck me hard from behind. It was rough and violent, and I usually felt it the next day. Those were also the nights I came the hardest and glowed the longest, so I guess I was as twisted as he was.

He'd always hold me close to his chest after, his hands soothing me from my stomach to my breasts. He would hold my jaw and kiss me, and I loved his possessiveness. I loved that before falling asleep, he would always check my palm for the tiny heart hidden there.

One night as I lay hugged against him, he held it up and placed his palm against mine. I reached out and touched his hand.

"What's the 21 for?" I'd promised not to ask about his ink, but this one was always in plain sight.

"It was the year my life changed." I could tell by his tone it hadn't been a good change.

"Maybe I can make it a 26?"

He opened our palms so he could run his thumb over my little heart. "I want this instead. I want them to line up when we do this." I watched him put our hands together again. "Then I want to tell you everything."

My heart jumped at that statement. "Name the day, and we can run over to White Lotus. I'm friends with the owner."

"Is that where you did yours?"

Nodding, I smiled, and he rolled me onto my back. His face hovered inches above mine, and he looked deep into my eyes. "I love you, Kenny."

Nothing kept us apart when he said that.

* * *

Before going to the gym the next morning, we hopped in Henry and drove to the tattoo shop. Wren was there, and she was happy to let us use her spare gun in the back room. She wore a black tank and *Love Hurts/Love Heals* was on full display.

"I really love your ink," I said, tracing my finger over one of the curled waves, thinking of our conversation at the gym.

She smiled and passed me two sheets of paper. "He needs to fill out all the usual forms, and I should probably have you pay me something small. A few bucks we can call rent in case anybody ever questions us."

"Of course!" I took the paperwork and handed it to Slayde. "Whatever you need just let me know."

"I'm only thinking about it because it's that time of the month." My mouth dropped, and she laughed. "When I do my bookkeeping, I mean. Although it makes me as cranky as PMS."

I laughed too. "We'll be out of your hair in less than ten minutes. I'm just doing something small."

She stood and walked over to Slayde, checking out the boxing gloves on his bicep. "That's some good work. You a boxer?"

"Ex." He glanced up as he filled out the forms.

"I've seen this before." She pointed to five dots on his right hand.

His eyes flickered to hers, but he didn't answer.

Wren didn't say any more, and I took his hand in mine. "Ready to get it done?" He glanced up, and my smile held all the love I felt for him.

He looked down and shook his head. "Yeah, I've got this all filled out."

"Come on then." I pulled his arm, and he handed the forms back to Wren, who now eyed him with suspicion.

Once we were in the back, I spoke softly as I prepped my workspace. "Sorry about that. You know how it goes. Everybody wants to talk about their ink."

His lips pressed together and he put his hand on my cheek. "This one is for us. It always will be no matter what happens."

I held a piece of tracing paper on my palm. "Outline it for me so I can be sure they match."

He took the black felt pen I had and quickly outlined the small heart. I took it and held his hand. "Mine is on the left, so yours should be on the

267

right." Holding his palm flat, I wiped it several times with an antiseptic pad before transferring the design to his palm. "Now it's just a matter of filling it in."

"You know I've done this before, right?" He grinned, and I laughed.

"I don't know why I do that." Shaking my head, my long purple ponytail danced around my shoulders. "I guess it's a habit."

He reached out and caught the ends of my hair, wrapping a lock around his finger. "Better hurry up or Rook's going to be pissed."

Leaning forward, I kissed him quickly before getting started. In less than ten minutes we were done.

* * *

Slayde went straight to the supply closet when we arrived at the gym, then headed to the men's locker room. His new ink only needed a small Band-Aid. It was tiny and I was a light touch, so it wouldn't take long to heal. Still, I made him wear a surgical glove while working.

Rook was at the juice bar when I finished with my last client, and he was pissed. Only it wasn't at us. The tanker had arrived in port, and the gym had been slammed all day with sailors taking advantage of the complimentary membership.

"Fuck, how long are these assholes in port?" He'd stormed into the juice bar speaking under his breath.

"Just a few days," Mariska said, making notes in her recipe book. "I'll make you a cucumber and ginger-root smoothie. It'll help you relax."

"They don't speak the language, they take breaks on the equipment, and they leave towels everywhere."

"Your Type A is acting up," my friend teased. "I think they're nice."

I ducked under the bar, hoping to diffuse the situation. "Why don't you take off? We can handle these guys."

He glanced at me. "I might. Tammy's been doing double classes, and I feel like we haven't seen each other in a week."

My lips pressed together as I tried to hold back my laugh. "Dude. Go home and fuck your wife. You know that's why you're so tense."

Everything went quiet for a beat. Mariska held her breath. Then Rook exploded with a laugh.

"Shit, Kenny." He jerked my ponytail and headed back into his office. "That's exactly what I'm going to do."

"We don't have to discuss it!" I called after him. "I finally got those images out of my head."

He was gone a few minutes later, and Mariska fell on me laughing. "You've got balls the size of Texas, girl!"

We both laughed harder. "What's the point of catching them twice if I can't give him a hard time about it?"

My gorgeous guy appeared around the corner then. "You two kittens are having way too much fun. What's up?"

"You are very sexist." I leaned forward to capture his lips.

"Thanks," he smiled, kissing me back. Then he frowned. "Oh, wait, you said sex-*ist*? I thought you said sexy."

"You're that too, Spinal Tap." I dropped back off the bar. "How's it going out there?"

"Overcrowded, but we can handle it." He took my hand and placed our palms together. I loved it. "I'm going to have to clean the locker room twice."

I didn't like the sound of that. "Want me to help you?"

"I would never want you to do that." He laced our fingers, and I thought about the two little hearts mirroring each other.

"I don't mind," I said softly. Never in my life had I been so completely and fully blissed out with happiness. It radiated in my toes.

Just then Pete called Slayde, and he kissed my hand before heading back to the weight room. "We're going to talk tonight."

"Okay," I nodded, anticipation hot in my chest.

"I'm trying not to hate you two," Mariska said once he was gone, but her giggle gave her away.

"You've got a lot of room—" I ducked out from behind the bar, but my words were cut off as two men strode through the glass doors.

It took me a second to register Patrick and Derek standing in the lobby of The Jungle Gym, completely out of context.

"Patrick?" I was confused, and I was pretty sure Mariska fainted.

"Hey, babe." Patrick caught me in his usual rough hug, but he wasn't smiling.

Derek waited, hands on his hips. He was a mountain of intimidating sex on two legs, blue eyes like steel. In typical form, I had no clue what to say to him. They were obviously here on a job. All at once, the realization of what it had to be slammed into me like a medicine ball.

"I need to know if you were working about a week ago," he said. "I think it was a Wednesday afternoon?"

"Oh, Patrick." I cringed with the guilt. I'd given up trying to call him about Stuart at Mariska's urging, but if something had happened to his brother… "I'm so sorry."

Patrick's expression grew more serious. "Why are you sorry? What happened?"

Mariska charged ahead, gripping the counter and practically crawling across it. "Is he okay? Tell me he's okay!"

Patrick's confused eyes moved to my friend. "I'm pretty sure he's okay — are we all talking about Stuart?"

I started to breathe again. "Oh, thank God. Yes."

Mariska collapsed against the wall as well, but Derek was impatient. "I'll step out and call Nikki, let her know he was here. Looks like we're only getting started."

He disappeared out the double-glass doors just as a voice I loved joined us. "Kenny? What's going on?" Slayde stopped beside me, but his eyes were on Patrick.

"Slayde," I said quickly, "This is Patrick. Lane's dad." Just as fast, I completed the circle. "Patrick, this is Slayde Bennett."

"Oh, sure," Patrick said. "So you're the guy who's dating my baby-mamma."

I was pretty sure I'd die on the spot, but Patrick wasn't through. He stood a little straighter, pulling his shoulders back. "Just so you know, punk, you hurt her, and—"

"Let me guess." Slayde cut him off, pulling his own shoulders back. "You'll rip my throat out and shove it up my ass."

Again, silence filled the juice bar. This time I'd forgotten how to breathe.

Until Patrick laughed. "Good guess. How did you know?"

I almost collapsed, but Slayde slipped his hand into mine, lacing our fingers. "I heard the warning the first night I met her."

I looked up at him, speaking softly. "It wasn't for you."

"Let me clock out," he said, kissing the back of my hand.

I smiled and watched him step around to the office. Once he was gone, I looked up at Patrick. His hazel eyes twinkled. "Damn, girl, you are so beautiful in love."

"I'm going to kill you," I groaned.

"It's okay if I say that, right? Because you are seriously glowing right now."

My cheeks were hot. "Will you knock it off? What's going on with your brother?"

His expression became serious. Derek rejoined us as Patrick explained. "He came back from Saudi a few months ago. He was running the Princeton office when Nikki, our office manager there, called and said he'd disappeared. Just went off the grid. I tracked a credit card transaction that led us here. Did he come to see you?"

"He did." I racked my brain trying to remember everything that happened that day, every word we said. "He was okay, but he seemed very focused—not in a good way."

272

Patrick's lips tightened. "Was his behavior in any way erratic or threatening?"

My eyes widened slightly. "Not at all. He gave me a medal... he said it was your dad's? He wanted me to keep it for Lane."

Patrick's face blanched, but Mariska jumped in, "He said he was going to your uncle's!"

Both men turned to her. "What exactly did he say?" Derek's deep voice was so serious, it made me afraid.

My friend was equally concerned. "He said it was out west, but he didn't get specific. Somewhere he could breathe?"

"I know where he is." Patrick seemed to relax a bit, and from the corner of my eye, I noticed Slayde returning to join us.

But something was wrong.

He was smiling until his eyes landed on the new addition to our group. At the sight of Derek, everything changed. It was as if he'd seen a ghost or something worse—something terrible. He paused and leaned heavily against the wall.

"Slayde?" I started to go to him, but Derek cut me off.

"What the HELL are you doing here?" Anger flared in his deep voice, hotter than his concern for Stuart.

His sudden rage made me pause.

Slayde appeared to be in shock. "I got out. They let me go on—"

"Of course they did." Derek's voice was disgusted. "Murderers always get out, don't they?"

"It was an accident—"

"The 'Slayer Death Attack' is no fucking accident. It's a trained fight move."

My heart beat too hard; it made my arms and legs weak. I'd never seen Slayde like this, and Derek was seething.

His words were like a foreign language to me—one I didn't want to understand. *Murderer? Slayer Death Attack?*

"It was a long time ago," Slayde's voice was flat. "I was out of control."

I tried to approach my love. I was afraid, and I wanted him to hold me. I wanted him to be okay, but Derek snatched my arm, jerking me back. "What are you doing?"

It was so sudden and violent, Patrick stepped forward, touching his shoulder. "Easy, partner. What's this about?"

"Are you *with* him?" Derek's grey-blue eyes flashed from me to Slayde. "Don't you fucking know who she is?"

Slayde looked at me, but he was crumbling. I could see it—as if he knew the answer before it was given.

His voice was barely above a whisper. "Who... is she?"

Derek stepped in front of me, his tall form and broad shoulders creating an unwanted shield between the man I loved and me. His voice was pure judgment.

"She's the widow of Blake Woods. The man you beat to death five years ago outside a bar in Princeton—"

Slayed doubled over. His fist went to his mouth, and those pale blue eyes met mine with such anguish. He stood up fast, pushing through the glass doors out of the gym. The noise of his abrupt departure echoed in my ears, but my heart had stopped.

My vision clouded over, and I couldn't seem to move. Everything was falling apart, shattering with my insides into a million pieces. Confused, I tried to look up at Derek, but I was blinded by his words.

"Why did you say that?" I couldn't breathe. I was drowning in the answers my brain was fighting to reject.

Patrick was with me, scooping me into his arms. "Hold on, Ken. I've got you."

Mariska's voice was far away. "I don't understand. What just happened?"

Derek answered her slowly. "Five years ago I helped put Slayde Bennett and his accomplice Stitch Alana away for the second-degree murder of Blake Woods and Max Marconi."

He paused for a moment before driving the meaning home. "Blake was Kenny's husband."

It was the last thing I heard before my world went black.

Chapter 27: "I am the architect of my own destruction."
Slayde

Five years ago...

Stitch was on his fifth beer, and I'd finished my fourth shot of whiskey. It wasn't working. Bitterness smoldered in my chest, ready to ignite. With every breath the burn grew stronger.

"They fuckin' invited Compton." My jaw was clenched. "He fights like he's on fuckin' Quaaludes."

"Fuckers are scared," my friend said. "They passed you over because they know you've got more talent than all those assholes. They're afraid of losing their careers."

He patted my shoulder leaning forward into my face. I pulled my arm back with a snarl. "Your breath stinks."

The bartender stopped in front of me. I pointed down. Another shot of whiskey. My friend laughed, and I raised the short glass. A skinny punk slammed into my arm, knocking it out of my hand.

"What the fuck?" The rage was burning behind my eyes now. Two steps and this asshole would be eating my dirt.

"You talking to me, motherfucker?" The idiot actually got in my face.

"Ah, shit." Stitch's low voice hissed beside me. "Keep moving, lowlife."

Too late. I was out of my seat. "I'm talking to you."

We were nose to nose. He was my height, at least twenty pounds lighter, and he wore a white tank that showed off skinny arms covered in ink. I couldn't wait to wipe the floor with this wannabe badass.

Stitch had my arm, pulling me back and speaking to the fucker with a death wish. "Take your drink and go."

The punk's eyes narrowed. He was a snake, I could tell it. A sneaky fucker. The type to pull a shiv out of his boot when your back was turned.

It didn't matter. The burn in my chest demanded blood. My fists clenched, and I had to get that release. I needed to pound his lights out. One more word, motherfucker.

Just as fast another chump joined him. This one was equally stupid. "What's your name, shorty?"

Stitch bristled. "Stitch."

Explosions of laughter flew in our faces. The skinny punks fell against the bar, and I heard the seconds ticking in my brain, the countdown.

"You some fuckin' Hawaiian alien, short stack?" *The new guy's arm was around Punk #1's shoulders, hanging on him like a loose coat.*

"I'm Hawaiian," *my friend growled.* "And when I finish with you, you'll have more stitches than skin."

"OUTSIDE!" *The bartender's roar was right at my face.*

"With pleasure," *Punk #2 said, leaning too close to my friend.* "I'll use shorty to clean the grease off my boots."

"Then you're gonna suck my dick." *The other one leaned into my nose.*

Stitch caught his friend by the neck, hauling him to the side exit. I grabbed #1 by the arms and threw him against the wall after them. He rolled through the exit, but I caught the sneaky gleam in his eye.

The alley was hot and dark, and it smelled like dog shit. It had been raining all day, and now the black asphalt was slick. Cigarette butts dotted the clumps of weeds against the brick wall.

Stitch had already landed several blows on Punk #2. To his credit, he was letting him stand, pretending he had a chance. I had no such inclinations, but the shithead who'd gone before me was ready. I'd just passed through the exit when a bottle exploded beside my temple.

"FUCK YOU, MOTHERFUCKER!" He screamed, using all the force of his skinny weight to fall on me as I stepped back against the wall. My fists were up just as fast, blocking his sloppy punches.

He landed one amateur, from the country strike to my cheekbone, and in the second it took me to regain my bearings, I saw him shaking his hand and cringing. He'd probably broken his hand.

"That all you got, tough guy?" My voice was crazy with laughter. The demon inside me was awake. He was roaring in my ears, and the flames were blazing from my chest into my brain.

Oof! The sound of my fist making contact with his torso was like hitting a thick piece of meat — solid and perfect. Gratification tickled in my brain. I needed more.

The punk was screaming insults now, elbows flailing, ribs unprotected. I wanted him to shut the fuck up. That stupid noise scraped against my satisfaction like rubbing a cat's fur backwards.

Spinning him around so his back was to the wall, my next strike went to his face. An arc of blood sprayed up my forearm as the satisfying crunch of bone echoed in my ears.

He screamed again, and my world went red. Vision tunneled, I was in that place. All that mattered was the swift movement of my fists, the pleasure of making *contact over and over, pounding this mass of flesh into submission.*

Right, left, right, left, right, left, right
Left, right, left, right, left, right, left

My fists flew like a machine gun. Every contact was a hit of the greatest drug. I was flying high. Bouncing back on my feet, my eyes closed. I let the pleasure roll down my shoulders like warm water. More.

"Aw, shit," I heard behind me.

I didn't notice the flashing lights. I only heard another noise come from the meat in front of me. That did it.

Right, left, right, left, right, left, right
Left, right, left, right, left, right, left

Beating him over and over, I kept going until he stopped making that fucking noise. Then I hit him again to be sure he was done.

"Speak again, fucker. One more word." My voice was sandpaper growling as I waited.

What used to be his face was now a black pulp in the dark night. My fists were black and sticky, but my entire body vibrated with adrenaline and satisfaction and everything I craved. It was so fucking good.

"Time to go." Stitch jerked my arm.

I took one step back, and the mass in front of me fell like a tree, straight and slow, ending with a shuffling thunk on the pavement.

My body was shaking and high. The only thing that would make this moment more perfect would be to find some chick and bang her senseless. Lifting my chin, I looked up to the sky as a large drop hit my face. It was raining again.

"Now, Slayer." My friend jerked my arm, and I took a few staggered steps into his car. I barely registered the sound of tires squealing and red and blue lights flashing into the parking lot.

Stretching back against the leather seat, I closed my eyes as we drove away.

Satisfaction.

* * *

Derek Alexander stood in that hallway, looked at me with those gunmetal eyes, and ended my life for the second time — this time for good.

The first time I'd seen him, I was a hate-filled shit who didn't care. I'd killed because I didn't value life. I had no respect, and I had no control.

Nothing in my life had given me a reason to believe in anything. I didn't believe in love. I didn't believe in the touch of a hand that could quiet the rage consuming my insides like the fires of hell.

I'd gone to that penitentiary ready to face my judgment. I was Slayer the death angel with fists of steel. I was the master of high-volume punching, and I wasn't about to be anybody's bitch. Let some asshole touch me. I'd see him in hell whenever it was my turn to bust that fiery hole wide open.

I had no soul. I had no heart. I was a shitless shell of human waste.

Doc took the time to change that. He saw in me something worth saving — not that I'd ever demonstrated any inclination toward goodness.

We shared the same cell for six weeks when I arrived in that hellhole in eastern New Jersey. For six weeks he got down on his knees every morning and prayed. He fucking *prayed*.

He asked God out loud to turn his wasted life into something that would make up for the sins he'd committed. He actually said that. Every goddamned day.

He wasn't a big guy. He wasn't intimidating or strong. He was older and skinny. Still, everyone looked up to him. The big guys went to him when they couldn't take it anymore, and because he had answers, he was protected. He'd found a path to peace in the evil that composed our lives on the inside. He'd found a way to control the rage burning in all of us, and he'd taught it to me. Therapy, mantras, steps to understanding my anger and controlling it...

It was already starting to rain when I got to the pier. I took off running down the shoreline in the direction I'd gone that night so long ago. Only it wasn't so long ago—it had only been a few months.

When I got there, I dropped to my knees. Then I fell forward on my hands, gripping the wet sand in my fists. Here was where I'd faced my first test on the outside. Here was where I'd passed that test, and here was where I'd found her.

"Why?" I whispered in a broken voice.

I didn't believe. I was too worthless to believe, but I followed the steps hoping to get some semblance of a life back. Now I was left with less than nothing. It was hard before. Now it was unbearable.

My stomach cramped with the truth. I looked up at the black sky, and the rain covered my face. I wasn't crying, but everything inside of me was breaking. I was coming apart at the seams, burning up inside.

I wouldn't recover from this, but I knew I had to face her.

* * *

Patrick Knight was outside her doorstep. I stood dripping wet, looking into his angry glare.

"You here to rip my throat out?" My voice was defeated.

He looked down at his arms crossed over his chest. A band of ink circled one of his muscled forearms. "I'm here for her. Whatever she needs right now is what I'll do."

With a nod, I reached for the doorknob and stepped into an apartment once filled with love. I stopped as rainwater dripped from me to the floor. I took off my shirt, then I took off my wet jeans. My dark boxer-briefs were all that was left as I crossed the living room, stopping at her door.

With a guilty hand, I opened it, and my heart broke. Her small body was curled tightly at the head of the bed. A pillow was clutched to her chest, and she was shaking with sobs. I almost couldn't hold myself back from comforting her, but I did.

I was the reason she was in that position. I had no defense.

Her eyes blinked, and she saw me. My chest twisted as she flew at me, fists raised. "Killer!" She screamed, hitting my chest over and over. "Murderer!" Her voice broke as she collapsed against me sobbing.

My head bowed. I couldn't change what I was, still my elbows bent as I held her, sliding to the floor with her as everything inside me shattered again.

She pushed against my arms and slapped me. It didn't even hurt compared to the pain twisting behind my ribs. She slapped me again and then covered her face with her hands as she cried more. Her knees bent and she pressed her eyes against them. Seeing her this way was tearing me apart.

I reached for her, and she shoved my hand away. "Were you *Slayer* when you killed him? Did you use your signature death move?"

Standing slowly, I let her see the truth, the ink I'd been so careful to conceal. On my left ribcage was a large teardrop—the life I'd taken. Below it were praying hands and the letters *R.I.P.*

Quietly, I answered her. "I was so out of control back then. When I went to the bar that night, I was gunning for a fight. He just happened to be the first punk to cross my path."

She blinked up at me then and stood quickly, hitting me again. "You beat him to death!" She cried. "You killed him like a dog. Just like *that* dog!"

Those words seared through me. It was true. I was as vile as the man who'd raised me. I would never move past who I was or what I'd done.

Yet I loved her. I loved her with everything inside me. For a short time, she'd saved me from being that person. She'd calmed the noise in my head and healed my rage with her love. She'd made me believe in second chances.

That's where I was the fool. It was never meant to last. I'd lost her before I even knew she existed.

CHAPTER 28: "WITH PAIN COMES STRENGTH."
KENNY

He stood there and let me hit him until I couldn't feel my hands anymore. He took my pain as I released it with all of the bitterness and loss and anger I'd held for so many years. Then with a quiet apology, he left.

It was over.

I didn't leave my bed for two days.

After all the years I'd spent alone, mourning, worrying about being true to Blake's memory, I took my first steps and ran straight into the arms of his killer.

My throat tightened as the pain tried to tear me apart again. I was grieving for him. Right or wrong, I loved him. He was a killer, a murderer, and from the first night when he saved me on that beach to every day after when he saved me from my loneliness, I couldn't live without him. We found each other; we fell in love. We were like pawns in some horrible, cosmic chess match, and we had no idea.

What kind of cruel joke would bring us together only to find out the horrible truth that would rip us apart? *Oh, god.* I clutched my knees tight to my chest. Closing my eyes, I still saw the devastated look on his face when Derek confronted him. It broke my heart.

But I had to fight. I couldn't lie in this bed and cry another day. I had a job. I had a little boy...

Ripping the blankets aside, I pulled open my door. Patrick was there on the couch in my living room, stopping me in my tracks.

"W-What are you doing here?"

He stood and walked groggily to me, pulling me into a hug. I fought against the fresh tears that threatened to return at his warmth. "You stayed with me when I thought I'd lost Elaine. Now I'm here for you."

The tightness in my throat made it difficult to answer him. "Oh, Patrick. There's no coming back from this."

His hands smoothed my back, and for a moment we were quiet. Still, I couldn't fall apart. I wouldn't let myself.

"You've got to get home to our little boy," I said. "Tell him I'll be there for a visit soon—give me a day or two. I don't want to cry in front of him."

Patrick nodded, wiping my hair off my cheek. "Okay." He hugged me again. "You're going to make it through this. You will."

I nodded, tucking my head against his shoulder. "I think I'll go back and lie down for a bit first."

"Your friend's been over a couple times. She left you some food that smells delicious—tomato-stuffed cabbage?"

"You eat it, okay? I might throw up if I eat anything."

His lips tightened and he nodded. "Get some rest."

Heaviness pressed hard on my shoulders as I walked back to my bedroom. I had to get back to work. I had to keep moving forward. Life didn't end because once again I made a wrong choice. No matter what, I had to survive this.

Picking up my robe, I staggered to the shower.

* * *

Mariska's eyes flew wide when she saw me walk into the gym. "Kenny!" She ducked under the counter and ran to me, pulling me into a hug. "I rescheduled all your clients for today. You basically have the day off."

My body was shell-shocked, but I shook my head. "I want to do something. Call somebody and tell them to come in."

She stepped back, still holding my hands. "I'd love for you to train me. Tell me what you want to do. I'll do whatever you want."

"I don't know. I only know I can't…" The idea of stepping into that boxing room made my stomach lurch. "Please let… *him* know he can take over my old boxing routine."

"Oh!" She blinked quickly. "You don't know?"

As much as I hated it, my heart beat faster. "Know what?"

"He's gone. He asked Rook to help him get on with the freighter crew. They pulled out last night headed across the Atlantic. Rook said they wouldn't be back for months. If at all." She chewed her lip, watching my face. "I'm so sorry, I should've told you sooner."

"He left on the freighter?" Nothing made sense anymore. "But he can't swim."

"You could've knocked me over with a feather, too. Remember at my house? The coffee?"

But I was struggling with a different memory. Ripples of pain clutched my chest as images of our last night together filled my mind. I'd hit him with my fists, but I'd destroyed him with my words. He would never come back. Not after what I'd said.

What was wrong with me? He killed Blake! Where was my loyalty?

My voice was quiet. "It doesn't matter."

"Oh, Ken," Mariska's voice was broken. "How can you say that?"

"I'm going to the steam room."

Walking away from her, I headed to the back. I'd never liked the steam room. It was dark and hot, and the steam made it difficult to breathe. I pulled the door open and went inside with all my clothes on. Sitting on the concrete bench, alone in the thick whiteness, I let the heavy, wet air flood my senses.

Inhaling a deep breath, I wondered how it didn't drown me. I put my elbows on my knees, looking at my palms for a moment—at the little black heart clear as a bell in my hand. Then I put them flat against my eyes, trying with everything in me to hold on, to take one more breath, not to fall apart.

One more inhale of suspended water—*please smother the pain in my chest.* I fought against the sob trying to fold me in half.

No matter what I told myself, it wasn't going to work. I'd never forget him. Still, I had to learn to live without him. Just like before, I didn't have a choice.

Climbing the gangway of the *Sea Empress* was a lot
like entering the gates of East Jersey State Prison.
Only, back then I was filled with rage. Today it was
only emptiness and pain.

When the men said they were heading out, this
ship was the only way I could think to try and
escape it. Twenty-six crewmembers were onboard a
600-foot vessel, transporting 4,500 containers.
Basically, it looked like an enormous aircraft carrier
holding the stacked backs of hundreds of semi-
trucks. It was also considered small by merchant-
ship standards.

I stood on the deck as we put out, watching the
waves below. Captain McKinney held a pipe in his
teeth as he spoke. "An oil tanker sank in the Bay of
Biscay on our last voyage."

A Danish captain, he was the man who traded
free gym memberships for miscellaneous furniture
and electronics deliveries. He would apparently
ship humans as well when he needed backup crew.

McKinney had been making this journey for
almost thirty years, and based on his reputation, my
parole officer allowed me contract-worker status
and provisional papers for the voyage to Hamburg
and back under McKinney's direct supervision.

I had no idea what all was onboard the *Sea
Empress*, and I didn't know what the hell I was

doing. I couldn't swim. I didn't care if I died, but I hadn't gone into those details with the captain. I'd only said it was my first time on a boat.

Listening to his story now, with three thousand miles of ocean ahead of us, it seemed like an appropriate sentence for me. "What happened?"

"Snapped in two. Just like that. *Crack!*" He turned his pipe over and slapped it against his wrist. His accent sounded French. "But you shouldn't worry. Cargo ships don't break."

"They blow up." A crewmember carrying a long, metal tube on his shoulder laughed as he passed us.

"We're not carrying explosives, Anders!" McKinney hollered back and started to walk, so did I. He wanted to talk, and I had nothing to do but listen. I'd be lying on my cot down below otherwise. "Our biggest concern is the weather. We'll make it to Hamburg in three weeks easy, but when the weather kicks up, a lot of the cargo can be lost overboard. That's our pay disappearing into the depths with every box."

"What do we do to stop them?"

"Nothing. Sometimes we have to cut them loose to avoid capsizing." He shrugged lighting his pipe. "Hazards of the trade."

We passed a quiet moment, and I looked across the bow at the thousands of containers, some twenty-foot in length, some forty. I wondered why I hadn't started at the shipyards in the first place. Looking down at my palm, I remembered why. Doc had told me to start over, to live my life. I saw where that got me.

"Many fatalities on these trips?" Something sick inside me hoped he'd say yes.

"Not at all." He puffed smoke in a blue haze around his head. "Collisions at sea can result in death. Or pirates. But we're not passing through narrow channels or dangerous lanes. We should be fine."

We were stopped again, and I was still looking at my palm, the heart. It was so small. I stared at it holding all the pain of what I'd lost.

"Why are you on this voyage, mate?" McKinney was watching me.

I decided to answer him truthfully. "Nothing left to lose."

"Ahh, so you'll be the one out in the storm trying to curb our losses?"

I shrugged. "If it's not that, it'll just be something else."

He slapped me on the shoulder. "In the past when I thought all was lost, that was when I realized what was most important."

It would've been good advice in some other situation. As it was, I only nodded and started walking again. I knew what was most important. I'd held it in my hands, and then I'd lost it.

Chapter 30: "Choice determines destiny."
Kenny

I wouldn't let myself think about him. I wouldn't let myself miss him. A month had passed, and running had become my new obsession. I would never step foot in that boxing room again, but there were loads of options when it came to getting outside and running as hard and as far away as I possibly could. The problem was coming back.

Rook was pretty patient in the beginning, but now he wanted me to turn it into a group fitness option. He said if I took that pain and used it, I might look up one day and find it was gone. I didn't bother arguing with him, but that was never going to happen.

I sat at a small table opposite the juice bar working out a trail route when an older fellow entered looking for me. He was thin with sandy brown hair. It was longish, in a style that used to be fashionable, and he had grey peppered at his temples. Kind brown eyes studied me from his thin face, but I had no idea who he was.

"He said his name is Gary Burden." Mariska spoke quietly as she stood beside the small table where I sat.

I frowned up at her. "I don't know anybody by that name."

"Do you know anybody named Doc?"

I was on my feet at once headed to the front where the older fellow stood.

"Are you Doc?" I asked, searching his expression desperately.

It was ridiculous for me to feel this sense of urgency. Slayde had known this man in prison. He wouldn't be here to give me good news.

His brown eyes lightened when he saw me. "You have to be Kenny. I feel like I'd know you anywhere from how he described you. Only your hair…"

The purple was gone, and now it was back to straight, dark brown. "Why are you here?"

"My number came up. I got out a few days ago, and I thought I'd visit my friend. Is he here?"

He was so cheerful, but that weight was back in my chest. I'd done my best to drown it in steam, run away from it until my lungs burned, pretend it never existed, but the reality was, it was always with me.

"He went away, I'm sorry."

Doc's brow lined. "Went away? But that's impossible. The last time I talked to him…" I could only assume he read my expression and realized with every word, he was killing me a little bit more. "Would you be willing to tell me what happened?"

How did I say this out loud? He was asking me to repeat words I wouldn't even say in my head.

"He… I guess you know he was in prison for murder." The man nodded. "We didn't know it at the time, but it seems the man he killed was…" I couldn't say it. That old pain sliced through my heart with a vengeance.

"It was someone you knew?"

I waited, turning the truth over in my mind like a sheet of paper. A sheet of paper that held what? Answers?

Quietly I said the words, "It was my husband."

Mid-afternoon was always a slow time at the gym, and for a moment we sat facing each other, the silence pressing hard inside my ears. He didn't speak, and as the seconds ticked past, I realized I wasn't going to break down. I guessed that meant I'd finally turned to stone.

"I'm sorry," Doc spoke at last. "I'm having a hard time wrapping my head around what you just said."

I wasn't about to repeat myself. "I don't have another way to say it."

He paced, rubbing his scruffy chin seeming lost in thought. I remembered how Slayde used to refer to Doc's mantras and words of wisdom. "That's a pretty strange twist of fate."

"That's all you got?" I was being shitty, but fuck it. I was so far past caring anymore. "You don't have some eternal truth for me?"

He nodded slowly. "Maybe. The Universe has a way of restoring balance. In some cultures, if you kill someone, you become responsible for their land, their family... their wife." He caught my look and continued. "It's a primitive system, I know. I'm only noting the comparison. Today we just kill you, widows and orphans be damned."

"I don't know what you're talking about." I was tired, and I didn't have time for this.

"I'm talking about forgiveness."

Turning the word over in my mind, I thought about what it could mean for me. "I was thinking about loyalty."

"I understand that." He nodded. "Tell you what, would you have dinner with me tonight? I think I'll stay at Slayde's place. He told me if I was ever in town to crash there, and maybe when he's back—"

"Does he still have it?" I tried not to think about what it could mean if he did. He'd be back one day.

"I'll find out, I guess. If not, I'll wait for you there. I'd like to talk to you some more."

I glanced at the clock. "I'll be finished here in a few hours. I'll drive over after."

"Good. See you then."

* * *

Being in Slayde's living room filled me with a mix of emotions. The finger paintings we'd made still hung on the wall in the kitchen, and I honestly couldn't look at them. It hurt too much. At the same time, being here, knowing Slayde still had the place... I wasn't comfortable with the flood of hope running through me that maybe someday he'd be here again.

"The door was unlocked," Doc said allowing me inside.

"He always left it unlocked." I thought about that a moment. "I guess he didn't like locked doors."

"More like he didn't have anything worth stealing," Doc laughed. "This place is empty."

Our first night here crept through my thoughts like a painful intruder. "He said if I ever lost everything, I'd be surprised at how much I didn't need."

"That's just the kind of thing he would say." Doc was energized. "It's why I wanted to talk to you a bit longer."

Glancing around, I raised my eyebrows. "Want me to order takeout?"

He seemed to remember we were meeting for dinner. "Yes! You probably know all the best places."

"I wouldn't say *best*, but I know places."

Thirty minutes later, we were splitting take-out Thai food and discussing twists of fate. Doc was clearly a frustrated philosopher, and from what I gathered he'd been something of a prison guru.

"I'm surprised they kept you inside so long," I said around a bite of spicy Pad Thai.

He shrugged. "The Universe works in mysterious ways. Things don't happen when you think they should or in the way you think they should, yet it's always right for you and your situation."

I shook my head, lifting the wine glass and taking a sip. Slayde still had a half-bottle in his fridge from the last time we'd been here. I was the only one who drank it.

"I'm amazed I'm not falling apart being here right now." Clearly the wine had loosened me up. It was a month old and not very good, but I needed something.

"Because you still love him?" Doc's gaze was pointed.

Not answering that. "I'm also surprised how direct you can be when you want to."

He leaned back in the chair, first studying the plate in front of him and then lifting his eyes to mine. "Five years ago, you didn't know each other, and I'm willing to bet you were both very different people. Yes?"

An image of me at twenty-one flashed across my brain—pale, black asymmetrical haircut, short black skirts over ripped fishnets and boots. "I was a little different. I've had a son since then."

"You're a mother. That's good," he nodded.

"It was actually pretty careless of me," I exhaled a laugh. "But I wouldn't take anything for my little boy."

He picked up his fork and moved a broccoli floret through the brown sauce on his plate. "I was in prison for the same reason as Slayde. High as a kite, I held up a convenience store needing money for more drugs. Clerk pulled a rifle... I don't even remember killing him I was so wasted."

Swallowing the lump in my throat, I tried to keep the stony look off my face.

"Oh, it's alright," he chuckled ruefully. "I deserve your hatred. I should have died in that cell."

"Yet here you are." I thought about Derek's bitter words to Slayde. He had a reason to be angry at the system. He had a baby boy and a beautiful wife to protect. Shaking that thought away, I put my hand over my eyes. "I think my head's all messed up."

"Do you believe people can change?"

For a moment, I pondered that question, trying to decide. "I don't know."

"When I met Slayde, he was a different person. He was driven by such rage... I'd never seen anything like it."

My mind flickered back to the story he'd told me about his dad. It was just as painful to remember now as it had been then. "I guess he had his reasons."

"I would pray every day." He paused for another laugh. "I was raised Baptist, so it was all I knew to do. Anyway, I prayed every day the same thing, 'God help me make up for my wasted life somehow.'" He took a deep breath and let it out slowly. "Slayde would get so pissed at me. Until the day he started asking questions. It all started to change then."

"He said you helped him." I circled the base of my wine glass with my finger.

"Slayde wanted to change. Otherwise he would've never gotten out." He was still looking at his plate. "I vouched for him to the parole board. He's got a good heart, and he wanted to make up for his crimes. I guess they saw something in him worth taking a chance on."

"That night on the beach, when he saved me..." I couldn't finish. I could still see his body vibrating with adrenaline in the moonlight, his fists clenching and unclenching. I had no idea the internal battle he was fighting.

"The night you were attacked." Doc nodded, looking down. "He called me after that. It was pretty significant for him."

Standing quickly, I pushed the chair aside. "I'm sorry. I've got to go."

I couldn't sit here and listen to any more of this. My past and his role in it were problems I couldn't solve. Maybe my soul would always long for his, but it couldn't be right for us to be together.

Doc stood quickly with me. "I'm sorry. I didn't mean to upset you."

"I've got to get home. I'm going to see my son tomorrow." Just like that, I decided on the spot.

"I don't think it's an accident that you found each other. Don't make up your mind so fast on what should happen."

Shaking my head, I pushed through the door. "Goodnight."

CHAPTER 31: "MAY YOU NEVER BE BROKEN."
SLAYDE

We made it to Hamburg without any real incidents at sea. A couple stormy nights had me vomiting like a pussy in my toilet, but nothing major cargo-wise. Captain McKinney declared me the ship's lucky omen, but I knew better. If my life was spared on this voyage, it was only because something crueler was in store for me.

Walking through the market near the docks, I couldn't stop thinking about Kenny. I didn't want to miss her as badly as I did, but I knew I'd never stop. She would always haunt my thoughts.

One of the merchants made miniature dolls. Not knowing any German, I couldn't speak to her, but she demonstrated how the tiny doll in my palm had moveable hands and feet. She had long purple yarn for hair. The part of my brain that wallowed in self-immolation imagined Kenny and me with a blue-eyed baby girl. She would love something like this. I pulled out the few Francs I had and handed them over.

The merchant was overjoyed, but I didn't know what I'd do with the doll. Its eyes were closed, and it looked so vulnerable in my hand. Something about it reminded me of that night on the beach. I wrapped it in tissue and slid it under my pillow when I got back to the ship.

As I sat with the crew waiting for us to leave port again, headed back for Bayville, I watched the crewman Anders twisting wire into different shapes. He was Finnish, and with a pair of needle-nose pliers, he took a thin piece of silver and twisted it until it was a tiny boat with sails.

"That's pretty good," I said, watching him.

"It's nothing," he laughed, handing it to me. "For our good luck omen."

He was something of the ship's philosopher, and he reminded me a little of Doc. He was also the same joker who liked talking about all the different ways cargo ships could sink.

"Who do you make them for?" I asked, watching him start another.

"Meh," he shrugged. "Wife and kids, mostly."

Nodding, I picked up one of the small silver rods and rolled it between my fingers. As he worked, I saw a thin red ring around his thumb. "Did you get caught in the line?"

He inspected his hand. "Oh, no. That's the Red String of Fate. Chinese legend. It's for those who are destined to be together no matter time, place, or circumstance—an invisible red string runs from her pinky finger to his thumb." Turning his hand, he smiled. "It might stretch or tangle, but it can never break."

My eyes ached and I curled my fingers to touch the little black heart in my palm.

"You believe in that stuff?"

"I'm a sailor, mate. I believe in omens, myths, legends, prayers." His gravelly voice was low when he spoke again. "What's her name? The girl who has your string? I can see it tormenting you."

Glancing up at him, I couldn't find a reason to hide it. "Kenny."

"She married?" I shook my head, and he poked his lips out. "The Japanese have a word *Komorebi*. It means 'The sunlight that filters through the leaves of the trees.' There's no English equivalent."

I thought of Kenny's smile as I watched him continue to twist the silver pin into an infinity knot. He continued working, and after a while, it was a heart. Finishing, he wrapped it around, and it was a ring.

"Here." Holding it up, he inspected it a few moments. "Tie a red string to this and give it to her."

With a sad smile, I shook my head. "It's going to take a lot more than a twisted piece of silver to fix what I did."

"The red string can never break. Now be our safe omen home."

* * *

The sunlight was too bright hitting the courtyard on that steamy morning, the grass too green. It stung my eyes, and I wiped the back of my hand roughly across my brow, blinking fast.

The older man in the blue cotton tee and matching blue work slacks clapped me gently on the back. "You got this." Deep lines on his face told of every hard lesson he'd ever learned, and I couldn't help wondering if I'd ever see him again after I walked out those gates.

"I got nothing," I said, rubbing an inked hand over my diminished midsection. Then I picked up the pack at my feet. "All I've got is this. What I brought with me."

"That's all anybody ever has in life." The man gave me a warm smile. His brown hair hung in his brown eyes. It was a style from another era, and the grey at his temples gave away his age. "But you're ready to pick up your life again. You're taking what you've learned."

My lips tightened, unable to force a smile. Yes, I'd learned coping skills, how to control the rage in my chest, how to walk away, but I had no life to pick up. Not anymore.

Still, I didn't want our parting words to be cross. "Thanks, Doc," I said with a nod.

"Don't thank me. I only helped you see what was inside you. You had to take the first step."

The first step.

"Right. Well, take it easy." I shook Doc's hand then put one foot in front of the other, slowly making my way to the waiting taxi.

Leaving this place wasn't like graduating from high school or college. Everyone would look at me differently now. They would question everything, from my trustworthiness to my ability to handle stress. Most wouldn't even want to be around me. The stigma would follow me wherever I went, and at twenty-six years old, that was going to be a long fucking time.

"Where to?" The cab driver's voice was wary. Or maybe it was disgusted.

My faded jeans hung a little looser on me now. I reached into my back pocket and pulled out the folded map I'd studied for the several days. My eyes had devoured the coastline, reading name after name, trying to decide which one felt right on my tongue.

I imagined living near the ocean would help. I could find a simple, low-stress job—maybe construction or maintenance—and if it all got to be too much again, I could go down to the water, practice the things Doc had taught me. Centering, breathing, green-light the emotions, name them, embrace them, let them go.

My mind had settled on Bayville. It was small and close to what used to be home. One thing about losing everything—it brought a definite sense of freedom.

"Hey!" The driver's voice was sharp. "You with me? I ain't got all day. Where to?"

My ice blue eyes flashed, and fear registered on the man's face. I'd have to adjust to that as well, I guessed. "Bus station."

Inside, the taxi smelled like old vinyl and stale cigarettes, and I wondered how many times this stocky, unshaven man in the dirty chambray shirt had driven from here to the Greyhound station. My pack was at my feet as I pulled the heavy metal door closed with a pop and a slam...

I jerked awake in my cot. Something slammed in the boat above me—crews working around the clock. Blinking into the darkness, I tried to get my bearings. It was just a dream.

Only it wasn't a dream. It was a memory. Was it possible to dream memories?

Yes.

It was the first time I'd dreamed of anything that wasn't Kenny. That painful thought sliced through my chest. Night after night I closed my eyes and I was in her arms. I'd touch her face, smooth back her dark violet hair, kiss her pale pink lips, hold her against my chest. I could hear her sigh as I sank into her warm depths, feel her legs wrapping around my waist, her fingers in my hair.

I wasn't sure why I thought climbing into the belly of a ship and sailing to the middle of the ocean would help me forget her. Every morning I awoke to the searing pain of losing her all over again.

Tonight was different, though. Maybe because of the story Anders had told me. The string. I remembered studying that map, looking at every city and thinking about the names. Of all the places to choose, I chose the one that would bring me to her. Did I have any control at all?

Shaking my head, I rolled over in my bed. I didn't believe in fate or Chinese legends. Yet, here I was, longing for her with every breath. I rubbed my forehead hard and tried to find a way through the pain.

In my mind, I heard Doc's words. *Without the darkness, you never see the stars.*

Chapter 32: "But the fighter still remains."
Kenny

Thanksgiving was four days away, and I'd promised my parents Lane would be with me for the annual Woods' family gathering. My dad and I had never seen eye to eye, and I didn't visit them as much as I should. But I tried to get Lane over to see them as often as made sense. It meant a lot to my mom.

Patrick and Derek had found Stuart and were with him in Montana. Something was wrong there, but I hadn't asked for details. Once Lane and I left, Elaine would fly out to join them for the holiday—or for a conjugal visit, more likely. I knew Patrick.

Lane snuggled in my lap until he fell into a deep sleep. Elaine and I stayed up a bit longer watching the fire and sipping red wine.

She chuckled. "If you'd told me three years ago I'd be sitting by a fire sharing a glass of wine with the mother of my fiancé's child, I would never have believed it."

"I guess it is sort of an awkward arrangement." I still wavered between feeling comfortable and feeling like I should apologize all the time when we were together. Still, I was so thankful Lane was here and not in New York with Aunt Laura. He would've been happy living with her, but our lives would be so different. I'd never see him.

"Oh, Kenny!" She sat up straighter, her eyes full of concern. "That's not what I meant, but even you have to agree life can take some pretty unexpected twists."

I couldn't deny that. "Sometimes I feel like the twists are all I get from life. Or the screws."

Elaine chewed her lip, her green eyes sparkling in the fire. "You and I have never had that kind of relationship, I know. But if you ever want to talk to me... I mean, we are Lane's two mommies."

In that moment, I knew why Patrick loved her so much. "Thanks, but I don't know if I deserve consolation. All the screw-ups in my life can be laid directly at my feet. They're all because of my choices."

She looked into her wine glass, and I could tell she was weighing her words. "From what Patrick said, this business with Slayde wasn't something you chose." Her eyes flickered to mine, and she quickly added, "Not that we were discussing you. I just... I knew something was wrong when you went a month without visiting Lane. You never do that."

Hugging my little boy closer to my chest, I felt the tears rising in my throat. "I didn't want him to see me cry. He's too little to understand."

She nodded, taking another sip. "Want to tell me about it?"

I exhaled a laugh. "The perfect mommy of my little boy? Not really."

"I'm not so perfect." She rested her head on her hand. "I'm a person just like you."

The fire crackled, and I stared at it a moment. "Blake was the first guy I ever loved. He was exciting, and he didn't give a shit about anybody. He had these sparkling green eyes and spiked black hair... he was covered in tattoos, and he was dangerous and sexy... I felt so alive when I was with him."

"I think I can understand that." She smiled, waiting.

"He was also a first-class asshole. He was a nineteen year-old former juvenile delinquent. He was the guy in the convenience store hassling the clerk. He was the idiot who'd be in your face if you tried to criticize him." Closing my eyes, I leaned my head against the chair. "If I met him now, I wouldn't give him the time of day."

The living room was quiet except for the hiss of the fire. Just then, Lane made a snarfle, and our eyes met. Then we both laughed. "Is my baby snoring?"

"Can't you see him being just like Patrick?" Elaine's voice was full of adoration.

I couldn't stop the smile crossing my lips. "Watch out preschool girls."

We both laughed more, and she picked up the gauntlet I'd thrown. "So Blake was a mouthy troublemaker. Slayde...?"

"Is a quiet killer." My eyes squeezed shut. "Jesus! I don't know what to do with this."

She took a deep breath and a sip of wine. "When you came back pregnant, and Patrick and I split up, I was so miserable. But I thought he had to be with you. He got you pregnant, he had to make it right."

"But Patrick never loved me. He loves you."

"And if you had married him, how long would it have lasted?" Her tone wasn't aggressive. It was thoughtful, building, and I was curious about her point.

"Until I stuck a fork in his head," I said with a smile.

She smiled too. "I guess what I'm trying to say is sometimes the 'right' thing isn't what we've been taught is what's supposed to happen. Life isn't neat or clean enough for that. We have to be willing to try a different way sometimes, take a risk to get to happiness."

I thought about what she was saying. "I feel like my life is one big test."

"And what if it is?" She sat up in her chair. "I give tests all the time. They're not judgments. They're an opportunity to show what you've learned."

Her eyes were round and full of heart, and a pain twisted in my chest. "I guess I've learned I'll never stop making mistakes."

"Does it have to be a mistake? I mean, look at us right now."

My eyes went from her to my happy little boy sleeping in my lap, and I thought about the twisted path we'd followed to get here. "You're really smart."

"I'm a teacher."

"A middle school teacher. The worst years."

"That means you should listen to me even more."

She grinned, but I couldn't talk about it anymore. I hugged Lane and stared into the fire thinking about tests and twists and finding a path to happiness through a life filled with wrong choices.

* * *

Lane was snug at my mom's house when I set out to do my usual jog on the beach the night after we returned to Bayville. She loved keeping him, and he was seriously in danger of being spoiled completely rotten.

Whenever I took him to visit my parents, she was beside herself with wanting to hold him and show him off to all her friends. Even my dad softened when my little boy's golden head appeared with me in the doorway. He might've been angry and disappointed when Patrick and I showed up that day with the news I was pregnant and had no intention of marrying the father, but he couldn't fool me. His love for his grandson was stronger than his lifelong frustration with his daughter.

The sun was just starting to set, and I parked my car at the end of the pier. As much as I didn't want to look toward Slayde's apartment, I couldn't keep my eyes from wandering in that direction. Doc was still there. He was determined to stay until his friend reappeared, and somehow that made the pain in my chest a little easier to bear. It gave me the slightest bit of hope that maybe there was a solution. I couldn't see it yet, but perhaps it would come to me.

Leaning forward, I stretched my hamstrings. Then I straightened and pulled my foot to my buttocks. The warm-up filtered through my quads, and I took off walking through the soft sand down to the firmer, wet sand by the shore.

Running in sand was tough. It was one of the hardest exercises I'd ever done, but it was nothing like being on these familiar beaches alone, trying not to remember Slayde's arms around me, him lifting me in the surf. I ran harder, away from the memory of finger paint floating around us in a loving rainbow as our bodies slid together.

More, faster, dig deep... I tried to outrun those feelings. If I kept going, the pain in my chest would dissolve into a burn that blocked out every emotion. The only room left would be for adrenaline to push me on, fighting the resistance low in my stomach begging me to stop.

I'd gone a mile, maybe farther when I saw the lights of a bar ahead. It was the boardwalk or it was one of the clubs on Toms River. I couldn't tell. I kept pushing until the burn in my chest lost out to the screaming of my lungs. I had to take a break.

Slowing, I dropped to a jog, then to a walk. I was breathing hard, but the pain was temporarily gone. No emotion could withstand the punishment of a sustained sprint.

There was no reason for me to keep walking toward the bar, but my legs kept moving putting one foot in front of the other. The night was completely black. Either it was a new moon or the clouds rolling in had obscured it. Self-preservation should've made me go back, but I kept walking until I slowed to a stop.

Above me on the beach I could just make out the dark shape of humans. I froze in place, fear gripping my insides. What was I doing out here alone? I was far from anyone who could help me, and worse, nobody knew where I was.

I didn't move. I didn't breathe. It didn't matter. The shapes further up on the shore weren't interested in me. First I heard a moan. It sounded like sex on the beach. Then I heard the scream.

"Let me GO!" A female voice.

Through the darkness, I could almost make out arms, waving like a pinwheel, but the larger shape clamped them down.

"Stop fighting me you little bitch, and you might enjoy yourself."

The words hit me hard, like lightening, fusing me to the spot. The voice.

I knew that voice.

More struggles, female wails. Then a second voice.

"Come on, Grif. Let's get out of here." The skinny guy. They were both here.

"Shut the fuck up and get out of here so I can nail this bitch."

It was the same thing all over again. Did they rehearse this sick stunt?

"Please let me go. Please." Her whining and begging twisted an ache of anxiety in the center of my torso. I was paralyzed with fear, but I couldn't let this happen. I had to do something.

"That's right," Grif snarled. "Stick that little ass up."

My stomach roiled, and I thought I might vomit. Her next words snapped me out of it.

"Help me! Somebody, plea—"

"Shut up." It sounded as if his hand was over her mouth the way her voice became muffled. Still it was enough.

Rage that had simmered long and low in my stomach for months boiled up and over. I remembered what Slayde told me, but I didn't have pepper spray or mace. All I had was the power of my body, my fists. He'd taught me how to throw a punch from the depth of my core all the way through the center of my fist, and I was ready to put my skills to the test.

Running forward, my hands clenched into tight balls as I rapidly crossed the sand, tilting my wrists slightly. I was just at him when the roar pushed out of my throat. "Let her GO!" I shouted in a voice I didn't recognize.

My first two knuckles plowed at an angle across his cheekbone and into his nose with the force of all my running and what little body weight I had to throw behind it. Pain exploded into my forearm when I made contact, but my form was good. I wasn't injured. I'd only made contact with bone, and he staggered dropping to his knees on the sand, releasing his victim. Fast as I could, I followed my one with the two, this time aiming for his throat.

"BASTARD ABUSING ASSHOLE!" Another roar tore from my throat, but no pain followed my second strike.

He fell flat, arching his back and gagging. As before, the thin man was nowhere to be seen, but I didn't care. I waited over Grif's body, fists still up, elbows tight. He struggled in the sand to breathe, and the girl crawled away fast, just like I had done the night Slayde saved me.

I looked up and she was limping and running back in the direction of the bar. "Wait!" I yelled, but she didn't stop.

I let her go. My rapid breathing moved my shoulders as I stood over the loser at my feet. I didn't have a phone. I didn't have any way to report this. He continued writhing and gagging, and at least I knew he wasn't dead.

"Look at me," I growled. He didn't move, and my voice grew louder, another roar. I was the tiger. "Look. At. ME!"

His head turned. "That was your second warning, fucker. Do you hear me?" I kicked him in the torso, and he let out an *Oof!*

"NEVER COME BACK." I pulled my leg back and kicked him again, harder. Another *Oof!* I dropped to my knee and grabbed the hair at the top of his head in my fist, jerking his head back as hard as I could. Blood formed a black mask over the lower half of his face in the darkness, and a sick satisfaction warmed my chest.

My voice was low and sinister. "If you ever come back here again, I *will* find you. And I *will* finish you. This is your last warning."

The sound of another person approaching snapped my head up. I released Grif's hair, and stood to face what had to be his accomplice walking toward us.

"Who's there?" I couldn't believe this asshole was going to try acting tough — again! He was going to try and spin it like the girl had asked for it.

Standing over the moaning body at my feet, I almost wished I had killed him. Then I thought about what kind of person that made me. I thought of Slayde — standing right here, fighting with all the inner strength he had not to kill this guy. I could still see his fists clenching and unclenching.

Pulling my foot back, I planted another, hard kick right in Grif's stomach, resulting in another grunt. This time, he curled forward.

"What are you doing?" Skinny was moving a bit slower.

I spun on my heel and started to run back the way I'd come. I heard his voice yell after me as my pace picked up. I was flying back toward the pier, toward Slayde's place.

When I got closer, I slowed to a walk. The burning in my chest was back, pushing out any fear or anger I felt. My run had burned up the adrenaline surging through my limbs, and now all I felt was the pain in my right wrist and forearm.

Looking up, I walked to Slayde's apartment. Doc would be inside, and I could only hope as a former convict, he'd know what to do with my battered hand.

"What happened to you?" Doc's eyes were wide, and his jaw slack as he took in my appearance.

I could only imagine what I looked like — hair slick with sweat, plastered against my forehead, blood on my hands. "I was running on the beach." My breath was still coming in quick gasps. "A man was attacking this girl, and I... I..."

"It looks like you handled it." His expression was cautious but prepared for what I might say.

I nodded fast. "She ran, but I got him. I left him lying on the sand."

"Get in here." Doc led me into the studio apartment directly to the sink where he straightened out my hand. "How does it feel? Any popping sensations? Numbness?"

I shook my head. "I did it right. I just hit him in the face. As hard as I could." Thinking about how it happened, I added. "The first hit was the hardest."

"Make a fist." He stood back and watched my fingers. "You're going to be okay, but you should ice it and wrap it. If you develop any numbness, you need to go to the doctor and get X-rays."

"You think I broke my hand?"

"I don't think so. You clearly know how to throw a punch."

My chest warmed, and I looked down at my throbbing wrist. "Slayde taught me." It was hard to say, but Doc didn't react.

I watched as he snatched the towel from the counter and went to the freezer. He took a few handfuls of ice and brought the makeshift ice pack back to me. "Hold your wrist in this. Keep it elevated tonight."

Watching him, I thought about the beach, my feelings and what I wanted to say and do. My voice was a broken whisper. I was on the verge of tears, but I fought them. "Will I ever see him again?"

Doc left my hand in my lap and wrapped his arms over my shoulders. I felt him take a deep breath and slowly let it out. "I think you will."

We didn't speak any more, and I knew I had to get back to my son. I could cover for my injury, play it off as some accident, but apart from all that, something inside me had changed. I needed to see Slayde again.

The night the storm hit, I was lying in my cot dreaming of her. It was the same as every night. I'd finish dinner, walk the deck, then head down to my cot to read more of that damn book about the French kid, or close my eyes and dream of her beautiful body. God those dreams were the most exquisite torment. I typically fell asleep pretty fast, since the crew enjoyed working my tail off.

As an Ordinary Seaman, I was at the bottom of the deck department ladder, which meant I got the all shit jobs. Didn't matter. I was used to it, and part of the reason I'd wanted this job was to work my mind and my body numb.

I'd spent the previous week scaling and chipping paint. Today, I'd sat on a board suspended by ropes over the starboard side painting. Never once did I fear falling into the ocean. If I drowned, it would be a welcome relief.

The few times I'd glanced up at the sky, I'd noticed the lowering clouds, but I hadn't paid much attention. At dinner I listened quietly as Anders swapped stories with the Boatswain about storms at sea.

"Wall of clouds rolling in portside." Anders had a knife, carving a thumb-sized piece of wood.

My eyes moved across my plate, and I remembered the small storm we'd encountered on our way over and the night I'd spent vomiting. I decided I was finished with supper.

"We're not in the Graveyard of the Pacific," he continued. "Winter storms there can have waves... seventy feet high."

The Bo's'n studied his boot, thinking. "On a China voyage, we hit seas so bad, four hundred containers were lost. Boat was in ruins when we pulled into Alameda. The judge called it an Act of God."

"God or no, we'll roll tonight."

Those ominous warnings were in my head as I lay watching the angle of my floor grow steeper with each passing wave. A banging on my door signaled the beginning of the worst.

"Water in the engine room," AB Nguyen yelled when I opened my door. "Get down and help bail."

Grabbing my windbreaker, I headed out, climbing the deck at an angle that seemed ninety degrees. The small, heart-shaped ring was still on my pinky finger, and I shoved it deep into the pocket of my jeans along with the little sailboat. By the time I reached the engine room, five guys were ahead of me with buckets and two with wet-vacs.

"Head up to the bridge," Nguyen shouted. "McKinney will tell you what to do."

My boots were wet, and I slipped on the ladder, but a month of lifting, scaling, and carpentry work had me strong enough to pull myself up the rungs. When I reached the bridge, papers were scattered all over the floor. McKinney was on the phone alternately yelling in German and barking commands to the first mate.

"Heave to!" McKinney shouted. "Turn the bow into the waves! Break the roll!"

Rain lashed the windows, and white flashes of lightening punctuated the black night. The bow of the ship went straight up, unbelievably high above the ocean surface before plunging straight down again throwing us all forward. White foam raced across the deck, covering everything with seawater.

"We've got to cut the big ones loose if we're going to come out of it," McKinney yelled to the Bo's'n above the noise of the storm. "Tie ropes around two of our guys, secure them to the line and have them take out the edges, one port one starboard."

"That's a suicide order," he shouted back. "They'll never come back from that job."

Another, taller wave threw us into the sky before dropping the bottom out again. A massive roller went clear across the bow, filling the bridge with shin-deep brine. All of us nearly lost our footing.

"It's that or risk losing the whole ship and everybody on it!"

Anders appeared from below. "We're barely keeping up in the engine room. We need more hands."

"We have to cut lashings on the heaviest boxes," McKinney answered him.

"I need two men."

Anders' face grew slack, and I could tell he was thinking what had already been said—it was suicide. Jerking his arm back, I pulled myself to McKinney. "I'll do it. Tell me which to cut."

McKinney's brow lined just as the ship dipped diagonally, throwing us all against each other.

"One more like that, captain, and she'll break," the first mate said. "We've got to get her lighter."

McKinney studied the glowing green radar. "Aim for there," he pointed. "It's out of the worst of it. Show him what to do."

He pointed at me, and Anders grabbed my arm, pulling me to the metal ladder leading down to the deck. "Wear this," he pulled a life vest over my clothes. "If you go over, I'm cutting the line. Swim away from the boat so you're not swept under it. We'll send the dinghy to find you tomorrow."

I didn't bother telling him I couldn't swim—there wasn't time, and it wouldn't have changed my decision. Instead I faced the tempest. "Which do I cut free?"

Another wave slammed us, causing us both to lay flat against the wall of the deck. It was smaller than the last two, but still powerful enough to increase the water filling the vessel.

"Go for the orange ones on each side," Anders shouted. "Forty footers. They're the heaviest!"

With a touch of my collar, I stepped into the storm. The noise sounded like something out of a war movie. The ship metal groaned and thunder rolled high in the clouds. Rain and seawater mixed to temporarily blind me, but I held on, making my way around the twenty-foot green and brown boxes to the forty-foot orange ones.

Starting portside, I made it to the first just as another wave hit, sending us splashing down, white foam shooting out like a rocket. My feet went out from under me, but I held onto the lashings with all my strength until the deck righted again, and I could find my footing. By the time I slashed the first straps, we were heading up again.

Two more cuts and it shot out from me so fast, I thought I'd go with it into the black depths. A quick grab, and I caught the rigging to my right. Pulling the weight of my body, my triceps burned with the exertion, and I yelled back at the blast.

White-hot lightening crackled across the sky like a spider web. It arched over my head, and I knew this was it. Pulling myself through the stacks, I made it to starboard, exactly parallel to the box I'd just cut. My strength was gone. I had to do this to restore balance to the ship, and I had to do it fast.

Another thirty-footer rose up before us. I didn't see it because that was how it was—the waves were felt before they were seen.

One lash. I followed hand over hand, shouting as the bottom dropped out and we fell, canting dangerously to starboard. She was going to roll if I didn't finish this lash. A dark-brown container shifted, pinning my boot against the rail. I couldn't reach my target.

The black waters stared me in the face as we leaned hard toward the depths. Frantically untying my laces, I loosened the boot enough to pull my foot out, and just as the water was headed straight at us, I swung the knife, cutting the final lash. The orange cargo shot out into the wave, and the boat shot up like a cork, throwing me back against the remaining boxes.

The same brown container slid forward, meeting the back of my head in a *SMACK!* that caused me to see stars.

Or perhaps it was a flash of lightening above my head. For a moment, I thought it was the light of the sun shining in Kenny's bright blue eyes. *Komorebi.*

My fingers fumbled and another rush of foam swept around my feet. I smiled as I reached for a lock of her hair—my hands felt warmth, just as I took the final plunge into darkness.

~ ~ ~

To sleep, to dream, to go to heaven, and pluck a strange and beautiful flower.
To awake, and hold that flower in your hand…

Chapter 34: "With brave wings she flies."
Kenny

All of my family was in Bayville for our annual Thanksgiving gathering. Lane was in heaven playing with his cousins. They were out in the yard throwing the football and running back and forth. I watched them for a little while, a sad smile on my lips.

My hand had only swollen a tiny bit, and no one had even noticed. The pain had receded by the day after, and tomorrow I wouldn't even be able to tell anything had happened to me physically. Emotionally, I was struggling. I'd used everything Slayde had taught me to save someone—just like he'd saved me. I'd fought that burning anger to finish my attacker—the way he'd fought it for me. I felt how strong it was. The thought twisted that old pain in my stomach.

Laughter met me from the family room, and I wanted to be alone. I wanted to walk down to the pier and look out across the ocean in the direction he might be. A few words with my mom, and I sneaked away to my car to make the short drive to the water.

Being the end of November, the air was much cooler. I only wore a light sweater over my orange tunic and leggings, and I knew I wouldn't be able to stay long or I'd catch a chill. My phone buzzed in my pocket, and I pulled it out to see Patrick's reply to my earlier text. I'd sent him a picture of Lane sneaking pieces of turkey when my mom wasn't watching.

That's my boy. Born troublemaker. He texted back.

More like that's your boy charming the pants off all his female relatives.

You can't fight genetics.

I giggled at the memory of Lane burying his little head in my aunt Patty's bosom and telling her she was "good to eat." *Watch how you talk to Elaine when he's in the room. He repeats everything.*

The noise of a wave caused me to glance up at the horizon. We'd had a series of bad storms the last few days, and everything was still grey and swirling as a result. The shoreline was brown and trashy with seaweed.

Patrick replied, *He's a freakin little ninja. I look up and he's there listening.*

He called my mom 'heaven on heels.'

It's better than 'hell on wheels.'

That made me laugh. *True. Will call later. Lane misses you, and I want to hear about Stuart.*

OK. Talk soon.

I shoved my phone back into my pocket and walked slowly down the length of the boardwalk. I tried so hard not to remember our last time here, the finger paint.

Doc had said the boat still hadn't arrived in port. He'd called the shipping lines, and they were scheduled to arrive a week ago. He got no explanation for the delay, and I couldn't help being afraid. What if something happened to him? Could I survive if he never came back? If the things I'd said, the angry words I'd shouted at him as I beat him with my fists...

Oh, God, those couldn't be my last word to him.

The pier posts were as tall as me, and I counted them as I walked. *One... two... three...* "Please come back to me," I whispered, feeling like a child plucking petals from a daisy. *Four... five... six...* "This missing... makes me sick."

Seven... eight...

With a sigh, I stopped at the last post and leaned my forehead against it. I was out of rhymes. My heart was broken, and even having Lane here with me didn't stop the hole in my chest from growing larger every day.

Turning my cheek to the damp wood, I closed my eyes and imagined it was him. He was standing here with me, his firm chest against my face. I spread my fingers against the post. "Slayde," I whispered. "Won't you please come back?"

"That depends." The familiar voice made my eyes fly open.

I wasn't sure I believed them. I wasn't sure I wasn't dreaming. He stood there in the same dark jeans and white tee, only now a long-sleeved red flannel shirt was on top. He was bigger somehow than the last time I'd seen him. His dark hair was longer, shaggy, and his beard fuller. One thing was the same—his pale blue eyes seared into me with an intensity that stole my breath.

Trying to calm myself, I asked the follow-up question. "Depends on what?"

"If there's anything for me to come back to."

I looked down. I couldn't answer that yet. "When did you get in?"

"Last night." He waited, watching me. I waited, unsure. "Doc's at my place."

I nodded. "He showed up a few weeks ago. Said you told him he could stay there."

"He certainly can. I just wish I'd known he was here when I crawled into my bed in the dark." He smiled that sexy, heartbreaking smile.

A gust of wind pushed my hair forward into my face, and I was glad because it hid the tears forming in my eyes. I reached up and caught the flying strands, holding them back and together in a fist at my neck. He only stood there, drinking me in as I did him. The sight of him was an image I could feel in my bones.

"It's been so long since I've seen you." He spoke quietly, trailing his eyes up my body. "You look... so good."

"You look... different." His brow lined, and I continued. "Bigger. Stronger, I guess — from working on the boat?"

"They worked me pretty hard, but it was good. Honest."

"I can't believe you left on a boat — I mean, you said you never would. You don't swim."

"Mariska is a fortune teller after all."

Smiling, I blinked down. "Don't tell her that."

In two steps he closed the distance between us. He only hesitated a moment before taking my face in his hands. "The entire time I was gone, I could only think of you. Every minute I was away. I tried not to, but it was pointless. I'd close my eyes, and you were there, waiting for me in my dreams."

His mouth hovered a breath above mine, and my lips throbbed with anticipation — but he pulled back. He lowered to one knee then dropped the other until he was on both in front of me. I tried to stop him, but he wrapped his arms around my waist, holding me so tightly, resting his cheek against my stomach. His face pointed down, and I carefully slid my fingers into his soft hair as tears burned my eyes.

"I can't change the fact that I put that tear in your hand." His voice was rough. "I broke your heart, and I don't deserve to have you or even to ask this. But if you could find some way to forgive me... I'd spend the rest of my life making sure you made the right decision. Please forgive me, Kenny. Please."

My heart ached for him as thoroughly as my entire body longed for him. "I have to forgive you," I said through the thickness in my throat. "I can't live without you."

He sat back on his heels and looked up at me. It was more than I could bear. I dropped to my knees in front of him, reaching for his cheeks. I kissed him with all the pain and longing that had consumed me since that horrible night, and without hesitation, he gathered me in his arms and stood, holding me in a breathlessly firm embrace just like before.

I wanted to cry. I wanted to laugh and cry and hold him and never let go. He was here, holding me, kissing me in a way I'd only dreamed of for so long. He was asking me to forgive him. He was asking me for everything.

Pulling myself together, I leaned back. "It's true. You put the tear in my hand." He watched as I took his right hand and spread it open. Then I lifted mine and pressed our palms together. "You're also the one who turned it into a heart."

His fingers curled through mine, sealing our connection where the little hearts mirrored each other. His brow lined, and his voice was low.

"I told myself I didn't need love. I didn't deserve it. That that part of my life was over—just like so many other parts. I was resigned not to look for it or even expect it. Then out of nowhere you appeared. You needed me, and I helped you." He leaned down and pressed his lips against mine briefly, his warm breath flowing over my cheeks as he spoke. "The thing that had ended my life, my ability to fight, saved yours. You gave my worthless life meaning, and when you looked at me with those beautiful blue eyes... I might as well have carved out my heart and handed it to you. You owned me from that moment forward."

Sliding his fingers into the hair behind my neck, he claimed my lips again. Mouths opened, our tongues met as a little noise ached from my throat. His arm went around my waist, and I was off my feet, holding him, chasing his mouth in a hungry, desperate kiss.

We moved together as desire and happiness flooded my body. Nothing could change the fact that I loved him. Wholly, entirely, and with everything in me.

Breaking away for air, I lifted my chin to look up at the grey sky overhead. He lowered me to my feet, and our eyes met again as he slid a hand between us, capturing my jaw in his palm. "I'm glad Doc's here, and I wish he were gone." Confusion lined my face, and he smiled. "I want to make love to you. Now."

Glancing around, I noticed a couple walking down the shore and cursed their hideous timing. Looking back, I ran my finger down that line in his chin. "Lane's with my mom. I need to get back and check on him." The frustration in his expression mirrored mine. "Come to my place tonight. I'll ask Mom to keep Lane for me, and I'll feed you turkey, fresh cranberries, and you can tell me all about life at sea."

"After we catch up with life on land." His gaze was so intense, heat flared between my thighs.

"Tonight." I stepped forward cupping his cheeks in my palms, kissing his warm lips. His elbows bent, and he crushed me to him again as our mouths opened and he kissed me deeper.

His lips traced a line from my cheek to my jaw the up to my ear. "I won't be late."

It had been so long, and I wanted him so badly, I couldn't bear to leave. I stepped forward and held him against me, my arms around his neck, his around my waist. We didn't move as our hearts beat together, our bodies again melting together. With my eyes closed, it was as if we were suspended in time.

"I can't wait."

Again it was raining as I walked up to Kenny's door, only this time there was no guard. She had forgiven me. Pain flashed in my chest at the memory of her crying and hitting me with all of her strength. It was a memory I'd do anything to purge from our past, yet at the same time, it was a memory I knew would make us stronger. Our scars would make us stronger.

She opened the door before I knocked, sliding her arms around my neck and meeting my mouth with her small one, parting her lips so our tongues could unite. She still wore the orange tunic, but the leggings were gone. I discovered everything was gone when I slipped my hands down and felt the soft skin of her body. Tracing my fingers up, I lightly touched the curve of her perfect ass and a ravenous hunger ignited in me.

In one swift movement, she was off her feet. Feverish, I carried her to the bedroom. I'd dreamed of this so long, every night, I wasn't sure if I'd make it. Her legs wrapped around my waist, and when we kissed, we consumed.

I lay her back on the bed and pushed the tunic all the way up, catching a tight nipple with my mouth, giving it hard pull before teasing it with my teeth. Noises came from her throat, and I held her narrow ribcage in both my hands, kissing the base of her sternum, inhaling deeply as I worked my way down.

She moaned and threaded her fingers in my hair as I licked her skin. Sugar and mint. It had haunted my dreams, my waking hours. She was a flavor that energized me, delicious and hypnotic. Lifting her thigh, I kissed my way down to the crease and lightly ran my tongue along that line.

"Slayde, oh god," she gasped, squirming in anticipation. Covering those lips with mine, my tongue circled her swollen clit before sliding down into her wet opening. I couldn't get enough of her taste, all of her. She cried out, and I knew I couldn't wait much longer. It seemed she couldn't either. Her muscles were clenching, and she pulled my shoulders.

"I need you in me," she begged, as if I had to be asked twice. Condom out, I opened it with my teeth, and it was on in record time. Slipping deep between her thighs, I closed my eyes and ascended to heaven. We rocked together, rolling so that she was above me. Her dark hair spilled around us in soft, flower-scented curtains, and she placed her hands on the headboard behind me, rocking her hips.

Shoving the tunic all the way up, I leaned forward and pulled a taut nipple into my mouth again. Her entire body convulsed, and I went off.

Breaking free, I leaned back and groaned loudly. "Oh, fuck." I couldn't stop the blinding orgasm taking me over the edge. Rolling us over again, I held her hips and pounded it out as she cried beneath me.

"Don't stop," she begged, and I didn't. I couldn't.

She worked me hard, holding me as her body trembled with her climax. Slowly descending back to this planet, I opened my eyes to my beautiful love. She was panting and lovely. Her dark hair spread over the pillow, and I lay my palm against her cheek tracing my thumb over her lips, her chin. As if waking from a dream, her bright blue eyes fluttered to mine, and my heart melted.

"I'm in love with you, Kendra Woods." I smoothed her hair back from her face. "Every night on that ship, I swore that if I ever got the chance again, I'd tell you how much I love you. How badly I need you to be mine. Forever."

She reached up to hold my cheeks, wonder in her eyes. "Every day you were gone I tried to make myself forget you. I did everything in my power to move on." Her words hurt, but she cancelled out all the pain with what she said next. "It was impossible. You're like air and water and everything I need to survive."

Kissing her once more briefly, I held her against my chest. "I wish I could give you some noble reason for what I did. I wish I could tell you it was self-defense or it was to save someone's life, but it wasn't. I was just a broken, lost asshole with too much money and too many people telling me I was the shit."

She touched my face. "You don't have to tell me anything. You've already told me enough. I know what you faced growing up."

"Still, I wish I could change what I was before I knew you." My eyes closed, and I felt the bitter pain of regret.

"And if you had, we probably never would have met." She traced her beautiful fingers over my brow. "I'm going to feed you Thanksgiving dinner, and you're going to tell me about being at sea."

"Deal." I rolled in the bed and quickly disposed of the condom as she stood.

"I never went off the pill." The twinkle in her eye about had me going again, but I shook my head.

"We won't do much talking if you keep that up."

"Okay!" She skipped out in only that orange tunic.

Smiling, I sat forward in the bed alone in that room. I thought about what Doc had said about making up for the shit heap I'd made of my life. I'd wasted all of my gifts, but it was possible this woman could help me find a way to at least try to make restitution.

When she returned, we had a spread of turkey, stuffing, cranberries, and bread. She leaned beside me against the headboard holding a glass of red wine.

My arm was on her shoulders, and I twirled a lock of dark brown hair around my finger. "Every night, I dreamed in violet, and now it's gone."

She leaned into me, kissing my cheek. "It can easily come back if that's what you like. Now tell me about being at sea. Did you see whales?"

"We saw sharks." Her eyes went wide as she set the wine glass on the nightstand and pushed a large pinch of roll into her mouth. I laughed. "And a lot of dolphins."

Next, she picked up a strip of white turkey and held it to my lips. I couldn't help remembering the first night we'd shared steak. "I'm so lucky to have you back."

That got me another greasy kiss. "Tell me a story."

"First…" I stretched off the bed, reaching for my pants and feeling deep in the pocket. "One of the sailors made these." I pulled out the small sailboat. "This is for Lane."

Her eyes warmed. "You got something for Lane?"

"And this is for you." The heart ring slid perfectly onto the third finger of her left hand. The little doll I'd save until the time was right.

She studied the twisted silver. "I love it so much," she whispered, catching my neck and kissing me. Holding her hand up, she tilted it side-to-side, and then she paused. "What about the necklace I bought you?"

I kissed the side of her jaw, taking a deep inhale of her sweet-flower scent. From there my lips moved behind her ear, and she shivered. "I love how your breathing changes when I touch you."

She reached for me, and we kissed deeply, tongues uniting. We held each other in an awkward embrace around the Thanksgiving dinner spread in front of us, and I wanted to be inside her. I wanted to make up for all the time we'd lost.

"I have my necklace," I spoke against her skin, "but it's not accurate. I'll never be free as long as you're in the world. Even after."

Her hand moved to my cheek, her thumb tracing the line in my chin. "I want you free from those old scars. I've forgiven you."

Kissing her once more, I turned my back to the headboard and pulled her against my chest. For a few moments, I only held her, feeling our hearts beating as one.

"We need to finish this dinner so I can make love to you."

She sat up facing me, eyes shining in that gorgeous way, and rested her head on her hand. "First tell me more about being at sea. Did you run into any storms? I've heard they can be really scary."

Taking a deep breath, I told her the news I'd been holding onto since I'd found her. None of it would've mattered if we hadn't made it to this place.

"We ran into a pretty significant storm on the way back." Her hand dropped, her blue eyes full of concern. "Yeah, it was a big one. McKinney guessed we hit thirty-foot waves."

"Slayde! Oh my god!" She sat straighter in the bed.

Reaching for her hand, I lifted it and kissed it. "You see I'm here, right? Still, conditions got pretty critical." Looking down, I decided just to tell her. "I wasn't sure you'd ever see me again, so I didn't think I had anything to lose."

Her voice was touched with fear. "What did you do?"

"The waves were so strong, the ship was in danger of breaking in two. They needed someone to lighten the load, cut some of the bigger boxes free so they'd wash overboard." Clearing my throat, I looked at the fresh, new scar across the back of my hand. "I volunteered."

Her eyes slid closed. "Oh my god."

"They tied a rope around me to help stabilize. I made it out to the bow, and I had to cut the lashes of the largest boxes on each side—enough so they'd slide off and lighten the ship."

"Oh, Slayde." Her shoulders dropped and I collected the plates from in front of us. Setting them on the side table, I slid down in the bed, pulling her tight against me.

"The first box was hard, but I got it free. The second one threw me back, and another of the crates flew forward and hit my head. I had a concussion."

Her head snapped up, eyes wide. "No!" She smoothed her hands on each side of my face, and I couldn't help but reassure her.

My voice was low and strong. "I'm fine. I was out for a few hours. We took a few days, the ship's medic was more than prepared."

"Why do I feel like you're holding something back?"

"Ahh," I growled, dropping back against the pillow.

She was on me in an instant. "What is it?"

Slipping my palms to her beautiful face, I held her. Then I rolled her onto her back. I kissed her left cheek, her right cheek, her nose. I moved higher to her right eyebrow, her left, then back down. "Do you have any idea how much I love you?"

She flushed soft pink. "Are you going to tell me?"

I kissed her mouth once more, tasting her. "They want to give me an award—I think it's a medal. They're saying I saved every man's life on the ship."

"There were no women?" Her dark brow arched, and I laughed.

"No, and trust me, you're glad."

"I think it's amazing that you're a hero. I'm so proud of you."

Her voice was quiet, and I knew she was serious.

"Will you be my date to the award ceremony?"

"I hope to be your date to everything forever as long as we both live."

When she talked like that, I couldn't help myself. I leaned down to cover her mouth with mine. I might never deserve the gift of this woman I was sent to protect on the beach one stormy fall night. The truth was, I'd spend my life doing my best to protect her, and to love her, and to try and prove to her I was the one to love. As long as she lived.

I smoothed my hands in her hair, thinking about what Anders had said. "I have a new idea for matching tattoos."

The corner of her mouth curled. "Okay, what is it?"

"Have you ever heard of the Red String of Fate?"

The End.

Epilogue: "Always Faithful."
Derek

The scene I left in Montana was heavy on my mind as I rode in the car from the Wilmington airport. Stuart was battling some serious demons, and I wasn't sure Patrick and I were enough to help him beat them.

Leaning forward, I rubbed my palms over my eyes thinking of Melissa and Dex. I had my own fucking demons to sort out, and the more time that passed, the harder it would be to negotiate a compromise solution. If there even was one.

Picking up the folded *USA Today* from the black leather seat, I flipped through Section A, not looking at anything until a small, black-and-white photograph under the headline "Hero at Sea" caught my attention.

I pulled the page closer to examine the postage-stamp sized image. I'd recognize those eyes anywhere. "What the *fuck*?" I whispered.

Slayde "Slayer" Bennett, former boxer-slash-ex-con apparently risked his life in a monster storm at sea to prevent the merchant ship *Sea Empress* from breaking in half. I quickly scanned the details. He'd been injured in the process, suffered a concussion, but was fully recovered. He received an honorary medal, an award of sorts...

What made me stop was the writer's editorial slant in her last sentences. A murderer, someone who callously took another man's life in a bar fight five years ago, went on to become a hero, to risk his life to save twenty-six crewmembers.

Leaning back in the car, I looked out at the changed scenery. I'd helped build the case against Slayer Bennett and Stitch Alana five years ago. Both professional middleweights, Slayer was in a rage after being passed over for an exhibition match, according to the story I'd put together. He and his buddy Stitch had gone to that bar looking for a fight. They'd waited for anyone to cross them. Blake Woods and Max Marconi had been the hotheaded suckers to follow their taunt into the parking lot where they'd fought a bare-knuckle street fight they were destined to lose. A fight to the death.

The court psychologist spoke for Slayer. I was wrong, she'd said. She argued he suffered from intermittent explosive disorder, whatever the fuck that was, and needed anger management therapy. He could be rehabilitated, she'd said. He was the product of an abusive home, an alcoholic father. I didn't give a shit about any of that. He'd broken the law, taken a life, and he had to be punished. Eye for an eye.

All of it was so long ago. Before I'd ever met Melissa.

The black-capped driver turned to the side. "We're here, sir."

Pulling out four twenties, I passed them through the glass and grabbed my large duffel before heading up the walk. I'd taken the red-eye, so Melissa and Dex were likely still asleep. Standing for a moment, looking out at the grey sky over the ocean, I thought about Blake Woods, the boy Slayer killed. He was a little punk who'd done time himself. *Did that change it somehow? Did the crime change if the victim was equally guilty?*

Rubbing my neck and those thoughts away, I unlocked the door, pausing to slip off my boots. Carrying my bag through the quiet house, I paused at a stack of thick bridal magazines in the living room. On the cover of one was a brunette model, who would never be as beautiful as Melissa, in white lace. After pushing the date back twice — once so Dex could be born and again so her mother could attend — our wedding was firmly scheduled for the spring, and she was so excited. I couldn't wait for the day she'd officially be my wife.

Continuing on, I stopped at the first door I came to and peeked inside. Dex's dark little head was sweaty, and his favorite blue blanket was twisted all around his legs, but he was out like a light.

I breathed a smile. My longing to see Melissa was the only emotion stronger than the swell of pride in my chest at the sight of our little guy. I pulled his door closed and went down the dark hall to our bedroom. Sunrise was lighting the light-green walls, and she was asleep on her side, curled in the center of our bed. A sharp ache hit my lower stomach at the sight of her long, dark waves spread on the pillow behind her. My questions of fate would have to wait. I wanted her in my arms with that soft cascade falling all around us.

Moving quickly, I shrugged out of my coat and pulled off the light sweater I wore underneath. Jeans gone, I placed a knee carefully on the side of the bed. The indentation rolled her forward, and her eyes fluttered open. She blinked quickly before pushing up against the mattress.

"You're back!" A flash of brown, and she was in my arms, kissing my cheeks and eyes, making her way up to my brow.

My hands moved to her thighs, catching the edge of the short, white nightgown she wore, sliding it up her body.

"Five seconds." She skipped away so fast I didn't have time to stop her before she was in the bathroom. In the half-minute it took her to brush, I lost my boxer briefs and arranged the pillows. She was running back, pulling the nightgown over her head and tossing it behind her as she crossed the room.

"I like how your mind works," I laughed, catching her slim torso as she dove into my arms. We rolled over so she was cradled against me, and for a moment, I simply looked down at her smiling face, blue eyes shining.

"I've missed you so much." She leaned up to kiss my neck. "You said we'd never be apart again after Princeton."

"I know." I leaned down to kiss her jaw, moving my lips up behind her ear so I could take a deep sniff of ocean-touched roses. "You smell so good."

My hand moved up to cup her firm breast, and she let out a little moan.

"Take it easy," her sigh mixed with desire.

She'd been nursing Dex for several months, but her breasts were still full and sensitive in the mornings. I knew this. Circling my thumb over her tightening nipple, I caught her mouth, pushing it open and getting a fresh blast of mint as our tongues collided.

344

Her arms were around my neck, holding me close, and the hand that was on her breast traveled down her stomach to the line of her panties and lower. Her mouth broke from mine in a moan as I slid two fingers inside her, using my thumb to massage her clit. She was already so wet.

"I've missed you," I breathed, rotating her all the way to her back as I gently kissed one nipple then the other before tracing my way to her stomach.

Her arms rose over her head as I quickly hooked my fingers through her lace bikini, pulling it down and off. "I like this, or I might've ripped it."

"Oh, god!" Her back arched as I opened her thighs, covering her with my mouth. My tongue swirled over the little bud that quickly sent her into spasms. She let out another, louder cry as I ran my tongue full over her, down and back up to make a circle, giving her a little suck. She tasted so good.

Her fingers were in my hair, and she was pulling, arching against my mouth. I couldn't help a smile as she started to come. She was gorgeous falling apart for me.

"Derek, please…" Her fingernails scraped against my shoulders, and I rose up to fill her with all the love and desire that had been building in me for the last ten days.

She cried out as I drove deeper, pulling her body up so that our chests were together. I held her as I sat back on my feet, letting her ride as I moved her. Her beautiful, full breasts were right at my mouth, and I gently caught one, giving it a light kiss rather than my usual, forceful pull. I'd have to save that for later.

"I want to go deeper," I spoke into her neck.

"Yes, yes," she nodded, dropping back onto the bed.

Turning her over quickly, my hands slid to her hips, lifting her so I could position myself at her entrance. She was on all fours, her beautiful ass perked, thighs parted. One hard push, and she cried out, arching up. I reached around, massaging her clit until she started bucking against me, sending me even deeper. Closing my eyes the intense need, that primitive hunger took over. It was relentless and strong and so fucking good.

Melissa and I usually made love, but sometimes, we'd let go and truly fuck. This was one of those times. Her hand stretched out to hold the headboard, and I continued massaging between her legs as the force of my orgasm rose in my pelvis, tightening my ass.

"Fuck," I shouted, my fingers closing over hers in front of us. I had to hold onto something or I'd crush her. The jerking in my cock had me going blind. Three more hard drives, and we were both flying.

"Oh, god, yes." Her body trembled, and I held onto her a moment longer, allowing the last remnants of our high to fade. We were both breathing hard as we slid down to the bed. Her face turned into my chest, a slender arm went around my waist. I wrapped both my arms around her before bending down to kiss her head and inhale another deep breath of her delicious scent.

Her voice was thick and sexy when she spoke. "I'll overlook the occasional separation if you make it up to me like that."

I laughed, tracing a finger down her back. "You're so damned sexy, how do I ever leave you?"

She lifted her head then, resting it on her hand. A dark curl slid over her cheek, and I wrapped it around my finger.

"How's Stuart?"

"He's not doing so good. He's got things... he hadn't told anybody about."

Her beautiful blue eyes were serious now. "How long before you have to go back?"

"I took the red-eye so I could be here as long as possible this weekend, but I need to head out on Sunday."

My chest ached as her brow fell. I knew she wasn't angry, but I hated to make her sad. "He's your friend, and he needs you. It's just, Dex misses you, and I..."

"Elaine's talking about coming back for Christmas. What if we all spent it there, together? His uncle's place is amazing."

"You think you'll be that long?"

I released an exhale. "Hard to know, but if I am, I want you and Dex with me."

Her eyes traveled around my face as she reached up to run her thumb across my cheek. "We can be there with you now if you want. My job travels."

Our last weeks on the horse ranch flickered through my mind — the late nights, the bad nights. The night I had to leave everything and ride across the plains until I found him alone, camped near one of the falls. Stuart was fighting everything right now, including his will to live, and our progress was slow and painful.

"I'm not sure he'd appreciate company yet, but a lot can change in a month."

A small voice squealed down the hall, and we both stopped. "He's awake," Melissa said with a grin, and I was up before she could move.

"I got this." Scooping my boxers off the floor, I jerked them over my hips. "Be right back."

Dex was holding the side of his crib, blue eyes bright and baby mouth grinning big when he saw me. A flash of love warmed my chest. "Come here, little guy."

Scooping him up, he jerked back toward the crib. I only paused a moment to grab his blue blanket, putting it in his arms before he lay his dark head on my shoulder. "I've missed you," I whispered, kissing him and taking a deep breath of sweet baby smell.

Melissa was in bed with her nightgown back on, but she was unfastening the tiny buttons down the front as I climbed in beside her.

"He's getting so strong." Dex reached for her as soon as I sat. "How long before he walks?"

She laughed stretching up to kiss my lips before taking him and sliding down on her side. "At least two more months," she said, pulling him close to her breast.

"Good. Don't want to miss that."

Dex latched on quickly, and I reached down to touch the tiny fingers now curled against her soft skin. "Even this is hard to miss."

"Give me a kiss," she whispered, and I gladly complied. Wrapping my arm around her shoulders as she gave our son his breakfast, I rested my chin on Melissa's head. My eye caught the eagle and SF tattoo on my bicep, and that old secret I carried, the one that could take me away from her for a very long time itched at the back of my mind.

I thought about the news article. Slayer Bennett had gone from criminal to hero. I'd done just the opposite. At the same time, the law, the right thing, these concepts grew nebulous when I thought about what was at stake, the choice that was taken away from me. Melissa had never pressed me for details about that night, and as yet I hadn't given her any. Patrick's advice was never to tell her. Not because she wouldn't understand—she'd be hurt, but she'd understand. Rather, it was because she'd blame herself, he said.

Happy baby noises were in my ear, and my beautiful future wife was safe in my arms. The secret I carried was an issue only if I let it be, Patrick said. Our one other witness agreed with him. Yet the idea of hiding my crime grated against who I was, my status as a Marine, a retired officer. I was sworn to defend our laws. I'd helped prosecute criminals for a living.

Exhaling deeply, I pressed my lips firmly against Melissa's head. My best friend was in trouble—his life could be on the line. My fiancée needed me here with her and my son. Questions of justice and atonement would have to wait. For now I had to focus on the ones I loved. My duty for today was with them, but that wouldn't be the case forever.

* * *

If you enjoyed this book by this author, please consider leaving a short, sweet review on Amazon, Barnes & Noble, and/or Goodreads!

Reviews help your favorite authors sell more books and reach new readers!

* * *

Don't miss a single SALE or NEW RELEASE by Tia Louise!

Get exclusive TEXT UPDATES straight to your phone or mobile device:

>> Text "TiaLouise" to 77948 Now! <<

(Max 3-4 messages per month or less; **HELP for help; STOP to cancel**; Text and Data rates may apply. Privacy policy available, allnightreads@gmail.com)

~ AND/OR ~

Sign up for the New Release Mailing list today! (http://eepurl.com/Lcmv1)*

*Please add **allnightreads@gmail.com** to your contacts so it doesn't bounce to spam!

* * *

BONUS CONTENT

-Hear some of the music that inspired *One to Love* on Spotify!

-See the images that inspired *One to Love* on Pinterest!

-Keep up with the guys on their Facebook Page: *The Alexander-Knight* *Files*! (**https://www.facebook.com/pages/Alexander-Knight-Files/1446875125542823**)

* * *

Dear Reader,

I hope you enjoyed *One to Love*!

Kenny has been one of my favorite characters since I was planning *One to Keep*, Patrick & Elaine's book. I knew her story would be heartbreaking and intense, and I hope you fell in love with her and Slayde as much as I did.

Up next, I'll be diving into Stuart's book. It promises to be intense as well, but I'm looking forward to it. I've never written a cowboy romance before, and I hope to have more Elaine and Patrick, and I'm sure Mariska will be there... (wink)

Be looking for *One to Leave* around the end of 2014 or early in 2015.

I hope you'll let me know what you think of my books! Email me your thoughts, feedback, what you liked—even what you didn't like! I really like hearing from readers. You can write to me at **allnightreads@gmail.com** or visit me on Facebook at **https://www.facebook.com/AuthorTiaLouise**!

Finally, if you enjoyed my books, I hope you'll leave a short, sweet review on Amazon, Goodreads, and/or wherever you purchased this book!

Reviews help authors so much, not only in reaching new readers, but also in helping secure advertising opportunities.

Thank you again for spending time with me. I hope to hear from you in the future!

Stay sexy,
<3 Tia

One to Hold
(Derek & Melissa)

Derek Alexander is a retired Marine, ex-cop, and the top investigator in his field. Melissa Jones is a small-town girl trying to escape her troubled past.

When the two intersect in a bar in Arizona, their sexual chemistry is off the charts. But what is revealed during their "one week stand" only complicates matters.

Because she'll do everything in her power to get away from the past, but he'll do everything he can to hold her.

* * *

One to Protect
(Derek & Melissa)

When Sloan Reynolds beats criminal charges, Melissa Jones stops believing her wealthy, connected ex-husband will ever pay for what he did to her.

Derek Alexander can't accept that—a tiny silver scar won't let him forget, and as a leader in the security business, he is determined to get the man who hurt his fiancée.

Then the body of a former call girl turns up dead. She's the breakthrough Derek's been waiting for, the link to Sloan's sordid past he needs. But as usual, legal paths to justice have been covered up or erased.

Derek's ready to do whatever it takes to protect his family when his partner Patrick Knight devises a plan that changes everything.

It's a plan that involves breaking rules and taking a walk on the dark side. It goes against everything on which Alexander-Knight, LLC, is based.

And it's a plan Derek's more than ready to follow.

* * *

One to Keep
(Patrick & Elaine)

There's a new guy in town...

"Patrick Knight, single, retired Guard-turned private investigator. I was a closer. A deal maker. I looked clients in the eye and told them I'd get their shit done. And I did..."

Patrick doesn't do "nice."
At least, not anymore.

After his fiancée cheats, he follows up with a one-night stand and a disastrous office hook-up. His business partner (Derek Alexander) sends him to the desert to get his head straight--and clean up the mess.

While there, Patrick meets Elaine, and blistering sparks fly, but she's not looking for any guy. Or a long-distance relationship.

Patrick's ready to do anything to keep her, but just when it seems he's changed her mind, the skeletons from his past life start coming back.

* * *

All books in the ONE TO HOLD series are complete, stand-alone novels. All are Adult Contemporary Romance. Due to strong language and sexual content, they are not intended for readers under the age of 18.

All books are available as
-eBooks on **Amazon** | **Barnes & Noble** | **iTunes** | **Google Play**| **Kobo** | **ARe**
-Print copies on **Amazon** | **Createspace** | Book Depository | Barnes & Noble
-Audiobooks on **Amazon** | **Tantor.com**

All of my books are part of the "Kindle Matchbook" program. If you purchased the print copy of any book from Amazon, you can get the ebook version *free*! One copy for you, one for a friend.

Acknowledgments

Mr. TL has been my number one cheerleader since *One to Hold* went live a year ago. In January 2013, when I was writing *One to Keep*, he named Kenny, and she became his "pet" character. I couldn't have been happier when he approved of Slayde, and I couldn't do *any* of this without his support and nonstop encouragement. All my love and gratitude goes to you, my wonderful husband. To my two precious daughters, who always want to know what story I'm writing... yes, they get the PG version. Thanks for being the best two kids on the planet!

When I decided to use tattoo quotes as title chapters, several faithful readers jumped on the bandwagon, sending me brilliant suggestions. Special thanks to Ilona Townsel, Mandie Jones, Jackie Wright, Pam Brooks, Mayra Statham, Heather Carver, and Kimberly Hulsey for all the rocking notes and pictures!

Ilona Townsel is my queen of feedback, encouraging notes, and thoughtful gifts, and of the Alexander-Knight Files. Love you, my friend! Huge thanks to Rebecca Bennett for giving Slayde her last name, and to Candice "Candy Love" Royer for Mariska. Two of my favorite characters from two of my favorite peeps! Christina Badder and Kimberly Hulsey are my queens of pictorial-book-love. I can't tell you how much your surprise teasers make my day. Squeezes to both of you. Mandie Jones, you keep me organized, you make my publicity sing!, and you helped me launch this baby. For all your hard work, I appreciate you so much. Couldn't have done it without you—chocolate and vanilla high-fives!

Every person who has helped me, from beta reading to cover feedback to general encouragement when I was feeling overwhelmed is so dear to my heart. My street team "The Keepers" — enormous thanks to Chrissy Fletcher, Jas de la Cruz, Angela Craney, Holly Leffler, Rebecca, Heather, Jackie, Kimberly, Melissa Jones, Autumn Davis, Hetty Whitmore, Jess Danowski, Daphnie Bennett, Karrie Puskas, Lisa Maurer, Amber Gleisner, Christi Curtis, Elizabeth Roberts, Jennifer Noe, Kendall Barnett, Nicole Huffman, Becky Barney, Angie Lynch, Lisa Gerould, Richelle Robinson, Ginger Sharp, Isabelle Berube, Katrina Boone, Lorraine Black, Melissa Tholen, Louise Iwanenko, Marie Cline, Zee Hayat, Evette Reads, Tamela Gibson, Jennifer LaFon, Jennifer Engel, Theresa Gomez, Lucinda Pillsbury, Debbie and Ali (that takeover cherry!), Maria Barquero, Ellen Widom, Laura Goff, Jennifer Marr, and Shirl Stewart. You guys are made of awesome. Christine with Books and Beyond Fifty Shades, all of the ladies of The Library, Fairy Book Club (Liz), Kinky Book Club (Ava), and Smexy Reads Book Club, my faithful book blogging friends Summer, Nadine, Ivie, Marissa, and too many more to name — you make my day every time you say "Sure! Glad to help out." Love you all so much.

Last but never least, thanks to Natalie and Mary at Love Between the Sheets for your amazing publicity services. Thanks to Steven Novak for the gorgeous cover design! And BIG love to my always-encouraging author-friends Aleatha Romig and Alisa Woods. To everyone who reads and loves my books, *Thank you!*

ABOUT THE AUTHOR

Tia Louise is a former journalist, world-traveler, and collector of beautiful men (who inspire *all* of her stories. *wink*)—turned wife, mommy, and novelist.

She lives in the center of the U.S.A. with her lovely family and one grumpy cat. There, she dreams up stories she hopes are engaging, hot, and sexy, and that cause readers rethink common public locations.

It's possible she has a slight truffle addiction.

Books by Tia Louise:
One to Hold (Derek & Melissa), 2013
One to Protect (Derek & Melissa), 2014
One to Keep (Patrick & Elaine), 2014
One to Love (Kenny & Slayde), 2014

Amazon Author Page: http://amzn.to/1jm2F2b

Connect with Tia:
Facebook
Twitter (@AuthorTLouise
Email
Pinterest
Instagram (@AuthorTLouise)
Goodreads
Tumblr

Keep up with the guys on their Facebook Page: *The Alexander-Knight Files*.

Exclusive Sneak Peek

One to Keep
By Tia Louise

Patrick & Elaine

We walked some more, then we took a place by the fire again. She told me about her brothers and her favorite aunt — her dad's younger sister who had moved in with them after her mom left. She talked about growing up with Melissa and about living on the coast.

We sat with our bodies touching, and we sat apart, with her feet in my lap. But that never lasted long before we were back to bodies touching again. Finally, I looked around at the deserted patio and realized how late it was. I could see she was tired, and I stood, holding out my hand to help her up.

"I'll walk you back to the spa."

She nodded slowly. We didn't speak the entire way, and all I could think about were her lips and covering them with mine. I'd been thinking about it all night, but I wanted to handle this one differently — right for a change.

Stopping at the entrance, I paused, lightly cupping her cheeks. Her green eyes met mine, and she smiled. In a flash I kissed her, opening her mouth, finding her tongue for the first time. My arms moved to her waist, pulling her closer. Our bodies molded together and a little noise escaped her throat. The sound sent a blaze of desire racing through me, focusing directly below my belt. But I wasn't rushing that. Not this time.

"Goodnight." My words should have parted us, but I held her closer.

Her arms held me tightly as well, and I knew this was different from anything I'd experienced before. All of this was tectonically different.

Forcing myself to let her go, I stepped back. I couldn't look in her eyes or I'd never do what I had to do right now.

"I hope I'll see you tomorrow." An ache was in my throat.

"I'll call you." Her voice was quiet.

I turned away, and my heart, my soul, everything stayed behind as I took the first step and then the second back to the main hotel where I was staying. I'd only made it three feet when I heard her rushing up to me.

"Patrick?" It was a high whisper, and I immediately stopped, turning to face her.

She was gorgeous standing in the moonlight, the dry breeze pushing her silky hair off her shoulders. I wanted to cover those shoulders with kisses, wrap my fingers in that hair. She reached out, and I caught both her hands in mine.

"Yes?"

"I don't want you to leave me." She was breathless. "I know this is fast. It seems crazy, but… I want to spend the night in your arms."

Her delicate pink tongue touched her bottom lip, and she didn't have to ask me twice. Two steps was all it took to have her body secure against mine again. I caught her cheeks and lowered my mouth to cover her soft, beautiful lips.

Our kisses came fast, hungry, and she held my neck, my face, her hands quickly dropping to my waist, making their way under my shirt to the skin beneath. I loved her touching me. I kissed her jaw, and another noise came from her mouth. The sound killed any hesitation on my part. Breaking away, I looked around for somewhere close I could take her.

"Come with me," I said, holding her hand and leading her back the way we came. We weren't far from the smaller pool, and while it was dark and locked, I'd noticed a break in the bushes when we'd strolled past it the first time.

Leaning down, I carefully stepped through, and it took me right into the dark courtyard. Going back, Elaine was waiting and when our eyes met, she smiled. My chest rose at the sight of her, and all I could think of was sliding that dress off her body, tasting her, being inside her.

I pulled her into the small pool area and into my arms again. Our mouths collided, and I only broke contact to whip my shirt over my head. Pulling her back to me, I eased the top of her dress down, allowing her bare breasts to meet my skin, and we both sighed.

"Mmm," she breathed, moving her hands to my back and pulling me closer. The little noises coming from her with every breath had my cock straining against my zipper. I wanted to lift her against the tiled column and sink inside her right then, but I stepped back, guiding her to the cushioned lounge chair hidden in the back corner. She held the top of her dress, as if trying to pull it back up.

"No," I whispered, taking her hand away and replacing it with mine. Her breasts were heavy in my palms, and I circled my thumbs over her taut nipples. Her eyes closed and she lowered her forehead to my shoulder with a little moan. "I want these out," I said, kissing her jaw, her lips, leaning down to pull a nipple into my mouth.

Another little noise, and she kissed my neck. "What if someone sees us?"

I looked around quickly, making sure we were well hidden in the locked courtyard. "Don't worry, we're safe here."

Laying her back on the cushions, my hands slid down the smooth skin of her legs. I kissed the top of her foot, and she sighed. Traveling higher, I lifted the hem of her dress and my breath disappeared. No panties, and her skin was completely bare.

"Gorgeous," I murmured, leaning forward and kissing the inside of her thigh before sinking my tongue between her folds.

"Oh, god!" Her back arched and she cried out, clutching the sides of my head as I tasted her sweetness. I pulled her up to me, her ass in my hands, and I sucked, nipping her clit then plunging two fingers inside.

"Patrick!" she moaned as her thighs jumped. Her noises grew louder the more I kissed and sucked her. She was sweet and swollen, a juicy peach I slid my tongue through, circling as she gasped and whimpered my name. My tongue explored every opening and crease, teasing and tasting, until I felt her coming hard against me. Her hips bucked, and I lowered her fast, condom in place. One last kiss and I plunged inside.

"Fuck me," I groaned. She was hot and tight and so slippery.

Her arms wrapped around my neck as her hips continued to rock, and I thrust again, harder. Inner muscles tensed, pulling and massaging my dick so beautifully.

"Elaine," I breathed as I kissed her shoulder, holding her body, trying to slow my pace. I didn't want it to end too fast, but I was powerless against my desire for her. My stomach clenched as need took over and my thrusting grew faster.

Her body surrounded me, tightened on me, and had me shooting over the edge. My ass tensed with each push and the sound of her moans filled my senses. Everything had gone dark, and my sole focus was the mind-blowing pleasure of my cock shooting off deep between her thighs, over and over.

"Jesus," I groaned as my orgasm slowed. My lips were on her neck and her hips moved against me. Her insides spasmed, drawing me out as she held me close, bonding me to her. I couldn't imagine letting her go.

I kissed her neck, cupping her bottom in my hands. "You are so fucking amazing," I murmured, and she started to giggle.

I leaned up to cover her mouth, smiling as I kissed her, tasting her peppermint kisses as she sighed happily and giggled again.

"Stop laughing and kiss me," I murmured against her cheek.

"Oh, god, I can't help it," she gasped, a smile in her voice. "That was fucking incredible."

I kissed her again. "Have I told you it's very sexy when you swear?"

She leaned forward to kiss me hard, quickly curling her tongue with mine before moving her lips to my ear as she whispered, "As sexy as your groans when you come inside me?"

My cock was stiffening again. "Damn, woman," I said with a grin, and she hugged me, her breasts pressing against my chest. "Keep that up, and I'll have to fuck you again."

"Mmm," she purred. "Please do."

I leaned back to remove her dress completely, but she slipped to the side. I disposed of the condom, and she took my arm.

"I want you in the pool with me." Her lips grazed mine. "Now."

* * *

Get *One to Keep* Today!

Available on Amazon, Barnes & Noble, iTunes, Kobo, ARe

Print copies on Amazon, Createspace, Book Depository, Barnes & Noble
Audiobooks on Amazon and Tantor.com

For updates, follow Tia Louise on **Facebook**, get Text Updates by texting "TiaLouise" to 77948, or to receive New Release Alerts, **sign up for her New Release Newsletter today (link)!***

*Please add **allnightreads@mail.com** to your contacts so it doesn't bounce to spam!

Made in the USA
Lexington, KY
30 October 2014